PROPERTY OF THE
Public Library of the City of Beverly.
PUBLIC LIBRARY OF THE CITY OF BEVERLY.
1855.

Also by Michelle Falkoff

Playlist for the Dead

PUSHING PERFECT

MICHELLE FALKOFF

HARPER TEEN
An Imprint of HarperCollinsPublishers

HarperTeen is an imprint of HarperCollins Publishers.

Pushing Perfect

For information address HarperCollins Children's Books, a division of HarperCollins Publishers, 195 Broadway, New York, NY 10007.
www.epicreads.com

ISBN 978-0-06-231053-8 (trade)
ISBN 978-0-06-249017-9 (int)

Typography by Ellice M. Lee
16 17 18 19 20 PC/RRDH 10 9 8 7 6 5 4 3 2 1

First Edition

FOR MY PARENTS

PUSHING PERFECT

1.

During the summer between eighth and ninth grade, I turned into a monster.

It didn't happen overnight; it's not like I woke up one day, looked in the mirror, and let out a dramatic scream. But it still felt like it happened really fast.

It started at the pool with my two best friends, Becca Walker and Isabel DeLuca. School had just let out for the summer, and though the weather still felt like spring, the sun was out and the pool was heated and Isabel had a new bikini she wanted to show off. Normally she hated going to the pool with us, since Becca and I spent most of our time in the water swimming laps to practice for swim team tryouts, but Isabel had gotten all curvy and hot and kind of boy crazy, and there was a new lifeguard, so getting her to come with us wasn't that hard.

We couldn't get Isabel to actually swim, but that was

okay; Becca and I spent most of the day racing. I usually won when we swam freestyle, but Becca always killed me in the butterfly. I was terrible at butterfly. We raced until we were exhausted, and then we got out of the water, dripping in our Speedos as we headed for the showers.

"Your butterfly's getting better," Becca said, stretching her long, muscular arms over her head. With her wingspan and power I'd never catch her in butterfly, but it was nice of her to say I was improving. Becca was always nice. Isabel was a different story.

"Thanks," I said. "Not sure it will be good enough to make the team, though."

"You never know. We don't have to be perfect to get on. We just have to be good enough. And if you talk to your parents, we'll be able to spend the whole summer practicing."

The goal was for me to stay with the Walkers for the summer, instead of going on the family trip my mom was planning. Dad had just gotten forced out of his own start-up once it went public, and Mom thought he needed to get away while he figured out his next move. She'd rented a condo in Lake Tahoe for the whole summer, and I really, really didn't want to go. I hadn't brought up the idea of staying behind with the Walkers yet, though, since I was having trouble imagining my parents saying anything but no. "I'll do it soon," I said. "I'm just waiting for the right moment."

We both rinsed quickly under the showers and then

pulled off our swim caps. Something stung as I removed mine; I reached up to my forehead to feel a little bump there. I ran over to the mirror to look at it as Becca shook her braids out of the swim cap. "I'm going to miss these when they're gone," she said.

"Are you sure you can't keep them?" The bump hurt a little, though all I could see was a spot of redness, not the protrusion I'd have thought based on how it felt. I took my hair out of its bun and brushed it over my face so Becca and Isabel couldn't see the bump. They'd always teased me for having perfect skin, and I knew they'd find it amusing that I didn't anymore.

"Braids are way too heavy for swimming. Besides, you promised we'd cut our hair off together. You're not going to bail on me, are you?"

"Nope. I'm in." I'd never had short hair before, and besides, what did it matter? I always wore my hair in a bun or a ponytail anyway. It was kind of handy to have long hair now, though, to cover this thing on my face, which was starting to throb.

We went out to tell Isabel we were done for the day. She was lounging on a towel near the lifeguard station, where some cute high school guy was sitting in a tall chair that gave him a perfect view of her cleavage. "Finally!" she yelled. "I thought you guys were going to stay in the water forever. I'm bored. Let's get frozen yogurt."

"Can't today," I said. It wasn't true, but I couldn't stop thinking about the red bump. I just wanted to go home.

"Suit yourself," Isabel said. "We'll just go without you."

Usually that was enough to get me to change my mind; I hated feeling left out. It wasn't going to work today, though. "Have fun," I said, and texted Mom to pick me up.

"Come over later," Becca said. "We'll be at my house."

"I'll see if I can," I said. Maybe the bump was just a temporary thing. I watched them walk away and then pulled my hair back into a bun as soon as they were gone.

"Oh, sweetheart, it looks like you've got a pimple," Mom said when I got in the car. "I can put some concealer on that when we get home."

Trust Mom to see a problem and immediately want to fix it. That was her job back then, after all; she had a risk-management consulting business and helped all the local venture capital firms decide what kinds of investments were safe. "Better to identify issues when they're small," she'd say, but I'd heard her talking to Dad about work when she thought I wasn't listening, and I knew a big part of her job was helping cover stuff up.

When we got home, she marched me straight into the bathroom, put the toilet seat down, and made me sit while she dug through her cabinets for makeup. I snuck a look at the bump, which seemed like a whole other thing from the whiteheads and blackheads Isabel and Becca complained about. Their zits were angry little dots, vanquished by a fingernail or an aggressive exfoliating scrub. Mine had begun to throb like a furious insect under my skin, just waiting for its moment to break through and escape. Maybe it wasn't even a zit. Maybe it was a spider bite. Or a parasite.

"Don't be ridiculous," Mom said when I suggested it. "Now hold still." She squeezed some concealer onto the space on her hand between her forefinger and her thumb, rubbed it all together with a delicate brush, and dotted it gently on my face. "You have to have a light touch, or else it will cake up."

I tried not to roll my eyes. Mom was just trying to be helpful, I knew, but all I could think of was what Isabel would say if she could see me now. She'd been begging her mom to let her wear makeup since we started middle school; she'd finally gotten permission this year, and now every time we went to the mall, she dragged Becca and me to the cosmetics counters in the makeup stores. One time she'd pressured one of the salesladies into giving us makeovers, one of those older women whose face looked like a smooth mask and who wore a lab coat, as if wanting to look prettier was some kind of science project. She'd covered Becca's face with foundation a shade lighter than her dark skin; she'd slathered me with bronze eye shadow and coral lipstick and made my freckles disappear. We were both miserable.

Isabel wasn't willing to concede defeat, though. "Okay, we'll have to try another place," she said. "But just wait until school starts and you see all those cute boys. We'll need everything we've got to compete."

She made it sound like a swim meet. "Meeting boys is not a sport," I said.

Isabel laughed. "It is if you do it right."

She would know better than we would. She was the first of us to get a boyfriend; Becca and I had just nursed crushes all year. "You guys need to ditch the Speedos and get some bikinis," she'd say. "You're totally missing out."

Missing out on what? I wanted to ask her. From what I could see, getting a boyfriend meant letting some kid who was shorter than me lick my face in public. When I imagined kissing a boy, it was more romantic, private. Less messy. I was happy to wait until high school, where I dreamed there would be boys who were at least as tall as I was. I was sure that in their presence my awkwardness would magically disappear.

"Perfect Kara wants a perfect kiss," Isabel would say.

I hated when she called me that. It was an old nickname, from back when one of my grade school teachers had used my scores on math tests to try and motivate the class. "Look at Kara—one hundred percent perfect, every time." I'd felt my face turn red under all the freckles and prayed that no one was paying attention. But everyone was, and I'd never lived it down. The only person who'd never called me Perfect Kara was Becca.

Well, I wasn't so perfect now. "There we go," Mom said.

"No, wait, it's not blending properly. Let me just put on a little something else." She went through bag after bag of makeup, which was kind of funny, since it wasn't like she wore so much herself. The bag she settled on had a bunch of shiny lips on it.

"No lipstick," I said.

"No lipstick," Mom agreed. "This is where I keep my foundation."

I was tempted to ask why she'd keep foundation in a bag covered with lips, but I didn't want to seem too interested in her makeup collection. Mom pulled tubes and compacts out of the bag, opening and closing them, grabbing my wrist and putting samples of skin-colored creams on them, frowning, digging back in the bag. Finally, she found a shade she liked. She patted some liquid on my forehead and cheeks with her fingertips, then smeared it around with a little triangle-shaped sponge. "Close your eyes," she said, as she opened a compact filled with beige powder and then reached for an enormous fluffy brush. I obeyed and tried not to sneeze as she swept the powder all over me.

"You can open your eyes now." I did, and then watched her inspect my face. She smiled, and I worried that meant I'd be dealing with another horrible mask, like the lab-coat lady had given me. I must have looked like I was going to freak out, because Mom laughed. "I promise it's not as bad as you think. Come on, check it out."

I stood up and turned to look in the mirror. At first I

was confused but relieved: there was no thick mask, no scary unrecognizable me. And no zit. But there were also no freckles; my skin looked smooth and soft. Really, it was kind of nice. If lab-coat lady had done something more like this, maybe I wouldn't have taken such a hard stance against this stuff.

"So?" Mom asked. "Was I right?"

She knew how much I hated admitting it, but at the same time, she'd made it easier for me to decide what to do. I'd rather Becca and Isabel make fun of this makeup than the horrible monster zit. "Yeah, you were right," I said. "Thanks."

She kissed the top of my head. "Excellent. This was fun, wasn't it?"

"I guess." It actually had been. It reminded me of when I was little, when Dad's first start-up had just taken off and he was at work all the time. Mom and I had spent hours at the kitchen table doing logic puzzles together. At first it had been great, having so much of her time and attention, when normally she was almost as focused on work as Dad was.

But then she'd figured out that I was really good at those logic puzzles, really good at math in general, and all of a sudden everything was about school. She started asking more questions about what we were doing in class, whether it was hard for me or whether I was bored, and when I made the mistake of admitting that I didn't find any of it all that difficult, she started giving me extra homework. "You're gifted," she said. "Pushing yourself is the only way to get better."

Better at what? I wanted to ask her, but I had a feeling I knew the answer. Better at everything. It would never end. At least not until I was perfect. Maybe that was why I was so freaked out about this one zit. I knew I wasn't perfect, but I didn't need my face to broadcast it.

"It'll be nice to spend more time with you this summer, when we can relax," Mom said.

There it was—my opening. But I felt bad trying to get out of the trip after she'd just finished helping me. There would be another time. I just nodded.

"I told Becca I'd go over to her house," I said. "Can I?"

"Of course," she said. "Let me know what the girls think about the makeup."

"I will," I said, though I hoped they wouldn't notice it.

No such luck.

"Something's different," Isabel said as soon as I got to Becca's house.

We were in her bedroom, where we always hung out. It was huge, almost more like a suite, and she'd set it up like a studio apartment: bed and dresser on one side, and a little lounge area on the other, with a love seat and two chairs. I sat in my usual chair and slung my legs over the side; Becca was in the other chair, her legs crossed. Isabel relaxed in the love seat like she was waiting for someone to feed her grapes. Becca had lit one of those big scented candles in a jar, so the room smelled like cantaloupe.

"I don't see it," Becca said. "T-shirt, Converse, cutoffs." Just like hers.

"We really need to go shopping this summer," Isabel said. "But seriously." She tilted her head and looked at me more closely. "Wait, I know. It's the freckles. They're gone. What did you do, soak your face in lemon juice?"

"Don't be mean," Becca said.

"I'm not. I'm evaluating. Stand up." I did, and she gave me the up-and-down look she was becoming notorious for. "Makeup," she said. "Kara Winter's wearing makeup." She waved her hand in front of her face as if it were a fan. "My stars," she said, in a fake Southern accent. "Our little girl's growing up." Then she collapsed back onto the couch. Always the drama queen. I sat down too.

Becca frowned. "I thought you hated makeup. You said you'd never wear it. What's changed?"

"Nothing." I hated lying to them, but if I told them about the zit, Isabel would make a Perfect Kara joke and Becca would feel bad for me, and neither one of those things was appealing. Isabel had a way of finding my most sensitive spots and poking them with a sharp stick, and I was getting tired of it. And Becca's pity just made me feel like I wasn't good enough to be her friend. I hated feeling like I wasn't everything people wanted me to be. Better to hide the feeling with a little concealer.

"Was it your mom?" Becca asked. "Did she talk you into this?" She made it sound like my mom had tattooed my face while I slept.

"Smart to try to soften her up," Isabel said. "Did you ask her?"

I shook my head.

"You missed the window," Isabel said. "You have to just do it. Be bold!" She raised her fist in the air.

If only it were that easy. "I still don't know what to say. They're making such a big deal out of this trip." No one knew how much my parents really needed this. They'd been fighting a lot lately; Dad was really stressed about finding a new idea, and Mom had taken on more work to make up for his lost salary, so she was exhausted. She'd been talking about our vacation for months.

"You just have to make it easy for them to say yes," Isabel said. "Tell them you've already worked it out, that Becca's mom already agreed to it."

"Tell them you've got a lifeguarding job," Becca said.

"I don't want to lie to them."

"You wouldn't be lying," she said. "My old camp counselor is in charge now, and she said we can work there if we want. We just have to go meet with her before camp starts in two weeks."

"Becca, that's amazing! Is there drama stuff there Isabel can do? Then we can all be together." I was getting excited enough that the idea of asking to stay home seemed less scary than it had just a few minutes ago.

"I signed up for a drama camp in San Francisco," Isabel said. "I'm not about to spend that much time in a pool with you losers. My hair will turn green." She blew us a kiss, which took away some of the sting of her calling us losers, though I already knew she was kidding. Isabel said stuff like that all the time.

"We'll just have to find a way to live without you," Becca said. "We've got a lot of work to do before swim tryouts."

I felt a wave of nausea. Swim tryouts. Becca and I had been practicing all year; keeping our schedule was one of the reasons I didn't want to go on vacation. But I had no idea whether we'd be good enough. What if one of us made it and the other didn't? I'd never been in that high-pressure a situation before, and just the thought of it made me anxious. The only way I'd feel better was if I spent the summer practicing, and for that, I had to be here.

And then a new fear kicked in. What would happen if they spent the summer without me? They'd been friends first; I'd met Becca through swimming, and Isabel through Becca. Though the three of us were close now, I'd always felt like it was temporary, like they could go back to being a twosome at any time. They'd done it before, after some stupid fights in middle school, and I remembered the ache of that loneliness. What if they had an amazing time with me gone, and didn't want me back? My thoughts started to spiral. What if they saw the zit and decided they didn't want to be seen with me at school? I was being ridiculous; I knew. It was just one zit.

"Don't worry," Becca said. "Your freestyle is amazing, and we'll keep working on your butterfly. We'll be great. We just have to make sure we aren't separated this summer. You have to sell it."

"I will," I said. "I promise."

When I woke up the next morning, the horrible monster zit had multiplied by five. I asked my mother to go to the store and get me some benzoyl peroxide, like I'd seen advertised on TV. I didn't ask her about staying with Becca; instead, I stayed in the bathroom and practiced putting makeup on by myself. It was a disaster.

The day after that, there were ten. They were hard and red and they hurt. I kept looking at myself in the mirror, hoping I was imagining them. But they didn't go away. I got back in bed and stayed there all day, trying to avoid envisioning showing up for my first day of high school looking like this.

With every day came more angry red bumps, throbbing away under my skin. The benzoyl peroxide didn't do anything. Becca called, and I told her I had a weird summer cold so I could avoid seeing her. I knew Becca probably wouldn't think the zits were a big deal; she'd be sympathetic and supportive, like she always was. But behind her support would be that pity, and I couldn't bear the thought of it. And Isabel—Isabel wouldn't want to hang out with a monster. Not if it would interfere with her social life. Becca would have to choose, and why would she choose me? She and Isabel had the history; all I had was swimming.

Maybe the monster face was just a summer thing. Or maybe Mom could help me find a doctor who could give me medicine to make the zits disappear. Or she could teach me enough about makeup that I could hide them myself. I just needed some time. I realized I wasn't just avoiding asking Mom about staying with the Walkers; I'd decided I wasn't going to ask at all.

Once I had so many red blotches on my face that my freckles had all but disappeared, I called Becca. "Mom said no," I told her. "I tried as hard as I could."

"That sucks," she said, not bothering to hide her disappointment.

"I'm sure Isabel will be fine with it."

"Don't say that." Becca knew I worried sometimes that Isabel just tolerated me. "She'll miss you as much as I will. Have a great time, and make sure to find somewhere to practice. And I'll make hair appointments for us when you get home."

"Sounds great," I said, though I couldn't imagine cutting off all my hair with this face. I'd worry about that when the time came.

I got off the phone and told Mom I wanted to see a doctor before we went to Lake Tahoe. And that I wanted to go buy some makeup.

By the end of the summer I had a diagnosis: papulopustular acne, which basically meant that my whole face and neck were covered with zits. I had a dermatologist I would see every week who told me chlorine might have triggered the initial breakout and I should give some serious thought as to whether continuing to swim was a good idea. I didn't get in the water all summer.

By the time school started, I had two new regimens: drugs and makeup. Every day I got up, took my pills, and counted the cysts to see if there were fewer than the day before, writing the numbers down in a notebook I kept in the bathroom. And then I slathered my face with foundation, along with a little eye shadow and lip gloss so the foundation didn't look weird. Self-evaluation, cover-up, and makeup.

SCAM.

2.

The Brain Trust was occupying its regular table when I came into the cafeteria with my brown bag lunch. As always, I had to walk by the drama table, where Isabel hung out with her theater friends, and the swim team table, where Becca sat. They didn't look up when I passed them by. They never did.

Mom had made me spinach salad with quinoa and feta and a lemony dressing. Brain food. She'd done a ton of research into my skin condition and had made me try a million different diets that, just like everything else, did nothing. She'd amped up her game in anticipation of the SAT exam. The test was coming up in a little over a week, and though I'd studied so much I'd worn my Princeton Review guide to shreds, I was terrified to actually take it.

Ever since everything went down with Becca and Isabel, I'd buried myself in schoolwork, spending all my time writing papers and studying for tests and making sure I did as well as I possibly could. It was all I had left. I was still hiding my face with makeup, but sometimes it felt like I was hiding my whole self, too. Or that I didn't have much self left to hide. By my count, it had been over a year since I'd talked to anyone about anything except school. Even at home, all my parents talked about was how well I was doing, how proud they were of my hard work; they didn't seem concerned that I was always alone. Sure, Mom had asked about Becca and Isabel at first, but I'd mumbled something about people changing in high school and she'd let it go. I'd convinced myself that everything would be different if I went to the right college.

But I could only do that if I killed it on the SAT.

I'd always been good at taking tests, but the SAT was different. I don't know if it was just the pressure of how much was riding on it, or if some secret part of me was convinced that standardized tests would somehow reveal how very not perfect I was, but I'd had a full-on panic attack when I took the PSAT—I hadn't even finished it. I'd left the room before people could see me freaking out. I was so spooked by the thought of the SAT that I'd put it off until this year, rather than taking it as a junior like everyone else in my classes.

The Brain Trust was a group of kids I'd met in the Gifted and Talented Program back in grade school. We weren't friends, exactly, but we had all our classes together, and we all shared the common goal of wanting to go to college on the East Coast. Harvard, specifically. Arthur Cho was a classical violinist whose parents didn't want him to go to Juilliard because they thought it would limit his options; David Singer dreamed of being an entrepreneur like Mark Zuckerberg, even though I kept telling him what my parents told me, which was that Silicon Valley was full of Stanford grads who looked down on people from Harvard. Julia Jackson, my nemesis, was gunning for a particular science scholarship and wanted to go straight from undergrad to Harvard Med.

As for me, I just wanted to get as far away from Marbella as possible. I liked the idea of Harvard because it seemed like the kind of place I could start over, where everything might be different. No one would know me as Perfect Kara there; at a place like Harvard, it would be normal to love math and to care about academics more than anything else. It didn't necessarily have to be Harvard; any good school out east would do. My last name was Winter and I'd only ever seen snow in Tahoe. I wanted red and orange leaves in the fall, tulips in spring, baking heat in summer. I wanted change.

"The National Merit Semifinalist list came out today," Julia said, her voice all sugary. "Didn't see your name on there." Julia and I had been in classes together since kindergarten and teachers had been pitting us against each other the whole time. Handwriting competitions in first grade, speed-reading contests in second, multiplication table races in third—by then it had gotten old for me, but it never had for her. Now I was first in the class, but she was right on my heels, and I knew she'd made it her mission to pass me by.

"Nope," I said, trying to keep my voice light. "I assume congratulations are in order?"

Julia nodded, as did the other two. Great. So I was the only one. "Well, I'm really happy for you guys." And I was, but I could also feel the anxiety kicking in. It had become a familiar feeling—I'd get this wave of nausea, then a weird thumping in my head, and then my pulse would start to race. I'd feel cold but get sweaty, which was usually the point when I'd take a walk or something to calm myself down. They were sort of my friends, but they were also my competition, as my guidance counselor kept reminding me. The problem was that they each knew exactly what they wanted, and everything they did was in service of their goals. I had no idea what I wanted, other than knowing it had something to do with math, and that put me at a disadvantage. The only way to make myself stand out—the only way to have a real chance at a new life—was to be valedictorian at one of the most competitive public high schools in the country, which Marbella High was. And to nail the SATs.

Basically, I had to be perfect.

I had to put the SATs out of my head if I wanted to avoid an actual panic attack, though, so I turned to the immediate task, which was staying at the top of the class. Which meant acing next week's calc and econ exams. "We should get out of here," I said. "I don't want to be late for class."

We all had calculus next, which was my favorite class, with Ms. Davenport, who was my favorite teacher. Today was a review session for a test we had coming up, and I was actually looking forward to it.

The thing I loved about math was that you could usually tell when you got the right answer. Like the logic puzzles I used to do with my mom that I now did on my own, for fun: if seven girls go to a birthday sleepover and each one brings different gifts and snacks and has to leave at a different time the next morning, how do you figure out which is which, given a list of clues? There was something so satisfying about creating a chart, with little boxes for Xs and check marks, and drawing inferences from the clues that let you put all the pieces together. Calculus, with its graphs and equations, was similar enough to be fun.

I finished the practice test quickly, secure in the knowledge that I'd gotten all the answers right. It took another ten minutes or so for everyone else to get done, and then Ms. Davenport started going over the answers. She was such a great teacher—she walked through everything so carefully, I couldn't imagine how anyone didn't get it after that. She'd been the same way when I had her for geometry as a freshman, a class I found much harder than calculus. And she was cool, too—she dyed her hair auburn and wore it in fancy rolls like she was from the twenties, with vintage dresses and cowboy boots. She seemed so much younger than the other teachers, though I knew she couldn't be as young as I thought she was, given how long she'd been teaching.

"Ready for the test?" she asked me, on my way out of class.

"Ready enough, I hope," I said.

"I'm so not," a voice said from behind me. "Ready, that is."

I turned to see Alex Nguyen, a girl who was in my calculus and econ classes. I didn't know her very well; she didn't talk much in class unless Ms. Davenport made her, and we'd never done more than say hi in the hallway once in a while. Last year she used to fall asleep in class a lot but this year she'd gotten it together.

"It won't be so bad," I said.

"Oh, you're just humoring me. This stuff is totally easy for you."

I hated when people said things like that. They had no idea how hard I worked, how much pressure I was under. Sometimes it felt like I was treading water all the time, working as hard as I could to stay afloat. I just wanted to swim. Alex didn't seem to mean anything by it, though. "I'm going to have to study all weekend," I said.

"Want to study together? You can come to my house. I can even bribe you with food—my dad is a really good cook."

My first instinct was to say no; my study habits were pretty set, and it wasn't likely that working with her would help me. But then I remembered how my dad would make me teach the class materials back to him when he helped me study, and how much better I understood things once I could explain them. Maybe it would be good for both of us. And then I remembered something else.

"How are you doing in econ?" I asked.

"Oh, econ," she said, with a wave of her hand. "Nothing to it."

"Can we study for that too?"

"Really? You want my help?" Alex clapped her hands. "Totally! It'll be fun. How about tomorrow?"

I had nothing but time. "Sure."

"Give me your number and I'll text you the address."

We traded info as we walked to econ. I couldn't help but feel kind of excited—the thought of going over to Alex's to study actually sounded fun. I hadn't gone over to anyone's house in more than a year, and it had been even longer than that since I'd studied with someone else. Maybe we'd even talk about something other than classes, though the thought of it made me a little nervous. What did I have to talk about these days? I only hung out with the Brain Trust, and almost always at school—I hardly ever saw them outside it. Once in a while I went to the movies or the mall with Julia, but we both knew it was because we didn't have anyone else to go with. Every time I swore I'd never hang out with her again; all she wanted to talk about was school, even after she and David started hooking up. I refused to ever study with her. The only person I'd ever had fun studying with besides my dad was Becca, and that was way back in middle school, before we got put in all different classes.

Of course, the minute I thought of Becca, there she was. It had been over a year since we'd last spoken, but I still missed her all the time. Isabel too, though not in the same way. Becca looked striking, like she always did; she wore smoky makeup around her green eyes and her dark skin was as clear and perfect as ever. She'd started to let her hair grow back, but just barely, so her head was covered in tight little black curls.

I still remembered the day she'd cut off her braids. I'd just gotten back from Tahoe, and as promised, she'd made us appointments at the same time. When she first suggested the haircuts, I thought it was a great idea; I liked the idea of us doing something together, something that would publicly mark us as friends. And it wasn't like my long hair was so fabulous; it was a washed-out brown and not particularly thick, and I never wore it down anyway.

But then there was the skin. When things got bad over the summer, I got in the habit of taking down my bun and wearing my hair over my face. There was something comforting about it, like I was doing a better job of hiding the problem even just by virtue of covering myself a little more. Mom had gently suggested that if I was going to wear it down, I might want to brighten it up a bit, so I'd gotten a trim and some super subtle highlights and started paying more attention to how I styled it. Becca hadn't seen it yet. She hadn't seen my new clothes, either, or how much makeup I was wearing regularly now. Mom said I looked like a new person, all grown up and ready for school. I was just happy not to look like myself, now that looking like myself had become so scary.

The appointment was scheduled for the day after I got back into town. "We need to do this like ripping off a Band-Aid," she said. "No chickening out."

I should have just told her then. Instead, I showed up at the hairdresser late. Becca was sitting in the chair covered in an apron, her braids already half gone. Even before the haircut was over, it was clear she could pull it off; she had a really great-shaped head.

"You're back!" she said, as I approached the chair. "I'd get up and hug you, but you see what's happening here." She pointed at the hairdresser, who held up a big pair of scissors.

"I sure do," I said. "You're really going for it."

"*We're* really going for it," she corrected. Then she paused and looked at me. "Come here."

I came closer. She reached out and touched my hair. "You got highlights," she said. "And layers."

I nodded.

"You're not going for it."

"No," I said, quietly.

"You're kidding. What happened? We had a plan."

The hairdresser moved the scissors away from Becca's

head. "I'm going to give you girls a minute," she said, and went into the back.

"I know we did, and I'm really sorry," I said. "But you know I've never had the same trouble with the swim cap thing as you, and I did that thing where you upload a picture and try out different hairstyles online, and I look awful with short hair." That was only kind of a lie—I'd done it, and I didn't look great with short hair, but that wasn't the real reason. It was time for me to just tell her the truth. I hated keeping secrets, especially from Becca; I never had before. I opened my mouth to say more, but I thought about having to tell Isabel, and I wondered whether I could ask Becca to keep my secret for me. Was that too much to ask her? I wasn't sure what to do.

I didn't have to decide what to say next, though, because Becca had already made up her mind. "You should go," she said. Her voice was cold, and I knew she was furious. Becca wasn't like Isabel, who yelled and screamed whenever she was pissed off. When Becca was mad, she got very, very quiet. "If you're not keeping your appointment, you don't need to be here."

That was the moment I should have said something. But I didn't. "I'll make it up to you. I promise." That was kind of a lie too, since I had no idea how, but I didn't know what else to say. And I didn't want to ask her to forgive me, because I was afraid she'd say no. So I just left.

We'd gotten over that eventually, just as we'd gotten over other things in the past. We hadn't yet reached our limits; it would take nearly two years and a lot more than a haircut for our friendship to end. But eventually, it did. So when Becca and I made eye contact in the hall, I saw the flash of emotions that passed over her face whenever she saw me: sadness, confusion, a little bit of anger, resignation. I imagined mine probably weren't all that different.

And then we both looked away.

3.

Alex lived in a subdivision not too far from mine. The only way to tell it was different was the style of the homes—in my neighborhood it was all ranch houses, but in hers there was a little bit of variation, though not much. Marbella didn't have a lot of architectural range. Alex's house was almost identical in layout to Becca's; it felt familiar, which made me nostalgic.

Alex's mom opened the door and welcomed me in. She wore the local mom uniform of yoga pants and a zipped-up track jacket, her thick black hair pulled into a high ponytail. "You must be Kara," she said. "Come on in—Alex is inside and my foolish husband is slaving over the hot stove."

She led me into the kitchen, where a short man in khakis, a denim shirt, and an apron that read TROPHY HUSBAND was frowning over a cookbook as several pans bubbled on the stove. "Hi, I'm Kara," I said. "It smells amazing in here." I meant it, too; the air was full of ginger and garlic and other spices I didn't recognize.

"Oh, it's a disaster," he said, cheerfully. "I've been taking classes and reading these cookbooks to try to reconstruct all these old recipes my mom used to make, but she took her secrets to the grave."

"I'm sorry," I said, though he hadn't sounded sad about it.

"I'm just sorry she didn't teach me how to cook. You can be sure I won't make the same mistake with Alex. Hi, honey! Come over here and give me a hand."

I turned around to see that Alex had just come into the kitchen. "You don't really want my help," she said. "I wouldn't want to get in the way of the fun you're having." She said it with a completely straight face, so it took me a second to realize she was kidding.

But her dad understood right away and stuck his tongue out at her. She stuck hers out right back. "Stop screwing around and help me," he said. This was obviously not the first time they'd done this bit.

"What do you need?" She gave me a nod to acknowledge she knew I was there and then went to read the cookbook over her dad's shoulder. "I thought you were just going to do pho. You can make that in your sleep."

"I got ambitious," he said, looking a little embarrassed. "Shaking beef with red rice . . . it's been a while since you had company."

Now it was Alex's turn to look embarrassed. "I *told* you, this is not a big deal!" She glanced over at me. "No offense."

"None taken." It was all pretty amusing. "Can I help?"

"No!" they both yelled at the same time.

Alex's mom laughed. "Let me get you something to drink, and then we can sit at the table and watch the show. It's usually entertaining, if messy. Last time they made shaking beef, I had to renovate the kitchen afterward."

I wondered whether she was joking. It was a really nice kitchen, with shiny sea-green tile that looked like little bricks lining the walls behind enormous stainless steel appliances. Even if she was serious, though, it didn't sound like she minded. Though she was wearing the Marbella uniform, she didn't seem as high-strung as some of the other moms. Mine included.

She handed me a glass of iced tea and we sat at the table and watched Alex and her dad prepare the food. They worked well together, only talking occasionally, trading ingredients and utensils back and forth like people who did this all the time, which they clearly did. I couldn't even imagine having that kind of a routine with my dad; he was so caught up in work that even my earliest memories were of him on his cell phone. The only time we'd really spent alone together was when he helped me study—he was really good at English and all the nonmath stuff that I wasn't so into—but that hadn't happened in a long time.

"Almost there," Alex said.

Once they were done, they stuck big spoons right in the pots and handed out bowls so we could all serve ourselves. Then we sat at the kitchen table and completely pigged out. I liked how casual it all was, but that they all ate together. In my house we mostly fended for ourselves or ate in front of the television; we only ate at the dining room table when my parents were having people over. Which happened almost never.

"This food tastes even better than it smells," I said, fighting the urge to talk with my mouth full so I could keep eating.

"He's a better cook than his mother was," Mrs. Nguyen said. "And he knows it, too."

"Don't be silly." Mr. Nguyen waved her off, but he looked pleased. "Cooking is just a hobby."

"A likely story," Alex said. "I keep waiting for you to tell us you're ditching work to open a restaurant."

"It's a great idea. Your mom can quit her job and take care of the books, and you can quit school to waitress."

Mrs. Nguyen laughed. "You're welcome to trade software for soft-shell crabs, but you'd have to carry me out of the office bound and gagged. And don't even joke about Alex dropping out of school."

There it was—that Marbella-mom edge to her voice. I wasn't the only one at this table with high-pressure parents, then.

"Speaking of school, we should probably get to work," Alex said.

I thanked her parents for dinner and then followed Alex to her room. Just as I'd expected, she had the same enormous bedroom setup that Becca had, though she'd done something completely different with the space. Her bed was in the same place, but instead of a lounge area she had a huge desk that ran the length of the entire back wall and then turned and tracked half of the rest of the room. That was where the computer monitors were. Three of them: one in the center and two at forty-five-degree angles on either side. Also huge.

"Are you an air traffic controller or something?" I asked.

She shook her head. "I guess you could say I'm a programmer." She sat down in a big fancy-looking desk chair and motioned to a smaller chair next to it for me.

I sat down. "What kind of programming do you do?"

She gave me a little smirk, like I'd caught her doing something she wasn't supposed to. "Well, maybe I exaggerated a little. I told my parents I needed all this stuff for programming. Can you keep a secret?"

If only she knew. "Sure."

"I need the screens for poker. I play online. Like, a lot."

"Isn't it illegal? I mean, not to sound like a goody-goody or anything . . ."

She shrugged. "It's, like, dubious. The playing part isn't

so much illegal, but the money part isn't something I want people to find out about, if you know what I'm saying."

"You make money? You must be good."

"Yeah, I am," she said, but she didn't sound arrogant. Just proud. "But that's also where the programming comes in. I wrote a bunch of tracking programs to help with my game, to run statistics, that sort of thing. It gives me a real advantage over some of the idiots who play online."

I was impressed. I'd thought she was just this random girl in some classes with me; it turned out she had this totally other secret life. My secrets weren't nearly as interesting as hers. "Why do you need so many screens?"

"Because I usually play about five or six games at a time. That's the nice thing about being online—you don't have to sit at just one table. Your avatar can be in lots of places at once." She clicked and her screen lit up with the image of a poker table covered in felt; she clicked again and I saw an image of a boy's face, with short dark hair.

"That's your avatar?"

"That's virtual me. I pretend I'm a boy so they'll take me more seriously. Sad, but poker's pretty sexist. It's weirdly not as racist, though—there are a lot of famous players with the same last name as me, so being Alex Nguyen is actually kind of helpful. Not that I use my real name, but some people I play with a lot know it. And they know my uncle, too—he was a professional poker player, a really famous one. Taught me everything I know."

"When do you have time to do all this?

"At night. I don't need much sleep."

I knew that couldn't be true; I remembered last year, when she used to fall asleep in class every day. "Don't you need a lot of math for programming? Do you really need my help? It sounds like you could help me more than I could help you—I'm way behind in AP Statistics, too." I'd loaded up my schedule with math electives, mostly to avoid having to take more science classes.

"Well . . ." She got that look again, like I'd busted her, and then started talking really fast. "I mean, yeah, calculus isn't my best subject, but I get by. It's just . . . most of my friends are guys, and you and I have been in classes together forever but we've never hung out, and I only see you with those Brain Trust kids, and in class you seem smart and funny and they're smart but not even a little bit funny, and they can't be a whole lot of fun, and you seem like someone who should maybe be having more fun than you are, and I thought maybe we should be friends."

She took a deep breath. I stared at her.

"Well, are you going to say something? Did I just totally humiliate myself? We can just study. No problem. I've got stats down cold. Took it sophomore year."

"No, wait," I said. "You just talk way faster than I can think. You're right."

"Right about which part?"

"Right about all of it. I do pretty much only hang out with Julia and those guys, and only at school, because they're not fun."

"I'm totally fun. We're going to start getting you out more."

I'd never met anyone so direct. It was kind of amazing. "That would be great," I said. I wanted to tell her that I used to have friends, that it wasn't always like this, but that wouldn't change anything.

"Oh, that is so excellent. I have such a good feeling about you, you know? And we're like twins." She pointed to our outfits, which were both variations on the hoodie/tank top/jeans/tennis shoes combo.

I raised my eyebrows at her. One minute into our friendship was too early to state the obvious.

"Oh, yeah, except for the Asian thing," she said.

Or maybe it wasn't. Even better.

Alex started her fast talking again. "Isn't it weird, how hard it is to make new girlfriends? It's like you hang out with the same people forever, and at a certain point that's all there is. Boys are so much easier. You can just go right up to them and say whatever you want, and either they'll be friends with you or they won't. Girls are so much more complicated."

"Is it really that easy?" I asked. "With boys, I mean?"

"It has been so far. Except for if they get a thing for you.

Then it gets complicated. But I bet you know how to deal with that, pretty as you are. God, it's so great to have someone to talk to about this stuff! We should tell each other everything!" She must have seen the look on my face. "Uh-oh. Is this not a good topic? Are you not into guys? Girls are good too. I mean, I've only made out with a couple, just to see if it was my thing, but . . ."

I couldn't help it—I started cracking up. She was so different than she came across at school. She wouldn't be the kind of friend Becca had been, but that was okay. "I'm not into girls. It's more that my experience with guys is kind of . . . limited." I was flattered that she thought I was pretty enough to have dealt with guy issues before, but of course she had no idea what I really looked like. Then again, no one did.

"Well, then, we've got some work to do. We'll have to strategize. Let's hang out next weekend."

"Saturday's the SAT," I said.

"You didn't take it yet? I got it out of the way at the end of last year," she said. "Such a relief."

I didn't feel like explaining about the whole panic attack thing. Besides, I'd studied my ass off and read a bunch of meditation books and eaten my mom's brain food for weeks. I'd be okay this time. "I put it off," I said. "I really need to do well." That much was true, anyway. So much for telling each other everything, though.

“Just come over after,” she said. “We can keep it low key. We’ll just hang out.”

“That would be great.” If all went as planned, I’d be in a good mood, and it would be fun to talk about it with a friend. Now that we were friends.

4.

The morning of the SAT I stumbled out of bed bleary-eyed and in desperate need of coffee. I'd resolved to get a good night's sleep to prepare, had even tried the stupid meditation techniques from the books I'd read, but nothing worked. I'd stayed up most of the night remembering that disastrous attempt at the PSAT, the one that had kept me from taking the test last year, when I should have. This time had to be different—if I didn't manage to get through it, I only had one more shot.

Mom was in the kitchen by the time I got downstairs, coffee brewed, a plate of what looked like green eggs at my seat. "Are we channeling Dr. Seuss today?" I asked.

"Scrambled eggs blended with spinach, kale, spirulina, and hemp seeds," Mom said, coming over and kissing my forehead. "That plus coffee should help you focus. I packed some baggies of almonds and blueberries for you to bring in with you. You're going to be terrific today."

"Wow," I said, picking at the eggs with my fork. They looked beyond disgusting. "Um, thank you?"

"I tasted them first," Mom said. "They're not as bad as they look. I added lots of salt and pepper. Give it a shot."

I took a very, very small bite. They tasted . . . green. Which was fine. Other than that epic dinner at Alex's, I'd eaten almost nothing but green food for a week in preparation for today. I was used to it. "Not bad," I said, though I loaded up my coffee with cream and sugar, just to have something that tasted good. "Where's Dad?"

"He's at work already."

"On a Saturday?" I shouldn't have bothered asking; lately he'd been working every weekend, and most of the time Mom had too, now that she was working with him. Weekends were irrelevant now that he was starting a new company.

"He's stressed about the next round of funding," Mom said.

"Should he be?"

"I don't think it matters. He'd stress out either way. Just like you."

And here we'd been doing so well. She was right, though; Dad and I did have a lot in common, and we both had a tendency to stress. But Dad's stress always seemed tied to work, while I managed to get myself anxious about everything. At first I'd thought it started with the skin, but then I thought about all the things I'd worried about before that—my friendships, school, my parents. Really, I worried about everything, all the time; the only thing that had ever helped me relax was swimming, and that was gone now.

I'd tried to talk to my dad once about how he managed, hoping he'd have a suggestion that would help me, but he'd told me he just tried to convert his stress to energy and put the energy into work, which to me seemed kind of circular. "I did go to a doctor once," he said. "He put me on some medication, but I had a really bad reaction to it."

"I don't remember that," I said.

"You were really young. And that was a good thing, because it was a very scary time. I was hallucinating and stopped sleeping. It was awful for your mother. She still doesn't like to think about it."

That did explain a lot, especially her emphatic "No!" when I'd asked her about beta blockers or Xanax. I knew lots of kids at school were taking them, but she wasn't having it. The whole brain food thing was her way of trying to make up for it, which I appreciated.

"When do you need to get going?" Mom asked, watching me pour myself another cup of coffee.

"Not for almost an hour," I said. "Can you pass me the crossword?" Better to keep my brain busy than to think about what was coming, I figured.

"Oh, I don't think it's here yet," she said, not looking at me.

"Mom. They drop the paper off in the middle of the night. You bring it in every day. The one time it wasn't here when you woke up, you called them to complain. I know you have it, so where is it?" I didn't mean to sound irritable, but I could hear the edge in my voice.

She sighed. "Can you just skip the crossword for today? You can do it when you get home. You have enough to think about as it is."

"Which is exactly why I need it." Why was she being so weird?

My question was answered as soon as she pulled the paper out from under a stack of magazines and handed it over. Marbella was small enough that the newspaper was half the size of a normal paper like the *San Francisco Chronicle.* And we had so little crime that the front cover was usually devoted to something related to local politics, or high school sports. Or good news.

JULIA JACKSON, NATIONAL MERIT SEMIFINALIST, WINS SCHOLARSHIP! the headline screamed at me.

Oh, great.

I skimmed the article. Julia had won the Silicon Valley Entrepreneurship Society's first annual prize, a ten-thousand-dollar-per-year scholarship to the school of her choosing. The prize was reserved for students of "exceptional promise," the article read. "'It's a new award, but it's a tremendous honor,' said an admissions officer at UC Berkeley, who wished to remain anonymous. 'It's certainly the kind of thing we'd take into account when choosing between students.'"

It was like they'd written the article just to mess with my head.

"I think I can see the steam coming out of your ears," Mom said. "That's why—"

"—you didn't want me to have the paper," I said. "I get it. You were right. You're right about everything." I got up from the table and took my plate and cup over to the sink. "Thanks for breakfast. I'll see you when I get home."

"Honey, I don't care about being right," Mom said. "I won't be here this afternoon, but I'll see you when I get home from work. Call and tell us how it went?"

Figures she'd go to work on a Saturday too. Bad enough when it was just Dad. "Yeah, I'll call. I'm going out tonight anyway."

"Really? With who?" Mom sounded excited.

"A new friend. No big deal."

"Well, you can tell me all about that too, when you get home. Don't stay out too late."

"I won't," I said. When had I ever?

Outside, the sun was shining and the sky was perfectly blue and free of clouds and it was like the day had been sent to mock me. I had a terrible feeling about how things would go; it would have been more appropriate for it to be raining. I got in my car and cracked an energy drink for the ride. It would probably be too much on top of the coffee, but I was too tired to do without it. By the time I got to school I was wired; I hoped that was the primary explanation for the jangling of my nerves.

Ms. Davenport was the SAT proctor, so the test was in her classroom. That was a good sign in more ways than one—all my associations with that room were positive. I'd aced lots of tests there, and just seeing Ms. Davenport at the front of the room was comforting. Maybe my feeling of foreboding was wrong.

Of course, the room was also full of seniors, since it was too early for even the most enterprising juniors to be taking their first shot at the test. But most of the kids in the AP classes I took had already taken it last year, so as I looked around the room, there were only a couple of really familiar faces.

Becca and Isabel.

Both of them were in their workout clothes, not much makeup, Isabel's long blond hair in a high ponytail. Both of them had big Starbucks cups in front of them and matching energy bars. They must have met up beforehand and come together. I wondered whether they still had the same favorite drinks: skinny vanilla latte for Isabel, and matcha green tea for Becca. Isabel and I used to tease her for that one; it smelled terrible, and though Becca insisted it tasted better than it smelled, we both refused to try.

I still missed them.

I couldn't let them get me off track, though. I had to concentrate on the good things: the luck of getting to be in this room, with its comforting smell of chalk dust; the fact that my usual class seat was open, so I could pretend this was just another test instead of the thing that was going to decide my whole life; the meditation exercises I'd practiced last night and that I had time to do now. So what if they hadn't worked before? Today would be different. It had to be.

I closed my eyes and breathed naturally, in and out, focusing on each breath. My pulse slowed; I could see patterns forming on the backs of my eyelids, white dots swirling like kaleidoscopes against a dark-red backdrop, and let them soothe me. Ms. Davenport's voice came into focus as she read the directions. I opened my eyes to see her passing out the exam packets.

I was going to be fine. I was ready.

Ms. Davenport gave the signal, and we tore open the seals holding our packets together. The first section was math, thank goodness. I started working through the early problems, the easier ones, and managed to get through five questions before I started feeling thumping in my head. *Breathe*, I thought. *Focus*. I calmed myself down enough to finish the section, which wasn't too hard. Just like I'd practiced.

I was relieved to know I could do this.

The second section was critical reading. Two fill-in questions, no problem. The words started to go blurry when I got to some analogies, but I reminded myself to think of them like ratios. I slowed down and concentrated, using the techniques I'd learned from the study guide to narrow my options. All fine.

Until.

The first paragraph took up the entire left-hand column of the page. I started reading it and got halfway through before I realized I'd only taken in maybe every third word. Something about global warming? Rain forests? Endangered species? I started over. I still wasn't getting it.

I held my thumb to the left side of my chin to check my pulse. It was speeding up.

My stomach clenched.

Beads of sweat formed on my forehead, even though I was really, really cold.

I looked back down at the test booklet and started reading the passage again. This time it was like I couldn't even see the words.

Come on, I thought.

My lungs were getting smaller, making it almost impossible to squeeze breaths in and out of them.

I had to get out of here.

I looked up to see Ms. Davenport watching me, brows lowered. She tilted her head as if asking me a question. I stood up to tell her I had to go to the bathroom, but I'd waited too long. The patterns from the backs of my eyes were back, the white dots and the maroon behind them, except this time my eyes weren't closed.

Then everything went dark.

5.

I opened my eyes to white. White with little black dots that it took me a minute to recognize as ceiling tiles. I was lying on a bed—no, a cot. Brightly colored posters with warning signs for eating disorders and sexual abuse covered the walls.

I was in the nurse's office.

I'd been here a couple of times, mostly to grab a tampon when I'd run out. The nurse was nice about making them easy to find, so we didn't have to bug her when we needed them. But I'd never actually gotten far enough into the room to explore the cot situation. It was extremely uncomfortable, with springs that poked into my back, and I wondered if that was on purpose, to keep kids from using the nurse's office to take naps.

I sat up and the springs creaked, loud enough to shock me, and apparently loud enough that they were audible outside the room because the nurse came rushing in.

"Kara, so glad you're up," she said. "You gave us a little scare but you're going to be fine. Good thing I was here!"

"What happened?" I asked. I remembered standing up to leave the room, but that was about it.

"You fainted. Just for a minute, but you had us worried—you were very agitated when you woke up, so we brought you here for a little rest. We left a message at your house but we don't seem to have your parents' cell phone numbers."

"I think I had a panic attack," I said. It was the first time I'd said it out loud; even when I'd talked to my parents about the things that had happened in the past, I never used those words. "My parents are at work—I don't want to call them."

"You may be right about the panic attack," the nurse said. "That's something worth talking to your doctor about. Are you sure I can't call your mom for you?"

I shook my head. No need to bring them into it. I wanted to manage my own disappointment in myself before I took on theirs. "I just want to go. My car's in the lot."

"I'm afraid I can't let you do that quite yet," she said. "I don't want you driving until I'm sure you're okay, and your teacher wanted to come by and chat after the exam. Should be done in just a couple of minutes, and in the meantime I've got some juice and crackers for you. Just to get that blood sugar up."

"But the test just started," I said. "I don't want to wait that long."

"Oh, you've been asleep for a couple of hours. You must have been wiped out. Here, have a snack and Ms. Davenport will be by in just a few minutes. Okay if I go man the desk outside? There are bound to be some post-exam meltdowns."

I nodded, and she handed me the plate of crackers and a little flowered paper cup of juice. The mix of carbs and sugar reactivated all the caffeine I'd had, and I started to feel less sleepy and more alert. Which brought the memory of blacking out in the middle of the classroom right to the surface. I started to shake as I realized that not only had I not managed to actually take the stupid SAT, but I'd fainted in front of Becca and Isabel. I couldn't remember ever feeling so humiliated.

There was a light tapping on the open door of the nurse's office and I looked up to see Ms. Davenport. "I came as soon as I could," she said. "Are you okay?"

I couldn't help it—as soon as I heard her voice, I started crying. Ugly crying, too, not just a few tears; I sobbed until I was almost hiccuping, burying my head in my arms. The cot creaked as Ms. Davenport sat down next to me and patted my back, waiting for me to calm down. Once I'd stopped crying long enough to try to breathe, she handed me a Kleenex. "Do you want to talk about it?"

I opened my mouth to say no, but instead all these words came pouring out, along with more tears. "I can't believe this is happening. I worked so hard and now I'm so embarrassed and I'm never going to get into college and I'm never going to get out of here and everyone saw and now they're all going to talk about me and my parents are going to be so disappointed and . . ." I started sobbing again, enough that I couldn't talk.

I couldn't believe I'd said all that to Ms. Davenport, but it made sense that if I said it to anyone, it would be her. She'd become more than just a teacher to me; we'd worked really closely together during geometry, and after a while I'd started telling her about all the pressure I was feeling, and she gave me advice on how to keep it from getting to me, reminding me that everything I was doing was for me, not for my parents, or for the competition. It didn't always work, but I did try to keep my eyes on the future. My future. I was thrilled to get her for calculus, and sometimes I'd stay after class or even after school and talk to her about colleges. She gave me a list of some of the East Coast schools with good math programs and said she'd write a recommendation for me for wherever I wanted to go. All the students loved her, so it made me feel special that she'd taken a particular interest in me.

I hated that she'd seen me like this, but I knew she wouldn't judge.

"All right, Kara, you're all about logic, so let's break this down together," she said. "I know you, so I have no doubt that you worked hard. And I understand you're embarrassed, but no one made fun of you; a couple of the girls asked if you were okay, but everyone else just went back to the test, because that's what people do—they worry about themselves. No one's paying as much attention to you as you think, and that's okay."

I wanted to believe her, but I also knew that the worst of it wouldn't happen in front of her. That would come later. I wondered whether Becca and Isabel were the girls who'd asked about me.

"You're also going to get into college, and you'll get out of Marbella too, if that's what you want. You're right that the SATs matter to a lot of places, so that's something you'll have to figure out some other time, but there are also schools that don't require them, and some of those schools are fantastic. You have options. And I met your parents at parent-teacher conference night back when you were a freshman, and they were very loving and supportive."

I did my meditation breathing while I listened to her. I liked that she knew me well enough to know that logic was the best way through this—if she'd just been all sympathetic and sweet, I'd have never stopped crying. "Okay," I said, and tried to blow my nose as discreetly as possible. I hoped my makeup hadn't smeared all over the place. "That helps."

"Now, do you want to tell me what happened in there?"

"Panic attack," I said from behind the Kleenex. It was getting easier to say it out loud.

"I've given you lots of tests and never even seen you break

a sweat," she said. "What's different about the SAT? Or is it just the SAT?"

"It's not just the SAT, but it's mostly that. I just get so stressed out about it, because my scores need to be perfect if I want to go to Harvard, since there's, like, nothing else interesting about me. I used to swim, but I don't anymore, so now all my extracurriculars are just filler, and all the schools will know it. I have to ace this test. But if I keep losing it every time I try to take it, I'll never get in."

"If you've convinced yourself that you need perfect scores, then it's no wonder you're panicking every time you think about this exam. Perfection is an unrealistic aspiration."

"That's what my mom says. I should 'just do my best.'" I made air quotes. "But we both know that's not always good enough. She just won't say it. She and my dad were both great students, killed it at Stanford, killed it in grad school. She can pretend that she doesn't want me to be perfect, but she doesn't mean it."

"Maybe she does," Ms. Davenport said. "Maybe you should take what she says at face value. Do what you can. Take the pressure off. All this pushing for perfection is damaging, you know. You've heard about what's happening in Palo Alto."

Of course I had. Everyone had. The papers were calling them suicide clusters. Kids who were scared of not getting into the right colleges didn't see any other futures for themselves. I bet a lot of them felt like me. I don't know what kept me from reaching that level of despair, but I felt lucky that I'd been able to avoid those kinds of thoughts.

"That's not happening in Marbella," I said.

"It could. Same circumstances—public high school in an affluent town, parents putting pressure on their kids to go to elite schools. I don't want to have to worry about you."

"You don't have to," I said. "Besides, I know I put a lot of the pressure on myself." Which was true.

"Well, you need to find a way to let yourself off the hook, then."

"I guess." It was kind of a bummer to hear Ms. Davenport talking like a typical grown-up, which wasn't usually her thing. She and Mom could say whatever they wanted about me not needing to be perfect, but I knew who I was competing with. My guidance counselor had basically admitted that if I didn't make valedictorian and get near-perfect scores on the SATs, all the good East Coast schools would be out of reach. And all the best math departments were at research institutions, as Ms. Davenport well knew, and they all required the SATs. There was no getting around it.

"I hear the skepticism," Ms. Davenport said. "Just tell me you'll think about it. And that you'll come talk to me if the pressure's getting to be too much. I'll do whatever I can to help."

“Thanks,” I said. “I will.”

“Now, can I call your mom to come get you?”

“She’s at work. I’m fine—I’ve got my car.”

“You sure you’re okay to drive?”

“I feel a lot better now,” I said. But it wasn’t true.

Alex texted as I was walking out to the parking lot: **All done? How did it go? When are you coming over?**

Good to know word hadn’t made it to her yet. Maybe Ms. Davenport was right; maybe people hadn’t been paying that much attention. I hated having to admit what had happened, but it was nice to have a friend checking up on me.

Disaster, I wrote. **Tell you about it tonight. When do you want me?**

Sounds like you need cheering up, she wrote. **Let’s go for ice cream instead. Meet me downtown at seven.**

I was about to suggest frozen yogurt, but then I figured, why bother? No need to keep up with the crazy health food diet if it wasn’t going to help anyway. Ice cream sounded awesome.

Now I just had to keep myself busy for the rest of the afternoon. If I kept thinking about the morning’s nightmare, I’d never stop crying. It was times like these when I really missed swimming. Being in the water, feeling the cool of it on my skin, concentrating on my arms and my legs and making them work together and nothing else—it was the perfect way to get out of my own head. My favorite stroke was freestyle, which had always come naturally to me; Becca was all about the butterfly, which made sense, given that she was more muscular than I was. She had so much power in her arms and shoulders, whereas I'd hit my growth spurt early and could use my long arms and legs to move through the water smoothly.

Swimming had been my only form of exercise. When I stopped, I missed the endorphins. I started getting depressed, though initially I'd assumed it was because high school was so hard and because Becca and Isabel and I were already growing apart.

Mom had seen what was going on. "Sweetie, you're going to need to get some exercise," she said one day, as I picked at my cereal, wishing I could just get back into bed instead of going to school.

"What, you think I'm gaining weight or something? Don't I worry about my appearance enough as it is?" I was really not in the best mood.

"Not at all," she said, unruffled. It took a lot to ruffle her. "You just seem unhappy, and I think you'd be surprised how much better you'd feel if you got in a workout."

"Well, that's impossible," I snapped. "I can't swim anymore, and I'm not about to go somewhere without the stupid makeup, and the stupid makeup is not sweat-friendly."

Mom paused, trying to decide which aspect of what I'd said to take on. We hadn't talked about my unwillingness to let anyone know about my skin problem, and back then she and Dad were just starting to work out their issues post-Tahoe, which I knew she hadn't told anyone about either. It's not like I'd have listened if she'd told me it was time to start sharing. "I understand," she said finally, and I thought that was the end of it.

I came home from school that day to find a brand-new treadmill in the guest bedroom. I had no idea how she'd made it happen that fast, but I recognized the gesture immediately. She wasn't even home from work yet; she must have come home to let the delivery people in and then gone back. My eyes teared up with embarrassment—I'd been such a jerk that morning, and this was how she'd responded. I changed into shorts, a T-shirt, and tennis shoes right away.

Ever since then, I'd come to enjoy running on the treadmill, at least as much as anyone liked running on a treadmill, and I used it to get away from being in my own head all the time. I cranked the stereo when no one was home (or blasted music through my headphones when they were), and for an hour I was free.

A long run would be the perfect way to get the morning out of my system. I put on the happiest music I could find and ran until I could barely feel my legs and my clothes were soaked with sweat. The feeling was exhilarating, and by the time I'd gotten out of a blissfully cold shower, I was ready to put the day behind me.

6.

Alex was waiting for me outside the ice-cream place when I got there, and I could tell she desperately wanted to ask me what happened; she was practically twitching with curiosity. But to her credit she waited until we'd both gotten big waffle cones filled with ice cream and topped with sprinkles—sea-salt caramel for her; mint chip for me—and walked over to the park nearby. Fall in Silicon Valley was almost more like summer—it was in the low eighties, even though it was October—and the store had been filled with people with the same plan as ours. Thankfully, though, the park itself was quiet.

We sat on adjoining swings and started on our cones. I liked to lick all the sprinkles off, giving the ice cream a little time to melt, but Alex just stuck her face right in there and took a big bite. "Oh my god, that hurts my teeth SO BAD!" she yelled, once she'd swallowed.

"At least you didn't get brain freeze," I said, but she was already squeezing her eyes shut. "Did I speak too soon?"

"If we're going to be friends, I mean real friends, you are going to have to teach me patience."

"You think I have patience?"

She pointed to my cone. "You're even patient with your ice cream. Not to mention that you haven't started talking yet and I am dying over here."

"I thought that was just the brain freeze," I said. "Maybe I can teach you patience by waiting a little longer."

She gave me a side-eye glare and I laughed.

"Come on," she said. "It couldn't have been that hard. Not for a member of"—she deepened her voice—"the Brain Trust."

"Hard wasn't the problem," I said. "The face-plant. That was the problem."

"The what now?"

"I totally blacked out. Fainted. In front of everyone."

"You're kidding," she said, and took another giant bite of ice cream, wincing as it hit her teeth. "Tell me everything."

And the funny thing was, I wanted to. Had it really been over a year since someone had been really, truly interested in what was happening to me? At lunch we talked about school, about our futures, but we almost never talked about ourselves. How we felt about things. That was what I'd had with Becca and Isabel, until I'd stopped wanting to tell them what was really going on with me. Or they'd stopped wanting to listen. Either way.

"Well, this wasn't my first panic attack," I told Alex. I didn't want to get into the specifics of the first one, but I told her there were some things that stressed me out and I'd started having these attacks, and then I told her about the PSAT.

"That sounds scary," she said.

"Totally," I agreed. "The thing is, there's only one more SAT before college apps are due, and I just have to nail it. I don't know what I'm going to do." I licked my ice cream, which was about two seconds away from dripping all over me. The perils of patience.

Alex had powered through hers and was now chewing on the last bits of cone. "So is it more about fear or focus?"

"Does it matter? I'm kind of screwed either way."

"Humor me," she said. "I might have some ideas."

I had to think about it. "I don't know. I mean, I think it's more about fear, but this time I got through that first bit, and then it turned into focus. It was like I forgot how to read—I finished the first section, math, but then when I got to reading comp it was like I couldn't see, and then I couldn't breathe, and then I was back to fear."

Alex kicked at some of the gravel under the swing. "So, I don't know if this is something you'd be into, but I kind of had some similar problems last year. It started out more as a focus thing—I was staying up all night playing poker, and I kept falling asleep in class. But then I was having trouble playing because my head just wasn't in it, and it started affecting school. And when it was clear the focus was gone, the fear kicked in—I didn't know if I'd ever get the focus back, and I was scared it was going to ruin everything. It was like this horrible cycle."

"But you got over it? And don't tell me it was like meditation or yoga—I've tried all that already. Total fail."

"No, I'm not into any of that crap. I'm more into better living through chemistry."

"I tried that," I said. "Well, I didn't actually try anything. But I asked my mom about getting some sort of medication. Adderall or Xanax or whatever."

"That's rookie stuff," she said. "I found something better. It's this new thing—it just got FDA approval, so not that many people know about it yet, but it's all over Canada and Europe."

I noticed she hadn't said the word "drug." "What does it do?"

"Everything! It's kind of a miracle. It keeps me focused and steady, but not hyper or jittery, and I know people who've taken it for anxiety who said it makes them totally calm. It's even helping my poker game—it's like I can keep more information in my head all at once without getting distracted."

"What's it called?"

"Novalert. And it's incredible."

It sounded like it. "I guess I can ask Mom about it. I don't think she'll go for it, though. How'd you get your mom to let you take it? Did you just have the right doctor?"

Alex laughed. "Oh, my mom has no idea. They're super antipoker—if she found out I was taking something because I was staying up too late playing, she'd kill me. I got it from some friends. I can hook you up if you want."

I didn't get why Alex's parents were so antipoker if her uncle was a professional, but I was way more interested in Novalert. "Let me think about it," I said. It did sound kind of like a miracle, and I really needed a miracle.

"No problem. But listen, seriously, you won't tell anyone, right? I just want to help."

"Of course not. Who would I tell?"

She started swinging back and forth, kicking her legs higher and higher in the air. "I'm so glad we're hanging out!" she yelled. "Swing with me!"

I hadn't actually swung on a swing set since I was a little kid, but this one seemed sturdy enough. "Sure, why not?" I kicked my legs until it almost felt like swimming, the breeze on my face almost like water. And I felt a whole lot better. For real this time. Alex was right—she was fun, and I was beginning to see how hanging out with her might make me fun too.

* * *

"You didn't call," Mom said, as soon as I opened the front door. "I was worried. Did everything go okay?" She was in the living room, watching TV on the couch, but she muted it once I came in.

"Not even a little bit okay." I flopped down in an armchair. I knew I should have called, probably even from school, but I'd wanted to put off the inevitable as long as possible. "It was awful."

"Awful as in difficult, or awful as in . . ."

"I fainted," I said. "That kind of awful."

"Oh, honey, I'm so sorry," she said. "You should have called me at work. I would have come right away."

"I know. That's why I didn't call."

Mom looked confused. "Why wouldn't you want me there?"

How did she not understand? "It's not that I didn't want you there. I didn't want me there. It was so humiliating. I can't do this."

"Of course you can," she said. "You can do anything you—"

"—set your mind to. I know. You've always said that. And that eating organic food would help with the anxiety. Or meditating. Or whatever. I don't buy it anymore. I can't do this. I need help."

Mom's mouth tightened. "What kind of help are we talking about?"

I knew that look. This wasn't going to go well. "Forget it."

"No, tell me. Do you want to talk to someone? I'm sure we can find you a good therapist."

"Talking won't do anything," I said. "It's not enough. And I've talked to people already. I've talked to you, I've talked to Ms. Davenport, I've even talked to—" I was about to say Alex, but I didn't want her to ask me the details of that conversation.

"Honey, I know what you want me to say. But your issues are mental, not medical. And you don't want to get dependent on something that could affect your brain chemistry. You're too smart for that."

"Dad tried medication," I reminded her.

"And he reacted terribly to it," she reminded me in return. "I don't want to see you go through that. I'll try anything else you want. Just not that."

"I don't get it. The whole point of medication is to help people like me."

"Not people like you," she said. "People who really need it. You're trivializing a very serious issue here."

"How do you know I don't really need it? Why are you so sure?"

"Because you're just like your father," she said. "You get anxious about some things, but you can work through them. Without drugs. I know you can."

I couldn't believe she was being so stubborn. Just because

Dad and I were similar didn't mean we had to handle everything the same way. Mom wasn't a doctor; who was she to say that therapy was better than medication? And even if she was right, there was no way a therapist could fix me in time for the next test. I was running out of time. I felt the nausea starting as I contemplated trying to get through yet another SAT without doing anything differently. "I don't know how you can be so sure about everything," I said, trying not to raise my voice. "I can't believe you're willing to risk my whole future on your opinion. You know how important the SAT is. This is the second time I've tried to take one of these tests and haven't even made it through the whole thing. I've done everything you suggested, and it's only getting worse. I have to try something."

"I'll do some research," she said. "I'll look at other alternative stress relief techniques. We'll try a different diet. We'll get you a therapist. There are lots of things we can still look at. And if the therapist thinks you need medication, then maybe we can get you a referral to a psychiatrist."

"There's no time for that," I said. The anxiety was subsiding, but I felt deflated. "Forget it." I didn't have the energy to fight with her anymore. She wasn't going to change her mind.

But maybe I would change mine.

7.

I'd been worried about going to school after the whole SAT debacle, nervous about what people might say, whether I'd hear whispers as I walked down the hall about how Perfect Kara wasn't so perfect after all, but I guess people had better things to do. If they were making fun of me, they were doing a good job of keeping it behind my back.

Which left me time to think about Novalert. I couldn't get it out of my head—I was completely out of ideas about how to handle my final shot at the SATs, and though I hadn't bought in to Mom's whole fear of drugs, I was still nervous. I peppered Alex with questions during our study sessions at her house: Were there side effects? Did people get addicted? How expensive was it, exactly?

"You're really making me work on this patience thing," she said, but she answered every question I had, and everything she told me worked toward convincing me that trying it might be a good idea. The only idea. "You know that the more nervous and freaked out you seem about all this, the more it seems like you should try it, right?"

I saw her point. Sort of.

Still, I was having trouble making a decision. It was one thing to get a prescription from a doctor, an expert who'd decided something was really wrong, but it was a whole other thing to make that decision for myself, and to do something illegal. I'd never done anything like that before; when Isabel had gone through her stealing-lipstick-from-Walgreen's phase, I'd refused to even go into the store with her, let alone participate. I didn't get a rush from that kind of rebellion; I really was kind of a goody-goody, even if I didn't want to admit it.

I admitted it to Alex, though. "Okay, so that's not your idea of fun," she said. "What is?"

"What do you mean?"

"Some people get off on doing the bad stuff—I think I'd still love poker even if it weren't a little off the morality scale, but I do get a kick out of having a secret. Lots of people do."

"I don't have any secrets," I said, but I had to look at my econ textbook while I said it. I hated lying, even though I basically did it every day.

"Everyone has secrets," she said. "I'm not asking you to tell me yours; I'm just trying to figure out what makes you tick. Let me show you something." She got up from her desk and walked to the other side of her bedroom. "Come on."

I followed her over, where, like at Becca's, there was an enormous closet next to a tiny bathroom. Alex opened the door and turned on the light, and I was shocked to see rows of shirts and pants and skirts and dresses, organized by color. "I'm so confused," I said as she flipped through the clothes, pulling things out to show me. "Did you rob Forever 21 or something? Where do you even wear this stuff?" Then I looked closer and saw some of the labels. This wasn't junk from the mall; all the clothes were designer. I ran my hands over one of the rows, stopping on a satin bandage dress in varying shades of silver, a crinkly black jumpsuit that felt soft as I rubbed it between my fingers, a minidress with a bright pattern that seemed to be made out of the same material as scuba gear. I couldn't picture Alex in any of them.

"The beauty of the internet," Alex said, holding a sequined sheath up to her body. "And I wear this stuff to parties, when I feel like it."

The only parties I'd ever heard about were keggers in people's backyards, and these outfits would be way out of place there. "It seems a little . . . fancy," I said.

"When I go out, I like to do it up right. It's kind of fun to dress up every once in a while. It's kind of like I play a boy online when I play poker, and I play a girl at night when I go out."

"And what are you during the day?"

"I'm just me," she said. "And besides, who cares what we look like at school? School isn't where the fun happens."

"That much I know." I was saving up my fun for college, where there would be more people like me, where it wasn't nerdy to care about school, where boys weren't the most important thing. Though they'd be important.

"You still haven't told me what you do for fun, and I'm getting the feeling that that's because either you're not having any, or else whatever you think is fun is not even a little bit fun."

"That's not fair," I said. "I like to do logic puzzles. They're fun."

"Logic puzzles? Like extra homework?"

"No, they're like games." I explained about the graphs and the clues and how they were basically like figuring out mysteries.

"You're proving my point," Alex said, pulling more dresses out of the closet, shaking her head, and throwing them on her bed. "You need to be around other people. And not at school. And not just me." She picked out a dress and held it up against me and frowned. "You're just too tall. Or I'm too short."

"What are you talking about?"

"There's a party this weekend," she said. "My friends have kind of an underground thing once a month, and we're going. It's what all the fancy clothes are for."

"Oh, I don't know." I remembered the last time I'd gone

to a party. It hadn't ended well.

"It's the best idea! You need to blow off some steam. Maybe that's why you're so stressed out—you don't have an outlet."

"That's not the problem," I said.

"Then what is?"

I didn't really have an answer to that. "I just . . . Being in situations like that makes me anxious."

"Then the party is the answer," she said. "Here's what we'll do. I'm going to give you a Novalert to try, just to relax you. If it works, the friend I get it from will be at the party, and I'll make sure he has more for you."

I wasn't so sure that was a good idea.

"Don't give me that look," Alex said. "You know I'm right. We'll have so much fun getting ready—I'll find something that fits you so we can get all dressed up, and you can help me with my makeup, since you're obviously way better at it than I am."

I'd never seen Alex wear makeup. Her skin was perfect; giving her a makeover would be kind of fun. Like painting on a totally clean canvas. "You really think I should try this?"

"It worked for me. Loosened me up, too. Much easier to flirt when you're not worried about whether it'll work."

"That might be going a little too far."

"We'll see," she said. "So, are you in?"

Maybe Alex was right. Maybe I did need to relax. Besides,

I'd already fainted in front of a bunch of people, so whatever happened at this party couldn't be any worse than that. And it was all in service of the most important thing, which was the SAT. If I didn't fix that problem, then I might as well trash any hope I ever had of getting into a good school and having a real future. When I thought about it like that, I knew I had no choice. I'd try anything.

"I'm in," I said.

The night of the party I told Mom I was staying over at Alex's, and I packed up a train case of makeup to take with me. I'd done the basic SCAM so she wouldn't see what my blank canvas looked like, but I saved the rest of it to do at her house, once we'd decided what I would wear. It would have been easier just to pick something out of my own closet, but I didn't have anything like Alex's Closet of Wonders, and she'd made it clear that this party was going to be capital-F Fancy.

Alex had already started decimating her closet by the time I got to her house. Her bed was covered with dresses in nearly every color. "I have to find the perfect thing," she said.

"For you or for me?"

"Both!" She picked up two dresses and held them out at her sides. "Me first. What do you think?"

One was a black cocktail dress, simple and beautifully cut. The other looked like a flapper dress from the twenties, short and spangly and adorable. "What are you going for?"

"Well, the plan was to be wingwoman for you. But I've got my eye on someone there too."

"Who?"

"Let's just call him the Prospect," she said. "I like to have nicknames when I'm on a mission."

"Gotcha," I said. "Okay, the black one isn't sexy enough. The other one's cute, but it's so short I think you'll be pulling on it constantly, which is probably not what you want."

"You're so practical," she said, but she sounded impressed. "I hadn't even thought of that."

"Do you mind if I—" I nodded at the dress pile on the bed. She gave me the okay and I started sorting through the mess, luxuriating in the fabrics: the soft-but-bristly feel of suede, the near-liquid sensation of running my hands through a dress made almost entirely out of fringe. I kind of wanted to just jump in the pile and roll around in it, everything felt so good. Finally I saw a silky red slip dress. It was short, but not as short as the flapper dress, and it had thin straps and a little swirl in the skirt. "What about this one?"

Alex squealed her approval. "Oh, I forgot about that one!"

Given how many dresses were on the bed, I could understand how. She shimmied out of her jeans and T-shirt before I had a chance to say I'd happily go into another room. Now that I'd seen her out-of-school wardrobe, I wasn't surprised she was wearing a matching set of black lace lingerie. I, as usual, was wearing faded blue briefs and a bra I'd owned for years that probably needed replacing. Alex slid the dress over her head, and it fell down her body as if it had always wanted to be there. The spaghetti straps emphasized her thin shoulders, the color was flawless against her skin, and the cut of the dress showed just enough cleavage and created the illusion of hips, which she didn't really have.

She slipped on a pair of shockingly high-heeled black shoes with bright red soles—I had no idea how she could walk in them—and twirled around. The skirt flared a bit, but not too much. "Yes?" she asked.

"Hell yes," I said.

"Now you." She kicked off the shoes and started going through the dresses again. "The height thing is going to be a problem. We might be better off with a skirt-shirt combo here—I've got some stretchy skirts that might do it."

"I'm putting myself in your hands," I said.

"I know! Isn't it exciting?" She grabbed a black pencil skirt with a slit in the back and threw it at me. "Try this. It's knee-length on me so it will be totally hot on you."

I didn't really want Alex seeing my old underwear, but she was so busy digging through the clothes for a top that I figured she probably wouldn't notice. I pulled off my jeans as fast as I could and put on the skirt. It was tight, but the material had some stretch so it fit okay, and she was right about the length—it hit me just below midthigh.

Before I could even look in the mirror she'd tossed me a black camisole and a sheer silvery sweater. The camisole was Lycra, skintight and low-cut, and made it look like I actually had boobs, which was inaccurate, and the sweater was lightweight and kind of slinky and amazing.

Alex looked me up and down. It reminded me of Isabel, but without the judgment. "Yup. Go look."

There was a full-length mirror hanging on the bathroom door. Alex had a good eye—the silver of the sweater made my gray eyes look almost silver too, an effect I could emphasize with good shadow, and the skirt made my legs seem super long. Except I was barefoot. "I didn't bring the right shoes," I said.

"Not a problem. Go in the closet and pick something. We're about the same size, aren't we?"

I wouldn't have thought so, given the height difference, but she was right—if anything, her feet were a little bigger, so I rolled up some Kleenex in the toes of a pair of metallic platforms and practiced walking around. "You won't let me fall over, right?"

"I've got you," she said. "Nothing to worry about. Your turn now—make me gorgeous." She pointed to the train case.

I'd never actually put makeup on another person before, but I figured it was just like putting it on myself, only mirrored. That turned out to be wrong—I knew how to keep my eyes still when putting on liner, for example, but with Alex

I had to get more aggressive, using my thumb to hold her lid flat. I gave her a modified cat eye that emphasized the fabulous shape of her eyes. "Open," I said, and checked my work, just like in calculus.

Perfect.

"Can I see?"

"Not yet. Close again."

"You're so bossy," she said with admiration.

White liner on the bottom to make her eyes pop, gold powder in the corners for emphasis, several layers of mascara for her almost-nonexistent lashes, and the finishing touch: red lip stain, covered with gloss.

"All done?"

"All done. Stand up." I stepped back to look at the full picture.

Nailed it. If I didn't get into Harvard, maybe I could get a job at a MAC counter.

"You're smiling! Show me!"

"Go look," I said. "But in the full-length, with the shoes—it's about the overall effect."

She put on her heels and tottered over to the mirror. For a second I thought she was going to be mad at me; she pursed her lips and turned her head from side to side, as if she wasn't sure what to think. Then she twirled around again and held her hands out as her skirt flared. "Dude, you're a genius."

"The Prospect will be powerless to resist you," I said.

"Eh, if not him then someone else."

I loved how casual she was about it—she was totally having fun. So different from the obsessive crushes Becca and I used to get, which, when I thought about it, weren't really fun at all. "Let me do mine real quick." I went back over to the train case, put on a whole lot more makeup than I usually did, and brushed out my hair.

"You need to show off your face more," Alex said. "Here, let me try something. Sit down."

I sat on the edge of the bed and she sat behind me, her hands moving through my hair and pulling at my scalp. I felt so exposed, my face open to the air; it reminded me of back when my hair was always in a ponytail or a bun, and I'd feel the breeze on my cheeks when I went outside. "Check it out," she said.

My turn to look. Alex gave me a hand mirror so I could see the back of my head in the full-length. She'd given me a fancy French braid, one that started on the right side of my head but then moved diagonally down my scalp until the tail of it sat on my left shoulder. It was loose and a little sexy and I loved it.

But that meant we were both ready, which meant we would be leaving soon. My stomach churned, the headache started, and my pulse started to speed up. I'd been kidding myself that this would be okay. So many things could go wrong, things I couldn't predict, things I couldn't control.

"What is it? You don't like it?"

"It's great," I said. "I just need to sit down for a minute."

"Oh, right," she said. "It's time." She opened a drawer in her nightstand and pulled out a little baggie with a few mint-green pills in it. "Here's the thing: it's all going to be fine. I know you're nervous, but think of it like a costume party. We're just playing dress-up, and it's all to help you with the test. It's going to be okay."

"I guess," I said, but my head was still hurting.

"I promise," she said, and handed me a pill. "You need water?"

"No, I'm good." Was I really going to do this? Had I thought about all the pros and cons, the things that could go wrong? Maybe I hadn't covered all of them, but I'd thought about them a lot. I always did. And where had that gotten me?

"Bottoms up," she said, and swallowed hers.

I had nothing to lose. Nothing I cared about, anyway. I put the pill in my mouth and swallowed mine too.

8.

The party was at the house of some guy whose dad was apparently employee number three at Twitter or something like that. Which meant they were loaded, even by Marbella standards. Usually when someone hit it that big, they moved to Atherton or Los Altos, but they'd decided to stay here, and had bought a bunch of land to build this ridiculous house, according to Alex. And "ridiculous" was definitely the right word. I'd never seen anything like it.

I pulled my car into a circular brick-paved driveway that was already filling up. Lots of little red Priuses like mine, along with some BMWs and Audi convertibles. The driveway was big enough that at least twenty-five cars could fit in it. But it was dwarfed by the size of the house itself, which stretched around the driveway and beyond, almost like it was wrapping the brick circle in an embrace.

Alex and I got out of the car and started the long walk

toward the front door. She was surprisingly confident in those heels; I could see she'd had a lot of practice. "This is not what I expected," I whispered.

"No need to whisper," she said. "We're not at a museum."

Maybe it was the sculptures lining the edges of the driveway that had made me feel like we were. Each was a carving of an animal, but not real ones—I recognized a gryphon and some other mythological-looking things. A pegasus? They fit the theme; the house had a sort of Grecian feel to it, with white columns lining the front. And it was quiet outside, quieter than I'd expected, given that we were going to a high school house party.

"Where's the music?" I asked.

"Just wait," Alex said. "All will be revealed in time. How are you feeling?"

"Fine so far," I said. But that itself was noticeable—the nausea was gone, as was the headache and the racing pulse. I didn't feel particularly good or anything like that; I just felt okay. Which, under the circumstances, was pretty terrific.

We walked between two of the white columns to the front door, which was unlocked. It was like entering a movie set, only for a movie I could never have imagined. The foyer was an expanse of white and silver: white walls with silver-framed paintings, white marble floors swirled with sparkling silver, an enormous white curved staircase with silver railings. It was huge, and it was empty.

"Are we in the right place?"

Alex nodded and led me through the foyer, past a statue of Pan, then off to the right, through a green dining room with a table that could have seated at least twenty people, decorated in green and gold. It was a warm contrast to the cool of the foyer, but I still didn't see anyone, though apparently people were treating it like a coatroom—there were purses and scarves and jackets everywhere.

"This way." Alex had clearly been here before; her heels clicked on the hardwood floor of the dining room, softening only when she reached a library, walls covered in books, floor covered in the biggest and most beautiful Persian rug I'd ever seen. In the back of the room was a glass door that led outside.

That's where everyone was.

The backyard was an expanse of perfectly manicured lawn, covered only in part by a stone patio where a string trio was playing. Waiters in tuxedos carried glasses of champagne and trays of canapés around to girls in sparkly cocktail dresses and guys in suits. I didn't immediately recognize anyone because they all looked so different from how they did at school, but after a while my brain started making the necessary connections. I saw a girl from my AP English class picking over hors d'oeuvres, a guy from the water polo team joking around with one of the girls who played lacrosse. The information settled in with almost a palpable click, and it was satisfying to put the pieces together. It was the same feeling

I got when I checked my work in calculus, or when I figured out the clue in a logic puzzle that opened up the whole thing. It was one of my favorite feelings in the world.

A middle-aged waiter came by and offered us champagne. Alex took a glass like she was used to people bringing her drinks at fancy parties, but I wasn't so sure that mixing booze and Novalert was a good idea, at least not for my first time. "Do you have anything nonalcoholic?" I asked, feeling my face get hot. The waiter gave me a silent nod and walked off, returning faster than I could have imagined with what looked like champagne again. Was I mistaking him for another waiter? "But I—"

"Ginger ale," he said, smiling. "I know how much you kids hate to stand out in a crowd."

I thanked him and took a sip, grateful that he understood this party better than I did. "This is so weird," I said to Alex, who'd already finished her drink and had snagged another. "But I think the Novalert kicked in."

"Yeah? What do you think?"

"So far so good," I said.

"Well, then, it's time to get in there." She grabbed my hand and pulled me off the patio onto the grass, where most of the kids were hanging out in small groups, talking. She stopped by a group of three guys who were standing near a statue of what appeared to be a Greek god. What was with this house and all the statues, anyway? I recognized two of the three guys—neither was in my classes, so I wasn't sure where I'd seen them before—but the third looked totally unfamiliar to me. The first thing I noticed about him was his eyes, which were super dark, almost black, the same color as his hair. The second thing I noticed was that I had to look up to see them, which was surprising given how high my shoes were. The third thing I noticed was that he was *hot*. I hadn't thought that about anyone for a really long time.

"You made it!" the cute guy said, and gave Alex a hug. My heart sank a little. He was probably the Prospect. "And you brought a friend, I see. Nice." He had an English accent, which was pretty much the sexiest thing I'd ever heard. Alex had good taste.

"Hey, Raj, this is Kara, who I was telling you about." She gave me a look, and I wondered what she'd been saying. "Kara, this is Raj, and Justin and Bryan."

Justin and Bryan were both cute—Justin was about my height, blond and wearing a very well-fitted shiny blue suit, and Bryan was short and dark and kind of uncomfortable in his suit, but in a charming way. Alex hung out with a good-looking crowd.

"That dress . . . ," Bryan said.

"Too much?" Alex did her little twirl again.

"Not at all," Raj said. "Just the right amount, actually."

Alex didn't react to Raj's compliment, though; she was

still waiting for Bryan. Perhaps I'd been wrong about who the Prospect was.

"Just tell her she looks good," Justin said. "It's not that hard. I'll show you." He turned to Alex and gave a little bow. "You look ravishing tonight, my dear." He held out a hand, and Alex spun into him as if they were dancing, and then he dipped her just a little. It was a cute bit—it kind of reminded me of Alex and her dad.

"I feel like I should applaud," Bryan said.

"No need," Alex said. "You can just go refill my drink." She handed him her champagne glass and watched him walk off.

"So you'll be lavishing your charms on Bryan tonight, then?" Raj asked. "Poor fellow. He won't know what hit him."

"I'm mostly here for Kara," Alex said. "Consider this her social debut."

"Well, it was lovely to meet you, Kara," Justin said. "Sorry to rush off, but I'd been planning to send Bryan to get me a drink before Alex so rudely coopted him for her own nefarious purposes."

Nefarious purposes? Who talked like that?

"You're leaving already?" Alex asked, but Justin was already gone. "He's such a performer."

Performer . . . that's why he looked familiar. He was one of the theater kids. Even though Isabel and I weren't friends anymore, I never missed a show—she'd gotten the lead every time since we'd started high school, just like she wanted, and she was fabulous. I looked around and sure enough, there she was, telling a story to a fawning group of theater kids. Always the center of attention. It had been helpful when we were friends; Becca and I could go out with her and be shy if we wanted to, secure in the knowledge that eventually we'd be surrounded by people no matter what. And she liked playing that role, liked being the one to find out who was interesting and introduce us to them. Maybe that's why I hadn't really known how to make friends myself, once she and Becca were gone.

I wasn't going to let her presence here bother me, though. I was here to hang out with Alex, to test my ability to make it through a social situation without disaster striking. So far so good.

"So, Kara," Raj said. "How is it that we've never met? Where has Alex been hiding you?"

"We just started hanging out," I said. "I wasn't hiding."

"Don't be such a flirt, Raj," Alex said. "We don't want to scare her off."

"I'm not a rabbit," I said. "I don't get skittish at the sight of sudden movement."

Raj laughed. "So I should keep flirting, then? Will it do me any good?"

"You're pushing it," Alex said. "Go make yourself useful and refill her—what are you drinking, anyway?"

"Ginger ale," I said.

"A sensible choice," Raj said. "I'll be back soon."

Alex turned to me. "Sorry, they can be kind of a lot, and Raj hits on anything that moves. But they're my friends, so I really wanted you to meet them. How are you holding up? Are you having fun?"

I was, actually, and I told her. I might have been a little disappointed that Raj was an equal-opportunity flirt, but it wasn't like I was really into meeting guys anyway, so it wasn't a big deal. Or so I told myself. The truth was that Raj was the first guy who'd sparked my attention in a long time, and that was kind of a scary thought. Was it just that he was the first cute guy to talk to me in forever? Maybe I just needed to meet more people in general. That's probably what Alex would say.

"Novalert still working?" she asked.

"I think so. I'm definitely not freaking out."

"Want it for the test? We can take care of it tonight if you've got money on you. It's sometimes hard to get, so if you want it, I'd get it now."

"Might as well," I said. I could always change my mind later. Better to get this part over with.

"Excellent. I'll make it happen. Look, the boys are on their way back. You okay if I leave you on your own for a bit? The Prospect awaits, and you seem to be doing all right so far."

"No problem." This would be a good way to test how well the Novalert was doing. But I could fend for myself. I was sure of it. Which was totally not how I'd been feeling earlier—maybe that was the first sign that it was actually working.

Bryan and Raj came back together, each holding two drinks. Alex took one from each of them and handed me the one she'd taken from Raj. "How do you know that's the right one?" I asked.

"Alex knows I don't really drink," Raj said.

"I know lots of things about you," Alex said. She reached up and pulled on his collar, bending him down so she could whisper in his ear.

"Gotcha," he said.

Alex turned around and started walking around the other side of the house, giving Bryan a little nod that he seemed to understand meant "Follow me." She was so good.

"It appears Alex and Bryan have gone off to do some exploring," Raj said. "How about I show you the rest of the party?" He touched my arm and guided me back to the house, chatting all the way. "I only moved here last year, so it actually makes sense we wouldn't have met."

"Where did you move from? Your accent sounds British."

"Got it in one," he said, as we crossed back through the foyer. I finally figured out the Pan statue—the half man, half beast linked the animal sculptures in front with the statues of gods and goddesses in the back. "I grew up in England, though my parents assure me I was born in India. We moved well before I was old enough to remember it."

"How do you like it here?" I wished I could come up with more interesting things to ask him. But it turned out not to matter, because once Raj led me around the enormous staircase and opened the door hidden behind it, I heard music so loud we'd have had to scream at each other to continue our conversation.

The music got louder and louder as we walked down the stairs, bass thumping so hard that I could almost feel my heartbeat aligning with it. When we reached the bottom, I saw that the house's lower level had been converted into a club. There was a long bar, complete with a bartender and a backlit wall of clear and colorful bottles of liquor; there was a booth for a DJ, where a girl with multicolored dreadlocks and a full-arm sleeve of tattoos was presiding over a computer and a bunch of electronic equipment I didn't recognize; there were strobe lights and smoke piping out of machines in the corners of the room; and of course, there was a dance floor. Packed.

"This is really someone's house?" I asked Raj, though I knew the answer.

"What?" he yelled.

"Forget it!" I yelled back, at three times the volume. "This is crazy!"

"It's fantastic! Let's dance."

I shook my head. I didn't even dance alone, in front of the mirror. "You go ahead."

"Just for one song," he said. "No one's paying attention, I swear. They're all out of their tree."

I looked at the dance floor, at the throng of improbably elegantly dressed teenagers throwing themselves around as if they really were at a club. Total abandon. I definitely wasn't the only one at this party who was on something.

"Come on, one song. Then we can chat." He looked at me with this little smile, like I was the only person in the crowded room. Maybe he was just a flirt, but he was really good at it.

One song wouldn't kill me.

Raj led me out onto the dance floor. Something about the touch of his hand made me feel secure, protected, and I liked it. The music throbbed as we started to dance. Raj really knew how to move, unlike most of the other people on the dance floor, myself included. His limbs seemed almost elastic; I wondered if he was high too, even though Alex had said he didn't drink. Just because he didn't drink didn't mean he wouldn't do other things. He was such an amazing dancer that I was okay with my own stuttering moves. He was right that no one was paying attention to me, but not for the reasons he'd said. It was almost like everyone else stopped to watch him, though they made halfhearted attempts to move back and forth as if to keep him from noticing.

One song melded into another, and then another, but that was okay; I was happy just to watch Raj in his element. His eyes were closed half the time, but he was always completely in sync with the music, as if he didn't have to think about it, he was so totally in charge of his own body. I had the vaguest memory of feeling like that, when I was in the water, but the closest I could come now was on the treadmill, when I could forget that my body was moving and hurting and I lost myself in the music, safe in the knowledge that I was in my own house and no one could see me. For a few miles I'd be free, like Raj was now.

As I danced, I closed my eyes and tried to get somewhere close to where he was, but I couldn't do it. It was almost like the Novalert kept me from daydreaming, kept me focused on what I was doing, even if I didn't necessarily want to be. That boded well for the SATs, but despite the respite it gave me from my anxiety, it wasn't helping me with the dancing at all.

Finally, Raj snapped out of his trance. "That was probably more than one song," he yelled. "Shall we go somewhere else?"

I wasn't sure if this was just more of his flirting, but it was entertaining. I'd be able to put him off if he tried something. Assuming I wanted to. He placed his hand on the small of my back to lead me off the dance floor, into a corner of the room that was far enough away to be just a little quieter, behind one of the smoke machines. I realized my heart was still pounding along with the music.

"This should do it," he said.

I wasn't sure how private it was, but at least there was smoke to shield us from view, broken up only occasionally by a strobe light, which flashed and broke the smoke into bits of sparkling dust that I could almost reach out and touch.

"So . . . ," Raj said, and leaned in toward me.

I wasn't sure what to do. Did I really want this? It was one thing to try to get into the social scene; it was another to make out with the first guy who was nice to me.

He leaned in a little closer. "So . . ."

I waited. If I didn't do anything, he could make the decision for both of us.

And then he said it.

"Did you bring the money?"

9.

How could I be so stupid? Of course that's what this was about. Just because Raj was a big flirt didn't mean he wanted to have some random makeout session at a party. Thank god for the Novalert, which was keeping my humiliation in check. That, and the relative dark.

"The money . . . ," I said. "I've got some, but Alex didn't say how much."

"It's not cheap," he said. "Twenty bucks a pill, so a thirty-day supply is six hundred. But Alex said you just wanted a couple, right? One for the SAT, plus a backup, just in case?"

Alex had gotten pretty chatty with Raj about this, given that I hadn't even decided to buy the pills before the party. "Right," I said, looking around.

"Don't worry, we're good here," he said. He reached into his pocket for a tiny plastic bag with a Ziploc closure. There were two glossy mint-green pills in it, like the one Alex had given me before the party. "You know how they work? Alex told you everything you need to know?"

I nodded, not mentioning that she'd given me one to test-drive tonight. I reached into my tiny purse and dug around, pulling out two crumpled twenties.

"That will do it," he said, handing me the pills. I put them in my bag as fast as I could. Raj might have been sure no one could see us, but I wasn't. I tried to wrap my brain around the fact that he was a drug dealer. He didn't sound like one; he sounded like some sort of British lord. But he also sounded like a friend who was trying to help me. Though wasn't that how drug dealers got you hooked?

"Got it," I said, my voice clipped. "Thanks." Whatever tone I'd used before, when I'd misread the situation, I had to get rid of. This was a business transaction.

Raj gave me a strange look, one I couldn't read. He'd heard something in my voice, though I wasn't sure it was what I'd meant for him to hear. "Do you have your phone with you?"

It was pretty much the only other thing I had, besides my license and keys. I took it out of my purse and held it up.

"Nice case," he said.

"It's practical." My phone was sheathed in a case that looked like a pastel rainbow of Legos. It was cute, but it was also indestructible, and I had a tendency to drop my phone a lot.

"Now type in my number and call me. That way you can

reach me anytime, and I'll know it's you." He read off the digits before I had a chance to ask why I'd need to get in touch with him. "Just in case you have questions. Or need more. Or if you just want to say hi."

I was losing the ability to tell the difference between him flirting and him trying to sell me something. Either way, he was smiling. And he had a really great smile. I needed to put that thought out of my head quick. "I won't need more," I said, sharply. "This is a one-time thing."

"I understand," he said. "Then you can just call to chat."

That was definitely flirting. I wondered if it was calculated. "Sure," I said, though I had no intention of ever calling him.

"I'm going to get back out there." He pointed to the dance floor. "Coming?"

"No, I'm good," I said. "I'll go find Alex."

"Good luck with that," he said.

I left behind his liquid movements and elastic limbs and went back outside, hoping that maybe Alex and Bryan had done whatever it was she'd decided they were going to do and that she'd be ready to go home. No such luck. I got out my phone to text her but my feet were killing me—how did anyone stay in heels for this long, even platforms? I found a bench next to one of the statues, sat down, and took my shoes off. Stretching out my toes felt incredible.

Outside, I wrote. **Ready to go whenever you are**

I waited a minute to see if she'd write back right away, but she didn't. Good for her—I loved that she was so in charge of what she wanted to happen. She had a plan and she'd executed it perfectly. I had my Novalert, and she had her Prospect. For her, I bet this was the best night ever.

For me? Well, I'd made it this far without completely flipping out, which was progress and which let me feel better about the upcoming SAT. I'd met some cute guys, even if I was a terrible judge of character, and I kind of liked getting all dressed up, even if I was wearing Alex's clothes. For the last couple of hours, I'd barely thought about my skin at all, which was rare. Maybe this wasn't my best night ever, but it was still pretty good.

And, as usual, the person I wanted to talk to about it was Becca.

Despite the fact that I'd bailed on cutting my hair with her, high school had started out okay. Becca, Isabel, and I were all in different classes, but we knew that was coming—they'd both focused on their extracurricular activities over academics even in middle school, but my parents would never have gone for that. Isabel joined the drama club pretty much the minute we showed up, but at first she still sat with Becca and me in the cafeteria at lunch, and we talked about the new people we were meeting and our teachers and how much fun we were going to have.

But everything changed when swim tryouts were announced. Becca kept talking about how excited she was, kept asking me to go practice with her, but I made every excuse I could think of. I faked a cold for weeks, complained about cramps, begged off to study.

"You know the team here is really good," she warned me. "I'm not sure that killer freestyle is enough. We really have to get some practice in."

"I will," I said. I knew I should just tell her, but I couldn't stand the thought of how disappointed she'd be. I really hated disappointing people. I hated being Perfect Kara, and yet I was terrified of people discovering my actual imperfections. Something would have to give eventually. And though it was inevitable that the first thing to go would be the swim team, I kept putting off telling Becca.

The day of tryouts I knew I couldn't go to school. I couldn't face Becca. So I stayed in my room after my alarm went off and waited for Mom to come pry me out of bed.

"Why aren't you up yet, honey?" she asked. "You know you're going to be late."

"I'm sick," I told her, with a fake crack in my voice. I'd debated whether to fake it with some proof—putting hot water on the thermometer, or making retching sounds in the bathroom—but I'd never pretended to be sick before, and I was counting on Mom trusting me. Which made me feel terrible, but which also made me sounding sick way more convincing.

"Will you be all right at home by yourself? I've got a lot of meetings today."

"I'll be fine," I said.

She came over to the bed and kissed my forehead. "You don't feel warm."

I got nervous for a minute. "But I feel awful. I just need to sleep."

"Okay," she said. "I'll bring home chicken soup from the deli tonight."

"Thanks." And with that, I was free. I had the whole day to think about what a horrible person I was, and to debate what to do next. Should I text Becca and tell her I wasn't coming, wish her good luck? Then it might distract her, throw her off during tryouts. Better to wait and hope she would call when they were over.

I watched the clock all day, imagining Becca powering her way through the water, beating everyone in her heat. She was a fantastic swimmer; there was no way she wouldn't make it. Maybe she'd be too excited to be angry with me. The clock chimed three o'clock, then four. I didn't know how long tryouts would last, so I kept checking my phone, waiting for a call or text.

By the time five o'clock rolled around, I knew it was over,

but I hadn't heard a word. Not from Becca, or from Isabel, who'd planned to go by the pool after rehearsal. Why hadn't they gotten in touch? Had something bad happened? Finally, I decided to send a text myself.

Home sick. Sorry I wasn't there. I'm sure you killed it!

I didn't know if I'd hit the right tone, but I had a feeling anything I said would be wrong. And I had no idea what would happen if Becca wrote back that she hadn't made it. She'd never forgive me for not being there then.

I waited all night for her to write back, or for Isabel to check in, through the chicken soup and Mom's insistence that I go to bed early, lying in bed with my phone next to me, switching it to silent mode after my parents went to sleep. Sleep wasn't happening for me, though; with every minute that passed without a text or a call, I sensed my friends moving further and further away from me.

I went to school the next day exhausted, practically sleepwalking through my early classes to get to the cafeteria. Isabel was in our usual spot, but Becca wasn't. "She's sitting with her new teammates," Isabel told me. "Swim team tradition, apparently. She made varsity, in case you were wondering. The only freshman who did."

Her voice was calm, but the hostile undertone was impossible to miss. She didn't ask me where I'd been, and I didn't volunteer it. "I'm not surprised," I said. "She's an incredible swimmer."

"Just figured I'd let you know," she said. "I've got to go run some lines with the theater kids. Didn't want you to think we'd abandoned you." She didn't say "like you abandoned us," but I heard it, loud and clear.

"I'll be fine," I said, though she hadn't asked.

Isabel walked away without turning around, and I sat there for a minute by myself, wondering if this was the end. I looked around the cafeteria and saw Becca laughing with the swim team girls, though she didn't catch my eye. At a nearby table were some of the kids from my classes, the ones I'd met when I was younger and who I now saw every day. Unlike Becca, they noticed when I looked over at them; Julia waved at me to come sit.

It was better than being alone, I figured. Anything was.

That's what I thought then, anyway. Hanging out with Alex had made me realize that there was a difference between being alone and being lonely. I was alone right now, but I wasn't lonely, and I was okay with it.

I wasn't alone for long, though. I looked down at my phone again to see if Alex had texted; she hadn't, but I looked up to see someone standing in front of me. Justin, the theater friend of Alex's I'd met earlier. "Mind if I sit for a minute?" he asked.

"No problem," I said. "You enjoying the party?"

"Oh, you know, same old thing." He sounded like he meant it.

"Not to me. Is this really normal for you guys?"

"Well, define *normal*," he said. "I just watched a guy in seersucker try to breakdance, but I guess that's normal for this crew. They're going for something; I'm just not sure what."

I wasn't sure either. But I was starting to like Justin. He was as cute as Raj, but not so flirty, and talking to him was comfortable. "Guess I missed that part," I said. "What I saw was fun, though."

"I don't know that you want to get used to this scene," he said. "I know Alex is your friend, but be careful. You seem like a nice person. This group could be dangerous for you."

What was that supposed to mean? Maybe I'd already misjudged Justin, like I'd misjudged Raj. Maybe he wasn't so nice after all.

"Thanks for the warning," I said, and tried to sound like I meant it.

"Happy to be of service." His phone beeped. "Sorry, got to go. My boyfriend's picking me up. I'll see you around."

It wasn't long after Justin left that Alex texted back.

Mission accomplished. Where are you?

Bench outside, in the garden, I wrote back.

After a minute I saw her running around the side of the house, heels in her hands. She flew over to the bench and sat down.

"Where's Bryan?" I asked.

"I sent him off to dance," she said. Her red lip stain was

mostly gone, I noticed, a little bit of it smeared on her cheek.

"Your lipstick has abandoned your lips." I pointed to my cheek to show her where she had a smudge, and she rubbed it off with her thumb.

"Perils of Prospect hunting," she said.

"I take it you had a good time?"

"Super fun. Bryan's adorable. He might actually be kind of into me, though, so we'll need to get out of here pretty soon. Don't want to give him the wrong idea."

I wasn't sure what she meant—wasn't it good for someone you'd just made out with to be into you?—but Alex seemed to know what she was doing.

"How about you? Everything all taken care of?"

"All set." I didn't tell her I hadn't realized Raj was the Novalert guy and had mistaken his casual flirting for something else. Something tempting. It was just too embarrassing.

"Did you have fun with Raj? He likes to come off all slick, but he's really kind of goofy and fun. And totally hot, right?"

"He's cute," I said. "Not my type, though."

"Really? He's not just cute; he's a really good guy, too. What is your type?"

I didn't really know what my type was, but I knew one thing. "My type is definitely not drug dealers, so that's one thing we can cross off the list."

"Oh, I don't think of Raj as a *dealer*," she said. "He just helps out his friends sometimes. No big thing."

"Not to you, maybe. But you know how easy it is for people to get reputations. And rumors can travel. I can't have anything interfering with college stuff. I have to get ready for the SATs and work on college applications. I haven't even started yet. Have you?"

"Early action MIT app is in. I'll hear in January, and I'm hoping that will be the end of it."

"Lucky," I said. "I wanted to go early at Harvard but I needed my scores before then."

"Harvard!" she squealed. "That would be so great! We'd both be in Cambridge and we could hang out all the time. Let's go get some food and strategize. I'm done with this party, and I'm starving."

"Sounds like you worked up your appetite," I teased.

"You have no idea," she said.

10.

I felt a whole lot better about the SAT knowing I had my two little green pills waiting for me. In the weeks before the test there was hardly any anxiety at all; I was too busy trying to keep up with school and hanging out with Alex. It turned out hanging out with her did mean hanging out with her friends sometimes; we didn't go to any more crazy parties, but I started sitting with Alex, Justin, and Raj at lunch, ignoring the dirty looks I got from the Brain Trust. Justin didn't make any more cryptic comments about Alex's crowd being dangerous, but I found myself wary of him anyway. He and Raj were really funny together, though, especially when they tried to outcharm each other. It was hard to believe they'd only known one another for a year; they acted like they'd been friends forever. Once in a while Bryan sat with us too, though he was still clearly a little moony over Alex, who treated him just like the other two.

Raj was pretty flirty, but I was starting to understand that he was like that all the time. It was almost like he wasn't sure how to interact any other way. "It's totally insecurity," Alex told me once. "He has no idea how hot he is, so he feels like he has to try really hard."

I wondered whether it was more that he hadn't had a lot of friends who were girls. In a way, I was glad that he didn't seem to be into me, or at least no more into me than he was anyone else. But a little part of me kind of wished he was, even though I knew he wasn't someone I should like. Still, he was fun to hang out with. They all were. They were more entertaining than the Brain Trust, anyway.

As strange as it seemed, though, I had the most fun studying at Alex's house, which I did at least once a week. It was nice having a real friend again, even if it would never be the same as it was with Isabel and Becca.

"Aren't your parents getting sick of cooking for me?" I asked once. "We could always go to my house. It's take-out central over there these days, though." Now that Mom worked at Dad's company, it was like they didn't see much reason to ever come home.

"Are you kidding? They love you. They're thrilled to see me hanging out with 'such a smart girl.'" She deepened her voice to sound like her dad. "You made quite an impression."

I wasn't sure how; it wasn't like I could get a word in

edgewise when Alex and her dad were putting on their kitchen show. But I was happy to be there. It was easier than being at home—my dad's new company had gotten its financing, but now they were full steam ahead toward the initial public offering, which meant my parents were either at work or talking about work. I wasn't sure which was worse.

First quarter ended in the beginning of November, and second quarter was already flying by. Before I knew it, Thanksgiving had arrived, and with it came our annual trip to visit my grandparents, who'd retired to Palm Springs. Mom always got a little stressed out around her parents—I didn't get it just from my dad, even if that's what she thought—but my parents managed to relax and not talk about work for the day, which was great.

I couldn't stop them from talking about me, though. "Kara is number one in her class," Mom told Grandma.

"For now," I said.

"For good," she said. "You've been working so hard, I can't imagine Julia's going to be able to do better."

"Your mom was number one in her class," Grandma said.

"Believe me, I know."

"There's no reason you can't hold your spot. You're smart and dedicated and eminently capable. You just need to keep doing what you're doing."

"No pressure," I muttered.

"What?" Grandma asked.

But Mom heard me. "I'm not pressuring you, Kara. I just want you to live up to your potential. Besides, I thought you wanted to be valedictorian. I thought that was important to you."

"It is," I said. That was the problem, in a way. "Can we talk about something else? Or can I be excused?"

"Aren't you going to thank your grandmother for dinner?"

"Thanks for dinner, Grandma." I got up and walked around the table to give her a kiss. "Everything was delicious."

"Hey, I was in charge of the turkey," Grandpa said. "Don't I get a little credit?" He held out his cheek and I kissed him too.

"Of course you do. The turkey was perfect, and I'm totally stuffed."

"Kara, you should go for a swim," Dad said. "The pool won't be too crowded today."

"That's the plan," I said. I did love the pool in my grandparents' apartment complex. It was an infinity pool, the kind that didn't look like it had an edge, as if it had emerged organically in the middle of the concrete. The pool here was the only place I felt comfortable swimming these days; my grandparents knew about my skin problem, though I'd never let them see it, and I didn't know anyone here except some friends of theirs I'd met. For just a little while I could go without makeup and immerse myself in the cool water. And one or two days a year of chlorine couldn't make my skin any worse than it already was.

The nice thing about swimming laps, especially when I was so out of practice, was that it kept me from being able to think too much. I had to use all my brainpower to make my limbs do what used to happen more naturally. I practiced butterfly and backstroke before settling into the more comfortable rhythm of freestyle, which came back to me faster than the other strokes.

Once I'd exhausted myself, I went back to the apartment, took a shower, and did a quick SCAM before anyone saw me. Even the idea of strangers seeing me without makeup was horrifying; I imagined I'd be able to see their revulsion, the looks on their faces reflecting just how I felt about myself.

I went into the living room, where Dad and Grandpa were watching football while Mom and Grandma cleaned up in the kitchen. "This is totally gendered behavior," I said, plopping down next to Dad on the couch.

"Not anymore," he said with a smile. "Your presence here subverts the dominant paradigm."

"I don't think that's how it works," I said, laughing. I was glad Dad had come with us; he'd been threatening to stay behind because he had so much to do at the office, but Mom had shut that down pretty fast. She was right, too—he was relaxed here, more so than I'd seen him in a long time. I was, too. Maybe it was the swimming; maybe it was just being away from school, from the constant feeling of pressure I felt every time I walked through the front door of the building. In a way, I dreaded going back.

But I did have to go back. Thanksgiving ended, with not much time left before my last chance at the SAT. As test day got closer and closer, I started getting more and more nervous. What if the pill didn't work? What if the pill worked and I tanked the exam anyway? Sure, I'd done well on the practice tests I'd been taking for over a year, but those were just practice. They weren't the real thing.

"You need to calm down," Alex said.

We were sitting at lunch. I'd convinced Mom to give up on the whole macrobiotic-green-food-whatever-it-was plan but was starting to regret it as I picked at a plate of limp spaghetti. "If I can't pull this off, my life is over," I said.

"God, you're more dramatic than I am," Justin said. "You're being ridiculous. Your life won't be over. Your current plan might get disrupted a little, that's all. A little disruption never killed anyone."

"This would be way more than a little disruption," I said.

"He's right, though," Raj said. "Did you know that British kids often don't even go to university right away? They take a gap year and work, or travel. It gives them time to figure out what they really want."

"Are you going to take one?" I asked.

He put his hand over his heart. "I'm an American now,"

he said. "Or I will be at some point. It would be unpatriotic of me not to conform. But you—you're a native. You can do whatever you like."

"Dare to be different!" Justin said.

"Or not," Alex said. "I know how important this all is to you. Just remember this isn't the only option. And you've studied as hard as you can, and you're doing everything you need to do. You're going to be great. Say it."

"Say it?"

"Say it. If you say it, maybe you'll believe it. You're going to be great."

"I'm going to be great," I said, trying as hard to believe it as I could.

"I'm going to be great," I muttered to myself, over and over, as I got ready for the exam on test day. I didn't really need to mutter; no one was home, since I'd told my parents I'd be less stressed out if they just went to work. That had the added benefit of giving me time to take the Novalert without having to worry about them catching me.

Mom had left a bag of bagels on the counter and a pot of coffee brewing—she must have gotten up super early to make sure everything was ready when I woke up. She'd left a note, too:

Good luck! I'll be thinking of you all day. Call when you're done.

I loved that she'd bought me carbs because she knew I'd want them, even though she was on a gluten-free kick herself. I ate my bagel with some eggs and coffee and then took out my minty-green pill. Such a small thing, but it could make all the difference in the world. This was my last chance to change my mind, to try one more time to make it on my own, but it was hardly even a serious thought. I had no other options.

I popped the pill into my mouth. It had a little bit of a sugary coating, like Advil, and it went down easy. Now I just needed it to kick in. On the drive to school I could feel the first hint of it, the little gears in my brain starting to whir, that feeling of confidence I'd had at the party, that I could do this. This is just a normal day, I reminded myself, as I had last time. It will be over in a few hours. But already things felt different. I felt alert and focused, and, more important, calm. No nausea, no headache, nothing. Of course, that could always come later, but I wasn't worried about it like I had been in the past. It was like the Novalert was my friend, whispering in my ear.

You've got this.

I was in the same room as before, which I already knew; Ms. Davenport was the proctor again, which I also knew. Seeing her at the front of the room was comforting, and in a strange way, so was the familiarity. It was like I was getting a do-over from last time. If today went well, I could pretend the last time had never happened.

Ms. Davenport read the instructions and handed out the test, just like before. I tore open the seal. Once again, the first section was math. But this time all the questions were perfectly clear right away, and the nausea and thumping in my head that signaled the potential for a panic attack never came. I kept coming up with answers that matched one of the options, and I was done with the section even before Ms. Davenport came around to collect it. Just like in calculus.

The other sections went the same way, even reading comp. No panic attack, not even a single symptom of one. And after four hours that went by pretty fast, it was all over. I'd stayed conscious, which was my biggest concern, and it was even possible that I had done well. Every single muscle I had unclenched in what felt like a full-body sigh—Novalert might have helped with the mental stuff and the basic physical symptoms, but my body still knew what all this meant, down to my muscles, and I'd been tensed up the whole time without even realizing it.

I hung around after everyone left and went up to Ms. Davenport. "I made it!" I said, unable to hold back my excitement.

"I know!" she said. "Listen, are you in a rush to get home? I could use a cup of coffee after this, and I'd imagine you could too. I'd love to hear more about how it went."

"Sure." I probably had enough in my system between all the coffee I'd drunk before the test and the Novalert, so I wasn't about to drink more caffeine, but Ms. Davenport didn't need to know that.

"I've got to get all the paperwork done—I'll meet you at Philz in about half an hour." She squeezed my hand. "I'm really proud of you, you know."

"Thanks." I was surprised to feel my eyes welling up, and I turned to go before Ms. Davenport could see. "Philz is perfect."

It was weird how much what Ms. Davenport said meant to me. I knew my parents loved me, and they were probably even proud of me too, but it wasn't the kind of thing they'd say a whole lot. They had such high expectations of me—they never stopped talking about how much they'd loved Stanford and how much I'd love it too, and Stanford was even harder to get into than Harvard, especially for someone from Silicon Valley. Sometimes I thought it would be nice for them to acknowledge that meeting their expectations was really hard work. Ms. Davenport was no substitute for my parents, but it was comforting to know there was a grown-up in my corner.

I got to Philz before her and ordered a gross green tea, thinking of Becca and her matcha. I really wanted hot chocolate, but I didn't want Ms. Davenport to think I was a little kid. When she arrived, she got an enormous mocha with whipped cream, which I eyed with envy. "I'm exhausted!" she said, collapsing into the chair in front of me. "I can only imagine how you kids must feel. How are you holding up?"

"Pretty well, actually. I mean, given what happened last time."

"I'm sure you did great," she said. "Something was definitely different this time. You were more confident, maybe?"

"I've been working really hard." Not like I'd ever tell her what had really changed.

She took a sip of her coffee, leaving a dark-pink lip print on the cup and a dot of whipped cream on her nose. I barely had time to decide whether to tell her when she wiped it off with her napkin. "Ugh, I love these things, but they're such a mess. What did you get?"

"Green tea," I said.

"How very proper of you. That's not very celebratory, though. Hold on." She got up and went back to the counter, then came back with an enormous almond croissant. "Here, we'll split it. You deserve something sweet."

It reminded me of my mom and the bagels. "Thanks," I said, and broke off a piece. I wasn't hungry, but I knew I should eat; I hadn't even taken a break to snack on the nuts I'd brought to the exam for energy.

"So now that you've got this out of the way, are you getting ready to work on your college applications? Have you talked to your parents about what schools you're applying to yet?"

"Not yet. I still don't know if my scores will be good enough. And they're so set on Stanford—I'm worried they'll be mad."

Ms. Davenport sighed. "It's entirely beyond me how you could think your parents would find Harvard inadequate."

"You don't know what they're like. It's like Harvard and Stanford were on opposite sides of the Civil War or something. They're not going to take it well. And it's not just Harvard—it's all those East Coast schools. They want me to stay here, close to home."

"You can always apply to all of them and decide later. I've already drafted your recommendation. It's the best one I've ever written, if I do say so myself."

I wanted to ask her why. I wasn't so special. "I still don't know what I'm supposed to write about in my essay," I said instead.

"Colleges like to hear about how you've overcome adversity," she said. "The story of how you got through these panic attacks to conquer the SAT might be a good one."

If only she knew. "I don't think it would be all that interesting," I said.

"Well, is there anything that comes to mind? Any struggles you've had with friends or family? You can tell me anything—I'll keep it between us."

Of course there was something that came to mind right away: the monster. But I'd never talked to anyone about it but family. I trusted Ms. Davenport, though, and maybe she would understand. She wore lots of makeup herself, bright lipstick and dramatically penciled-in eyebrows. Maybe she needed it, like I did.

"I've got this skin problem," I said, and then the words came out faster than I could contain them. I told her about that first zit, when I should have told my friends but didn't, and how much worse it had gotten, until telling anyone seemed impossible, and all the ways it had kept me from being honest with my friends, until I had no friends left. "I don't think I could write about it, though. If anyone found out, I think I would die."

"You wouldn't," she said. "And you'd be surprised how many people are keeping their own secrets, secrets they think are the worst thing in the world but wouldn't necessarily matter if they belonged to someone else. But it's up to you to decide how to handle this. I don't know that it's a good topic for you quite yet, though—I think you still have a lot to work out first."

"Any suggestions?"

"Anything I'd say would sound like a cliché to you. But honesty tends to be the best strategy. You have more control over the story that way."

I had a feeling she'd say that. "I'm not ready for that."

"Not yet," she said. "But maybe someday you will be. Telling me was a start."

"I guess," I said. It didn't really feel like one, though. I'd thought that maybe saying it out loud would be a relief, the first step to being more open with everyone, and not just about my face. But while it did feel good to tell Ms. Davenport, all I realized was that I viewed her in the same way I viewed my family—I could trust her, and she'd never tell anyone, but my secret wasn't any less secret for her knowing it. She was right about me having a lot to work out, that was for sure.

We went back to talking some more about what colleges I was planning on applying to, and how things were going at school, which was easier than thinking about my whole skin thing. I supposed I really did feel better having told her, though—she didn't seem shocked or grossed out or any of the things I was worried about, though she hadn't actually seen the horror for herself.

"I hope you're going to celebrate tonight," she said. "You've worked really hard for this."

"I'm going over to a friend's house," I said.

"Have a great time. You deserve it."

"Thanks again," I said. "For everything. See you in class next week."

"Count on it," she said, with a wink.

Next stop was Alex's, but first I texted Mom. **Made it through this time. Feeling optimistic. See you at home tonight.**

Alex's mom answered the door when I arrived. "She's

been holed up in there all day. Get her to stop looking at all those screens, would you? She's going to need to change her contacts prescription again if she keeps this up."

I knocked on Alex's door and she called for me to come in. Her mom was right; all three screens were on, and they were covered with images of green tables with a mixture of people and animals sitting around them, cards and chips on the table. "Gimme a few minutes," she said, and I watched as she clicked furiously, moving from screen to screen.

"Which one is you?" I pointed at the players, not seeing the boy avatar she'd shown me before.

"Bottom center," she said without looking away.

I laughed when I saw that she'd changed her avatar to a scanned-in picture of a screaming baby with a Mohawk. My phone buzzed. I figured it was Mom texting me back, but when I looked down, I saw three new messages from a blocked number. Odd.

I opened the messages and realized they were all photos. The first was a picture of Raj and me from that fancy party. It looked like we were talking. How could anyone have even taken pictures, with all that smoke? Then I remembered the flashes of light, the dust in the air that looked almost like glitter. I'd thought they were strobe lights, but maybe they weren't.

My heart started to pound. I guessed the Novalert was wearing off.

I scrolled down to the next picture. Raj was holding the baggie of Novalert.

Uh-oh.

And then the final picture. Me, with money in my hand. This wasn't good.

My phone buzzed again.

Want me to erase these?

I'll need a favor. Or two.

11.

This can't be real, I thought. I looked at the pictures again and tried to clear my head. I must have been having a negative reaction to the Novalert. Maybe there was a side effect Alex hadn't mentioned: paranoid hallucination. I closed my eyes as tight as I could and then opened them again, sure that the pictures would be gone.

They weren't.

I had the strangest feeling—my stomach wanted to churn, and my head wanted to pound, and my heart wanted to thump, but I still had some Novalert in my system. I wanted to panic, but physically, I couldn't.

My rational self could, though. Strange how I'd taken Novalert to keep irrational anxiety away, and now it was making it hard for me to freak out when I legitimately had something to freak out about. I'd spent so much time imagining all the downsides of taking Novalert—having a bad reaction, liking it too much, finding out that it didn't work and passing out in the SAT again, even getting caught buying it—but once I'd actually tried it and then gotten some myself, I'd thought the danger had passed.

It hadn't.

Now I had to think about a whole other set of terrible options, including the possibility of getting arrested. If the idea of people seeing my skin was the worst thing I could imagine, then the thoughts swirling around my head now were the second worst, and getting close to catching up.

"Your phone's blowing up over there," Alex said. "Just give me a minute. I'm almost done."

"Just my mom checking in," I said, trying to keep my voice from shaking. I didn't know what to do, but my first instinct was to keep the pictures a secret. Apparently that was always my first instinct. Which didn't necessarily make it a good one.

After a couple of minutes of me silently spiraling, Alex turned around in her chair. "Finished!"

"Did you win?" I asked.

"Did I win?" She snorted. "Please."

I couldn't imagine ever sounding as confident as Alex did. And I couldn't imagine her getting into this kind of mess. She could handle anything—she had lots of secret lives, but I got the sense that she kept her secrets to make herself feel powerful. My secrets did the opposite.

"So how did it go? Did the Novalert help?"

"It went great," I said, relaxing even as I said the words. The test was what was important, after all. I decided not to think about the pictures right now, though in my mind they were all I could see. "It was like the polar opposite of last time. I was focused and calm and everything made sense. And I didn't pass out."

"That's a win," she said. "Want to let loose tonight? There's another one of those crazy parties. The boys are going. And Raj asked specifically if I'd bring you. I think he's actually into you, which is just so great. You guys would be perfect for each other."

"I told you, he's not my type." Except he totally was. He was smart and funny and sweet and so, so cute. Except for the whole drug thing, which I had to keep reminding myself was a very good reason to stay away. Still, I'd found myself thinking about him a lot, no matter how much I tried not to. And now I had another reason to think about him—he was in those pictures with me, after all. I wondered whether I should tell him or whether that would just make him as panicked as I was.

Or maybe he already knew.

He couldn't have taken them, obviously, but that didn't mean he hadn't set me up. I felt my brain spinning again, but the Novalert in my system kept shutting down my body's desire to react.

"I think you're being ridiculous," Alex said, oblivious to my internal freakout. "You guys totally get along, and I know you think he's hot. You could have a little fling and see how it goes, just for fun."

"I can't get past the drug thing," I said.

"You got past it with me," she said.

I stared at her.

"I'm the one who told you about it in the first place. And I gave you some, and I think we both know I didn't get it from the doctor. But we're still friends. Why hold the fact that Raj hooked you up against him? Besides, maybe he's got good reasons for doing it, just like you had a good reason for taking it."

She didn't have to say that I was just as guilty as Raj; her tone and the photos I'd just received did the job. "I see what you're saying. But I just can't right now."

"Someone else, then," she said. "There are going to be a ton of cute guys at this party."

"Not tonight. Tonight I'm staying in."

"All right, I'll stop pushing. I don't know what you're waiting for, though."

"College," I said.

"You're waiting for college to date?"

"Yeah."

"Why?"

"What do you mean, why?"

I couldn't help it—my brain went right to that last night out with Becca and Isabel, the house they'd dragged me to, and how awful it was. Sometimes I felt like I spent more energy trying to block it out than it would take to just think about it for even a minute. But I still didn't want to. "In college the guys will be more like me. Everyone will. I can start over. I've screwed up so many things here, and spent so much time thinking about what other people want from me. In college I'll figure out what I want for myself."

"What did you screw up? And what exactly do you think is going to be different?"

It was hard to explain. "I won't have to deal with my parents, or this school and all the crazy pressure. I'll be able to relax."

"That's about way more than just the guys," she said. "That pretty much covers everything. Are you really waiting for college for everything?"

"Maybe." I hadn't really thought about it that way before.

"Kind of sounds like it. Look, I don't know what you think is going to magically happen when you get to Harvard or wherever you end up, but I can tell you this much: those schools are full of kids just like us. And when you get there, you're still going to be you. Why not just live now?"

It was a fair question. But living now hadn't exactly made things better for me. I'd thought I was having fun at that party she'd taken me to, and look how that was turning out. "I'll think about it, I promise," I said. "But tonight I'm staying in because I'm wiped out from the SAT, not because I don't want to have fun. I'll go to the next thing, I promise."

"I'm going to hold you to that. I've got energy to burn, though, so I'm still going. Help me pick out an outfit?"

That much I could do.

My parents were still at work when I got home, no surprise there, but I was glad—I wanted to be alone. I needed to think. I needed to treat this like a logic problem and reason it out. I went up to my desk and got out a notebook and pen—I didn't want anything on the computer, where someone could find it.

The first thing I did whenever I started a new logic problem was to make separate lists for all the categories. I arranged the clues by category, and then I started to unpack them. A clue might seem to be about one thing, but it could unlock the secret to something else.

First list: Who knew about me and Raj and the Novalert? That was easy: me, Raj, Alex, and whoever took the pictures. Unless that was Alex, but she would have had to ditch Bryan. Or else Bryan would have to have been with her. That was all too convoluted, not to mention that Alex just didn't make sense as an option. Which meant the person who took the pictures was someone at the party.

Second list: Who was at the party? That one was harder. There were a ton of kids there, and I didn't know all of them—some of them didn't seem to be from my school, and some of them I just hadn't met. So I made a list of everyone I knew: Raj, Alex, Justin, Bryan, Isabel, and some other kids I recognized.

Third list: Who would want to blackmail me? I stared at the page for a while. I had no idea. But maybe I'd phrased the issue wrong. Who would want to hurt me? I knew I was kind of naive, but I still couldn't imagine who'd fall in that category. I had to try again.

Who had I hurt?

This list, unfortunately, was a little easier to start. I'd hurt Becca and Isabel. Sure, they'd hurt me too, but they'd hurt me through honesty, and I'd hurt them by lying. That was worse.

The doorbell rang before I could make myself even more miserable. I checked my phone—no one had called, and it was already after eight and dark outside. Who would come over at this hour? Could it be Blocked Sender?

I ran downstairs and looked out the windows that ran along each side of the door. Pacing on my doorstep was Raj, wearing the same suit he'd worn to the last fancy party and holding a big paper bag. I opened the door.

"Surprise!" he said.

"No kidding. What are you doing here?" I tried to sound more curious than rude, but he'd kind of scared me. Or I'd scared myself, thinking Blocked Sender would just come here.

Unless Raj was Blocked Sender.

It was possible, if he'd had someone else take the pictures. But he was just as implicated as I was, if not more—he'd have to really trust the person he was working with. I couldn't imagine him taking that kind of risk; he wasn't stupid, after all. Still, I'd have to be careful, just in case.

"Alex told me she hadn't managed to convince you to come to the party. I'd been counting on seeing you."

"Oh, come on," I said.

"Did I hear you say 'Come in'? I'd be happy to." He walked past me into the living room. "Lovely place you've got here. Very . . . beige."

That was accurate. The living room was basically all beige, with gold accents on the coffee table and throw pillows and gold frames on the pictures hanging on the walls. "It's just this room," I said, not sure whether he was being judgmental. And not sure what to think about him basically barging into my house. Though it was nice to have been interrupted from making that list.

"Tasteful," he said. "You should see my house—colors everywhere. It's dizzying, really. Can I sit? I need to empty this out." He gestured to the bag.

"Um, sure." I sat in an armchair and left him the couch. No need to encourage the flirting by sitting too close.

He reached into the bag; I heard a clinking noise, and then he pulled out two bottles of soda. "Ginger ale. Reed's extra spicy." Fancy soda—no Quik-Stop cans here. "You were drinking ginger ale at the party, weren't you?"

"You remember that?"

"I've been paying attention," he said, and dipped his hand back into the bag, emerging with a handful of candy bars I'd never seen before. "I trust you like chocolate?"

"You are correct. But what are those?"

"I'm here to introduce you to the wonders of British chocolate. Cadbury, in particular."

"We have Cadbury here."

"Not anymore, you don't. Hershey has banned it. You have but a poor imitation in a Cadbury wrapper. Trust me when I tell you it's not remotely the same."

I looked at the candy bars. They all had names like Flake and Wispa. "What's the difference between all of these?"

"Mostly texture," he said. "Flake is kind of hard to describe—it's like they took one long super-thin layer of chocolate and then kind of rolled it up and smooshed it together. Wispa is airier, like someone took a regular chocolate bar and then hollowed some of it out. The texture is almost like a malt ball in the middle, but it still tastes like chocolate. And Wispa Gold is the same thing but with caramel too."

They all sounded weird but also mostly wonderful. "What's your favorite?"

"I like Flake bars myself," he said. "The process for

making them is a secret, kind of like the formula for Coke. Very mysterious and appealing."

He made it all sound so sexy and romantic. Which was totally not how I wanted to be thinking about him. I opened up the Flake bar and took a bite. He was right about it having an unusual texture; little pieces of it literally flaked off as I sank my teeth into it. "This is really good."

"Try the Wispa," he said. "Same chocolate, but a very different experience."

I peeled off the wrapper and tried it. Right again—it was gritty, and the inside of it once I'd taken a bite looked like coral.

"You like it?"

"I think I like the Flake better."

"Is that why you saved some for later?" Raj tapped his upper lip, and I licked mine to find a crumb of the Flake bar there. So embarrassing. Except Raj hadn't taken his eyes off me the whole time. Maybe Alex was right; maybe he really was into me. For a second my heart jumped at the idea of it—apparently the Novalert had finally worn off—but then I remembered the things that kept me away. The things about him, and the things about me.

"Wispa Gold now," he said.

"I'll pass on that one," I said. "Too much going on. I like things simple. Plain."

"Unadulterated, you mean. Plain sounds boring, and I don't think you're boring."

"You don't know me that well, though," I said. "Maybe you're giving me too much credit."

"I don't think so. I like to think I'm a pretty good judge of character."

I felt my face turning red under the makeup. I hoped he couldn't see. "This is all very nice, but I don't understand—"

"What I'm doing here?" He smiled. "We're celebrating. I'd hoped to celebrate at the party, but you're not at the party. You're here, so we're celebrating here. Alex told me about the SAT."

I was flattered that he'd given it—me—this much thought. I didn't know what to say. "Thanks. I feel bad that you left the party, though."

"Don't. Those parties get old quick. It was all lovely and novel when it started, but now it's just an excuse for the ladies to buy formalwear. I keep suggesting they spice things up a bit, maybe have themes or secret passcodes or something more than just fancy drinks and fancy DJs and the like, but so far I've not been very convincing, I'm afraid."

I thought about Alex's Closet of Wonders. He was probably right about the clothes, at least. I held up my bottle and tilted it toward his. "Well, cheers."

We clinked bottles and I took a sip of the ginger ale—I'd

never tried that kind before, and I was surprised to find that it burned my mouth a little. It was like I finally understood what ginger ale was supposed to taste like. "You were right about the spicy," I said.

"Good, isn't it? Let's see if it goes with the chocolate."

It didn't, really. Raj made a face. "Should have taste tested that one."

I took another drink. "It's not that bad. It gets better after the first sip."

"So you weren't crazy about it at first, but then you got used to it? Kind of an acquired taste?"

He wasn't the most subtle. And he'd gotten it all wrong. I decided to ignore it. "Thanks for the Novalert," I said. "It really did help." Which was true, at least with respect to the test. No need to get into anything else.

"Glad to hear it," he said. "Did you have any problems? Any side effects? They're not usually too bad, but it's worth being aware."

"You sound like a doctor."

"I get that from my parents," he said. "Along with the prescription pads, of course."

That explained some things, at least. "You seem to know a lot about this stuff. Have you been taking it long?"

"Oh, I've never tried it," he said.

"No mixing business with pleasure, is that it?"

"I wouldn't really call this business. I just help my friends out on occasion." He looked over at me; I was trying to hide my skepticism, but apparently I wasn't doing a very good job. "I'm not some nefarious underworld figure, trying to hook all the children on drugs so they'll be in hock to me forever. Is that what you thought?"

The way he said "figure" kind of melted me a little. That accent! I hated all this going back and forth I was doing in my head—it wasn't like I could ignore how cute he was, or his voice, or how I hadn't realized he had such nice lips until he'd pointed to them, but nothing he was saying really changed anything. He might not be a nefarious underworld figure, but I'd bought the Novalert from him, and now bad things were happening to me. I didn't see that fact changing anytime soon. "It just seems like a dangerous thing to do."

"Not if I'm careful. Besides, I like being someone my friends can count on."

How had I ended up in a position where the person I'd bought drugs from made me feel like a bad person? A bad friend? "It sounds like you have a lot of friends," I said. "For someone who just moved here."

"Well, I'm quite social, in case that wasn't obvious."

"Not me," I said.

"I've noticed. Alex will put an end to that soon enough, if you let her. And I'm happy to help as well."

"Thanks," I said. My phone buzzed from where I'd left it on the coffee table. I really, really hoped it was Alex, telling me about the party, or that she'd found a new Prospect, or that Bryan's puppy dog eyes were having an effect on her. I picked it up and read the text.

First favor: get more Novalert. Instructions to follow.

Oh no. I started to feel sick. The Novalert was definitely out of my system now.

I had to get Raj out of the house before I lost it. "Listen, I'm really wiped out. Thanks for coming by. You should go back to the party. I'll see you in school, okay?"

"Okay," he said, though he looked a little bummed. "Until Monday, then."

"Right, Monday."

As soon as the door closed behind him I looked at my phone again. Instructions to follow? What kind of instructions? When were they supposed to follow?

I had to go back to my lists. Raj had distracted me from what was really important: figuring out what was going on. I read over what I'd written and realized it was all stupid. The real question was simple: Who was Blocked Sender? I'd now received texts when both Alex and Raj were in the room with me, and though it was possible either one of them was working with someone else, it just seemed too crazy. And risky. Would a blackmailer really take that kind of risk? I didn't think so. Then again, what did I know about blackmailers?

I felt a little better at the thought that Alex and Raj were unlikely suspects, but that left me with no idea who the likely suspects were. I couldn't do this myself. I had to trust someone. But my track record in that area was not so great.

I had to try. I had to be better now. I steeled myself, then got out my phone and texted Alex.

Something's happened. Call tomorrow morning as soon as you get up.

12.

The phone rang at seven the next morning, much earlier than I'd expected, given that Alex had probably had a late night. "Love the cryptic text," she said. "What's up?"

"I don't want to talk about it over the phone," I said.

"Coffee?"

"Too public. Can I come over?"

"No problem," she said. "My room's still trashed from last night, but you don't care, right?"

"Not even a little bit." Her room was the least of my concerns.

I stopped at Philz on the way over and got us coffees and two of those amazing croissants I'd had with Ms. Davenport. "I'm cleaning," Alex said when I got there. We'd left a pile of clothes on her bed after choosing her outfit for the party, and apparently she'd just pushed them all onto the floor before going to sleep. Now she was moving them back onto the bed.

"That's not exactly cleaning," I said. "Cleaning would be putting them back in the closet."

"Too time-consuming," she said. "Ooh, treats!" She grabbed a croissant and started eating it right away, crumbs getting everywhere.

"More like bribery," I said. "Looks like it's working, too. How was the party?"

"That is so not the topic at hand. I mean, it was fine. It would have been more fun with you there, though. Did Raj end up coming over? Is that the news?"

"He did, but that's not what this is about. Although it is kind of about him." The easiest thing to do was just to show her, so I got out my phone and pulled up the texts from Blocked Sender.

She took the phone. I watched her face as she scrolled through the texts and tried to read her expression.

First shock, then recognition.

She looked up at me. "So he got you too," she said.

That was not what I expected. "What do you mean? Do you know who Blocked Sender is?"

"Is that what you're calling him? I just went with Asshole. No, I don't know who he is. But I got some texts like this a few months ago. Nothing to do with the Novalert—just someone who knew a little too much about me. Scary threats, just like you, then requests for favors."

"The same favors?"

"No, different for me. It was like the person knew me

well enough to know what to ask for. The favors were mostly about setting up offshore bank accounts and how to move money around online."

"How do you know about all that?"

She pointed to her computer. "I told you about the poker, but it's a little more serious than I let on. I make a lot of money. Like, all those clothes in there? I bought them myself. And I have enough saved to pay for college."

"You're kidding," I said. "I knew you were good, but I had no idea you were that good."

"Well, I learned from the best," she said. "My uncle made millions before all that bad stuff happened."

"What bad stuff?" I asked.

She took a sip of her coffee. "He was doing great, and then he threw it all away. He had a problem, though. It wasn't just about poker for him. He gambled on everything, and not all of it was legal. He spent some time in jail, and other than some money he'd socked away overseas, he lost everything. Including this family. My parents totally cut him off, and I never see him anymore."

"I'm so sorry," I said.

"Yeah, it sucks. We email sometimes, but if my parents found out I was in touch with him they'd kill me. And if they found out about the poker, they'd cut me off too."

I didn't want her to get mad at me, but I had to ask. "Why do you keep playing, then?"

"Because it's the only thing I'm really good at. It's the only thing I love. And I don't have my uncle's problems—I don't gamble on anything else, and poker isn't really gambling, anyway. My parents don't understand that now, but I think someday I can make them see. I just have to wait until they've calmed down about my uncle."

"How long has it been?"

"A couple of years," she admitted. "They're not getting over it quick."

"I still can't believe they'd cut you off, though. You guys are so close."

"You only know their happy, everything's-going-well-so-let's-cook-dinner side. You haven't seen what I will diplomatically call their other qualities. Let's just say embarrassing the family is not on the agenda."

I could relate. Back when my dad got kicked out of his start-up, he'd get in his car and leave at the same time he normally would every day, so no one would know he didn't have anything else lined up yet. He'd rented a little office a couple of towns over to work on new projects, but he kept the same routine. And I heard Mom on the phone, talking to her friends or her parents, never mentioning any of the trouble she and Dad were having. Family problems stay within the family, they'd say. I wanted to note that their parents were also their family, but I didn't think they'd appreciate it. "I know what you mean," I said. "My parents can never find out about this." It's not that I thought they'd cut me off, but the weight of their disappointment would be more than I could bear. And them finding out was the best-case scenario, at this point—there was still the risk of the police. As far as I knew, Marbella High had never had a felon as valedictorian. I'd never get into college, either.

If this came out, my life was over. My heart started thumping away. So much for Novalert making things better.

"My parents can't find out either," she said. "But if it makes you feel better, I did what your Blocked Sender asked me to do, and it was over. I never heard from him again. If you do it, maybe that will be it." She didn't sound convinced, though.

"Maybe," I said. "But I still have to figure out how to get more Novalert."

"That part's easy. Just ask Raj."

"I told him it was just for the test, though."

"Who cares? Besides, he's so blinded by his crush on you, I'd bet he'd do anything to make you like him back."

I wanted to tell her that wasn't true, but last night had made me think that maybe she was right. "I don't want to get him involved."

"You're assuming he isn't already. If this Blocked Sender person is after you and me, who's to say he's not after other people, too?"

She had a point. "He's never said anything about it to you, though, has he?"

She shook her head.

"Let me think about it," I said. "I'm supposed to wait for instructions, anyway. I don't want to do anything until I know what Blocked Sender actually wants me to do."

"Fair enough," she said.

"And besides, we're acting like it's a given that I'm going to do it. Did you just decide to do what he asked right away?"

Alex looked over at me, brows pulled together. "It never occurred to me not to. Not if it meant my parents would find out. Or the police. Blocked Sender never said who he'd tell, but none of the options were good."

That was true. "Who would do this to me? To us?"

"Good question. I've thought about it a lot, and I haven't been able to come up with anyone. I've kept the poker thing pretty quiet—a few friends know, but that's it, and I can't imagine anyone would tell."

"I started making lists. But I got stuck too."

"Can I see? If we talk through it, maybe I can think of something you didn't."

I got my notebook out of my bag. "I was hoping you'd say that."

We started with the first category, the people who knew I was getting Novalert from Raj. "I think this list is probably longer than what you've got here," Alex said. "If you include people who knew Raj was selling Novalert in general."

"Well, it has to be a longer list, unless you took the

pictures." I wasn't really asking, but I was curious what she'd say.

"No, that was when I was with Bryan. But if we're going to be all logical about this, like I know you are, it makes sense to consider me. Now, Raj is in the pictures, so he can't be the one who took them, but he might have told someone else. Or set up a camera somewhere."

"I thought about that. It's partly why I don't want to talk to him about it yet. Or ask him for more Novalert."

"It's just hard to imagine, though. He's usually good about this stuff, so it's not likely that it's him, but I don't know where he actually gets it, or how, so there might be other people involved."

"Prescription pads," I said. "He steals them from his parents."

Alex tilted her head, nodded. "Got that out of him already, did you? Wow."

"We were just talking, and it came up. I don't even remember how."

"Well, I still don't think he'd run around telling people in general, but I'm sure there are other people who know. And it might be that someone was taking pictures at the party and put the pieces together, then told someone else."

This was starting to get really scary. I'd thought this was all between me and Alex and Raj, but now it turned out anyone could know about it. How had I been so clueless? How could I not have realized what a big risk I'd taken? For someone who was supposed to be smart, I really was an idiot. "So anyone at the party could have taken the pictures," I said, pointing to my second list. "Those are the people I know. But there were a ton of people there. Is there any way to narrow this down?"

Alex read the names I'd listed, but before adding more names, she looked at my third list, in all its forms. "People who'd want to hurt you, people you've hurt . . . are you sure these are the right questions?"

"I assumed it was personal. Do you think that's wrong?"

"I don't really know. It was different when I thought it was just me—someone knew what I could do, and they figured out how to make me do it for them. Now that you're involved, though, it doesn't really make sense. I mean, it's not like we've been hanging out that long. Not long enough for someone who has something against me to also have something against you."

"So we need to think about it more practically," I said, feeling even dumber than I already did. Practical thinking was supposed to be my specialty. "This is really about someone using us to help them get what they want."

"I get what he wants from me," Alex said. "I basically taught him how to hide money."

"You said *wants*," I said.

"What?" She looked down at her hands.

"You didn't say wanted. You said it was over, but then you said *wants*. For someone who's a professional gambler, your poker face kind of sucks."

She paused. "Well, I do only play on the computer. I haven't had to hone my physical skills. But you're right. It's not over. I send money, too. Every month. A cut of my winnings."

I understood the pause now. "Alex, that's really serious. That's illegal."

"So's everything else," she said.

"I know, but money seems worse. I don't know why, but it just does."

"Maybe all of this is about money," she said. "Squeezing it from as many people as possible, however he can."

"So he'd be making me get Novalert so he can sell it?"

"Or he'll ask you to."

"No way," I said. "I would never do that. Besides, why ask me? Raj is already selling—why not blackmail him?"

We both sat quietly for a minute, neither one of us wanting to say the obvious. But I knew we were both thinking it. Either Blocked Sender was already blackmailing Raj, or else Raj was involved. Nothing else made sense. At least nothing I could think of.

"Where does that leave us, then?" Alex said, finally.

"I don't know," I said. "Waiting for instructions, I guess."

13.

I thought the waiting might kill me. At first I assumed I'd hear something right away, so I checked my phone constantly, fearing I'd have a new text, hoping I wouldn't, but in a way wanting to get whatever it was over with. The longer I waited, the more possible it seemed that maybe this would all go away.

The wait seemed endless, but it wasn't like I didn't have anything to do. Second quarter was winding down and I had finals to study for in all my classes. Not to mention college apps—I'd started filling out the Common Application, but I was twitching waiting for my SAT scores to come back, and I still had no idea what I was going to write about for my essay. Ms. Davenport was right that I didn't have a good enough handle on what my skin problem meant to me, and it wasn't like I wanted to advertise to colleges that I was secretly hideous. I'd have to come up with something, but I still had a little while to think about it.

Exams were in full force when Blocked Sender finally contacted me again. The text arrived in the middle of the day this time, while I was eating lunch in the cafeteria.

Get a Novalert prescription for 30 pills and await further instructions.

My head started to throb, and I knew if I didn't calm down I'd have yet another panic attack. It almost made me want Novalert. It would be ironic if this whole blackmail situation ended up turning me into a drug addict. I giggled at the thought of it.

"You okay?" Alex asked quietly. Raj and Justin were sitting with us too, debating the difference between effective strategies for hitting on men versus women.

I could understand why she was asking; laughing out loud for no reason was not a thing that okay people usually did.

I passed her the phone.

"That's not very specific," she said after reading the text.

"And I don't see how I'm supposed to get it," I said. "I'm not asking Raj." Alex and I hadn't talked any more about whether we thought he might be involved in some way, whether as blackmailer or blackmail victim, but either way, getting a prescription from him did not strike me as a good idea.

"Any chance you could try again with your mom?"

"I've asked her a bunch of times already. She's convinced that I'm just like my dad and will have a negative reaction to drugs. I can't tell her I already know I won't."

Alex thought for a minute. "It doesn't have to be a prescription for you, as far as I can tell."

"But I don't know anyone else who has one. Or who'd be willing to give it to me."

"You do know someone with a prescription pad, though."

For a second I wished I hadn't told her about Raj. "But how are we supposed to get one if we can't ask him?"

"Leave that to me," she said, and then straightened up and started talking in her normal voice. "Hey, guys, fascinating as it is to debate the concept of gendered flirtation, Kara and I were just saying that we kind of need to chill out this weekend, in a nonparty environment. I vote movie night."

"I'm out," Justin said.

"Yeah, we know," Raj said.

Justin punched him in the shoulder. "Wiseass. I mean I've got other plans."

"Do you have a date?" I asked. I remembered him talking about his boyfriend back at the party.

"As a matter of fact, I do."

"Are we ever going to get to meet this guy?" Alex asked. "You've been hiding him for kind of a ridiculously long time. I bet he's some adorable closeted sophomore." Her words were light, but her voice was sharp. Almost like she was jealous. Weird, since there was no reality where Justin was a feasible Prospect.

"My lips are sealed," Justin said.

"That won't make for a very fun date," Raj said. "We'll have more fun watching movies. My house, as usual? My parents will be out Saturday night."

"Excellent," Alex said. "Your place is perfect." She nudged me with her elbow.

"I'm in," I said. Clearly Alex had a plan. I had a feeling I wasn't going to like it, but that wasn't going to stop me from going along.

I picked up Alex on my way over to Raj's—she knew where it was, and Raj had put us on snack duty, so it made sense to go to the Quik-Stop in between her house and his. When she came out, I immediately realized I'd picked the wrong outfit—I'd gone with casual-but-cute, with colored skinny jeans, a tank top, sweater, and flats, but she was basically wearing pajamas, hair tied up in a ponytail, no makeup.

"I'm totally overdressed," I said.

"You look great. This is what I always wear to movie night."

"It's very seventh-grade sleepover," I said. "You'll have to warn me next time."

"I bet Raj will appreciate the effort," she said, and elbowed me as I started to drive.

"Don't get your hopes up. I'm not in a dating frame of mind right now. Are you going to tell me what the plan is?"

"Just follow my lead. Better that you don't know the details."

We pulled into the Quik-Stop; it turned out we'd both skipped dinner, so we were starving. It didn't take us long to pick out three different kinds of Pringles (plain, barbecue, and pizza-flavored), three different kinds of M&Ms (plain, peanut, and pretzel), and an assortment of the weirdest sodas we could find. We'd brought a Whole Foods reusable grocery bag to put everything in, which struck us as hilarious, since the food we'd brought was pretty much the opposite of Whole, and we were still giggling about it when we rang Raj's doorbell.

"Hello, ladies," Raj said when he opened the door. He was wearing jeans and a short-sleeved green T-shirt over a long-sleeved black one. He looked as good as ever, and I felt a pang of guilt about whatever it was we were about to do. Except, I reminded myself, there was no reason to feel guilty if it turned out he was the reason why we had to do it in the first place. "Kara, you look lovely. Alex, you forgot your teddy bear."

"I was going to borrow one of yours," she said, and handed him the bag of snacks.

He took it and pretended to collapse under its heft. "Did you spend your body weight in money at Whole Foods?" he asked, then peered in. "Ah. The bag is just a ruse. I sense Kara's influence in all the plain variations here."

Alex smirked at me. "Raj seems familiar with your taste in snack food," she said. "Interesting."

"That's the kind of thing friends know about each other. What are we watching?" It wasn't a subtle way to change the subject, but it was the best I could do.

"Come in and get settled and we'll go through the Netflix queue," Raj said. "Alex made her own list last time. Apparently my selections were insufficient."

"Wait, aren't you going to give Kara the tour?" Alex asked. "This is her first time here. Unless you guys aren't telling me something."

I rolled my eyes at her. But I'd said I'd follow her lead, and this was most likely part of the plan.

"Happy to oblige," Raj said. "Follow me, ladies." He led us down the hall. "Kitchen and dining room over here to your left. Note the predominance of takeout menus on the fridge. Workaholic parents equals a lack of home cooking."

"It's like being in my own house," I said.

"What's your favorite restaurant?"

"Alex's house," I said, and she laughed. "What's yours?"

"I'm partial to Thai Palace myself, not having gotten an invitation to dinner from Ms. Nguyen lately. But after living in England, I'll eat just about anything—I basically survived on takeaway curries for years. The only thing I'm picky about in the States is Indian food. Once you've had Indian food in India, there's no going back."

"I am so doing that someday," I said.

"Into travel, are you?" Raj asked.

"Anything to get away from Marbella."

"Well, you can't get much farther than India."

We passed a couple of closed doors—"Parental office and the bathroom, respectively," Raj said—before we reached the end of the hall and a staircase. "Bedrooms on the next level. Are you sure you ladies will be able to contain yourselves?"

"We've managed so far," Alex said as we followed him up the stairs.

He led us to a foyer surrounded by three doorways. "Parents' room to the left, Priya's room to the right, mine in the middle," he said. "Explore at your leisure."

All three rooms were tidy and simply decorated—his parents' was navy and cream, his sister's was pink and yellow, and Raj's was white. But where his parents' walls were covered with art, and his sister's were covered with pictures of British boy bands, Raj's walls were bare.

Or were they? I walked in and peered a little closer. I could see the edges of some pieces of tape, as well as pin holes. I turned to Raj, who was trying to keep from cracking up. "I wondered if you'd be able to tell," he said. "I did some editing."

"No kidding," Alex said, emerging from Raj's parents' room. "Aren't your walls usually covered with soccer players and swimsuit models?"

"Guilty as charged," he said, holding up his hands. "But I wanted to make a good impression."

"Way too late for that," Alex said.

I thought it was sweet, actually, but I wasn't about to say so. "Let's go pick the movie," I said.

We went back downstairs into the living room, all fluffy rugs and comfy couches and brightly patterned blankets, though hardly the explosion of color Raj had told me about, along with a huge flat-screen TV. Raj went to the kitchen as we got settled in, putting snacks into bowls and ice into glasses for our sodas. "We can watch whatever suits your fancy," he called out. "You can go through Alex's list or pick a category."

"Quick, come here, while he's busy," Alex whispered.

I scooted over on the couch.

"I did a quick scan of his parents' room to see if they kept their doctor stuff there. Didn't find anything. One of us is going to have to get into their office."

"We can't do that!" I whispered back.

"Sure we can. The office is right by the bathroom. We'll just say we have to go, and if he catches us, we'll say we went into the wrong room by accident. I'll do it if you want."

I got the sense that she kind of wanted to—her eyes were all shiny and she looked excited. But it was too much of a risk. "I'll do it," I said. "It's my problem; I have to deal with it. But why the office? Why not get the ones Raj already stole?"

"He might notice," she said. "And we already know his parents didn't notice when he took theirs."

"What's all the whispering?" Raj asked, setting snacks and drinks on the coffee table and sitting at the other end of the couch.

"Just picking the movie," Alex said. "How about a nice conspiracy theory? Have you guys seen *The Usual Suspects*?"

"About a million times," Raj said, at the same time as I said, "No."

"That's the one, then," Alex said. "Raj, you don't mind watching it again, right?"

"It will be a pleasure to introduce it to someone else," he said.

"Are you sure?" I asked. I didn't know what Alex was thinking, bringing attention to conspiracy theories right now, but I'd rather have watched something else. Something light and fun. "Wouldn't a comedy be better?"

"Trust me, this will be worth it," Alex said.

Raj grabbed the remote from Alex—"Such a guy move, Raj. Not cool."—and started the movie. I was afraid at first I wouldn't be able to concentrate now that I knew what I'd have to do, but the story grabbed me right away. I was usually good at figuring out who the bad guy was in movies like this—the logic problems came in handy—and I had a pretty good idea this time, too. But Alex nudged me just as the cop started accusing the narrator of lying, and I couldn't wait any longer.

"Can we take a break for a sec?" I asked. "Raj, the bathroom is that way, right?"

He pointed toward the hallway. "I'll pause it," he said.

"No need. I'll catch up in a minute." I didn't want to risk the quiet, even if Alex could probably cover for me.

I walked down the hall and started opening doors, figuring out which room was the office and which one was the bathroom. I turned the bathroom light on and closed the door, then went into the office and closed that door too, using my phone as a flashlight.

Being there was creepy, and not just because it was dark, though that was part of it. The office was a mess, with stacks of paper all over the floor and on the ornate wooden desk. I had no idea how I was supposed to find anything, though it was a comfort to know that not everyone in the house was perfectly neat all the time. How his parents actually got work done in here was beyond me.

I moved the flashlight toward the desk and sat in the desk chair so I could start going through the drawers. They were all full of junk, though—pens and notebooks and toys embossed with drug company logos. There was a stress ball with a smiley face on it and Novalert's logo, which seemed appropriate. I was tempted to steal it, but I reminded myself of the task at hand.

Digging through the drawers didn't get me anywhere—there wasn't a prescription pad in sight. And it was taking me longer than I thought. I had to get back to the movie. Besides, I really wanted to know who the bad guy was.

I stood up to push the chair back, but my shoe caught in the wheel, and when the chair rolled back on the hardwood floor faster than I expected, it took me with it. Why couldn't there have been a fluffy rug in this room? Then I wouldn't have wiped out loudly enough for Raj to hear. Because I'd barely managed to stand up again when the door opened and the light went on.

"This isn't the bathroom," he said. And he sounded mad.

14.

Busted.

But maybe I could cover. "Um, no, I just got a little lost," I said. Just like I'd planned. Except I'd been gone way too long for that story to work now. I tried to pass it off with a joke. "Good thing you showed up or I'd have peed in the closet by accident."

He didn't look amused. "You'd have figured it out a lot faster if you'd turned on the light. And the light in the bathroom is on. So you must have found that first. What's going on, Kara?"

"I can explain." But I didn't know where to start, or how much to admit.

Raj stood in front of me with his arms crossed over his chest. "Go for it."

"I just— I have to—"

"She needs a Novalert prescription," Alex said. She'd

come up behind Raj and I hadn't even noticed.

"I don't understand. I thought you didn't want any more Novalert after the SAT."

"I don't."

"Then why do you need a prescription?"

"I don't, exactly."

"But Alex just said—"

"It's complicated," I said. "I don't need a prescription for myself, but I do need one. I remembered you said you got prescription pads from your parents, so I thought it might be easiest to just get one of theirs, if they were just lying around." No need to tell him this was Alex's idea; he was clearly furious, and his fury might as well be directed at me. They'd been friends longer, after all.

"Let me see if I understand." His voice was quiet, but in a scary way. "You needed a prescription but not for yourself, so you thought it would be easier to steal from my parents?" Getting louder now. "Rather than just asking me?"

"I had my reasons," I said. True, they didn't feel like great reasons now that I'd been caught, but still.

"You want to tell me what they are?" He looked over at Alex. "How about you? I'll take an explanation from either one of you."

"It's complicated," she said.

"Yeah, I think Kara covered that already," he said.

I didn't know what to do. He seemed genuinely angry,

which indicated that he really didn't know why I was doing this; if he was Blocked Sender, or was working with him, he'd know why I needed the prescription. Maybe telling him was the right thing to do; then we'd find out whether he was in the same boat we were.

But what if I was wrong? What if he was a better actor than I thought, or there was something else we hadn't considered? I stayed quiet.

"So this whole movie night was just a cover," he said, finally. "This was the plan all along."

I looked at Alex, helpless. She didn't know what to say either. I felt awful. How could we ever have thought this was the right move? "I'm really sorry," I said. "We'll go."

"That's probably a good idea," he said.

I grabbed Alex's arm and practically dragged her out of the house. "That was a disaster," I said.

"I know, I'm sorry," she said as we got in the car. "I thought it would be easier. And I thought I'd be able to keep him from going after you. But he was so worried when you were gone so long. It was kind of sweet, really. I almost forgot that there was a possibility he was behind all of this. I kept alternating between wanting to tell him and wanting to kill him."

I wanted to get out of there, but I felt too shaky to drive, so we sat in the car for a minute. "Do you really think he's part of this?" I asked. "I mean, now? He didn't seem to know what was going on."

"I know," she said. "I kind of feel like the worst person ever for even thinking such bad stuff about him."

"What do we do now? Should we go back and talk to him?"

"We should give him some time to cool off," she said. "Give him the weekend. He'll calm down, and we can explain everything."

"I don't know what I'm supposed to do in the meantime. I have to get that prescription, and I have no other way." If we weren't going back in, then we needed to leave. I pressed the button to turn the car on and the stereo started screaming at us. We'd been in such a good mood on the way over, listening to music and singing as loudly as we could, windows down in the cool Northern California evening air. I turned the radio off and the silence was eerie. The Prius was in electric mode, so even the car wasn't making any noise.

"We'll think of something," Alex said. "After we've talked to him."

"I don't think he's going to want to talk to us. What we did wasn't very cool."

"Trust me, I've known him longer than you have."

"Not that long," I said. He'd only been here a year, after all.

"Yeah, but we kind of bonded early. He showed up at a rough time for me."

I glanced over at her, but she was looking down. We'd

never really talked about what our lives had been like before we started hanging out. I wasn't about to get into all the drama with Becca and Isabel, and I'd assumed Alex was exactly what she seemed to be: a fun party girl with lots of guy friends but no one she was really close to. "What was going on?"

"It's not worth getting into right now. But he was a good friend to me. He's got a really big heart, for all his flirty goofy stuff."

"And we tried to take advantage of it," I said.

"We had reasons. And if we're right that he isn't Blocked Sender, then there's a pretty good chance he's in the same position we are. Which means he'll definitely understand."

"I hope so," I said.

"I'm sure of it. Besides, we still haven't finished the movie."

I looked over at her again. She was smiling now. "We're never going to get to finish it," I said. "Maybe you just need to tell me how it ends."

"It's the person you least expect," she said. "It always is."

Raj glared at Alex and me as we walked into the cafeteria on Monday. "I don't think the weekend was long enough," I said.

"You may be right," she said. "But I don't think we should wait too long. Let me go over there and see if he'll meet us after school. You lie low for a bit."

"What makes you think he'll be willing to talk to you? He's mad at both of us."

"Yeah, but I've got the history. Let me try, anyway."

"Good luck," I said, and went to go sit with the Brain Trust.

They looked surprised to see me, which was understandable. "What an honor," Arthur said. His black hair was as disheveled as ever, though he still constantly ran his hands through it to try to smooth it out. Julia and David had discovered the joy/grossness of PDA and ignored me to make out.

"I've just been branching out a little," I said. "Is it okay for me to sit here?"

"Sure. It's not like I have anyone else to talk to." He glanced over at the liplock. "Things have escalated, as you can see."

We started talking about classes, as if I'd never left. But it was different now. I saw everyone through the filter of Blocked Sender: Could this person be capable? Could this person hate me? Arthur and I had never been anything more than acquaintances, and his parents were Harvard alums so I probably wasn't even competition for him, really. He had a big crush on a girl in orchestra with him, so it wasn't like he was pining away, angry at me for not being into him. Julia had tried to get us together a while back, when she and David were sneaking around thinking the rest of us didn't know, but he'd made it clear I wasn't his type. Which was fine; he wasn't mine either.

He was safe. He wasn't Blocked Sender.

"I heard SAT scores are coming out this week," he said.

"They're supposed to. Here's hoping I didn't tank it." I raised my carton of milk in a mock toast.

"You didn't." He sounded confident. I wished I could be too.

"I'll find out one way or another soon enough," I said.

He reached over to Julia's lunch tray and started eating her fries. "What?" he said when I made a face at him. "She won't notice. I've gotten double fries for weeks now."

He was right that Julia and David didn't seem to notice anything. Or require air. I could see over their heads to where Alex and Raj were sitting. I could tell they were arguing, though their heads were low and close together. They were probably whispering to keep Justin from hearing. I hoped she was able to convince him to talk to us. The more I thought about it, the more sure I was that he wasn't involved, that I'd been wrong to ever think he was. It made me feel terrible.

"You should go back over there," Arthur said. He didn't sound mean about it, just matter-of-fact. "It's where you'd rather be, isn't it?"

"I'm happy here," I said.

I wasn't getting any better at lying.

Alex met me at the door of the cafeteria on my way out. "He's still mad but he's coming around," she said. "He said he'll meet us later this week or over the weekend. You around?"

"Doing nothing but waiting for my stupid SAT scores," I said.

"You're going to do great," she said. "I'll let you know when I hear from him."

At least he was willing to talk to us. For that, I could be patient. I was just worried that Blocked Sender would give me more instructions when I hadn't managed to pull off the last ones yet.

Back to waiting.

I spent so much time checking and rechecking my phone for texts that I wasn't at all prepared for Wednesday afternoon when the email popped up from the Educational Testing Service. My SAT scores were available, it said, and told me where to log in.

I'd been home from school a couple of hours, sitting on the living room couch surrounded by books, trying in vain to study for finals but really chewing my nails over what Blocked Sender would tell me to do next. But the ETS email jolted me back into reality, or at least the reality I wanted to be in. I wanted my only source of stress to be finals and SATs and college applications; I already missed the days when I thought those were my biggest problems.

I ran upstairs and got on my computer. I clicked through all the menus, typed in my username and password, and waited for the page to load. Normally the internet around here was lightning fast—we were in Silicon Valley, after all—but with every high school student who'd taken the SAT online at once, things were bound to be slow.

Finally, though, the page showed up.

READING: 750

MATH: 780

ESSAY: 23

Holy crap, I'd nailed it.

NAILED IT!

I couldn't believe it. I hit refresh a couple of times to make sure what I was seeing was real, then logged out and logged in again to check that I'd given the right information, that it wasn't some sort of mistake. But there it was, over and over again.

The Novalert had really worked. All I'd needed to do was get over my own anxiety and fear. I didn't know who to call first. Mom? Dad? Alex? They'd all made me promise to get in touch as soon as I'd heard. I decided to be a good daughter and check in with Mom. She must have been waiting to hear from me—the scores were supposed to come out after two weeks, and it had already been two and a half—because she picked up her cell right away, a rarity when she was at work.

"Honey, I'm so proud of you!" I could hear her beaming over the phone. I loved hearing her say it. "You're a lock for Stanford now. Make sure to call your father, and we'll go someplace nice for dinner tonight."

"On a school night?" I asked, in mock horror, ignoring the Stanford comment.

"You'll survive one night without studying through dinner. See you when we get home."

I called my dad next, then Alex. I even texted Ms. Davenport, who'd made me promise to tell her how things had gone. Everyone wanted to celebrate with me, which made me feel great, though it also made me want to call Becca. She'd seen me through the disastrous PSAT sophomore year, and she would understand exactly what this meant to me in a way Alex and Raj never could. But I couldn't call her.

Dinner with my parents that night was actually kind of fun, at least until they started getting all excited about Stanford and reminiscing about their time there, how they'd met, what all their friends were doing now.

"You realize I'm applying to more schools than just Stanford, right?" I said.

"Of course," Mom said. "You need a backup plan. Berkeley, maybe UC Davis, just in case?"

"She doesn't have to live in our backyard," Dad said.

Finally, I thought. He understands.

"Los Angeles isn't so far. UCLA is always an option."

Or not. This was as good a time to bring it up as any, given what a good mood everyone was in. "I was thinking about applying to some East Coast schools," I said.

"Oh, you don't want to do that," Mom said. "You'd be so far away. And you've never had to deal with that kind of weather. You'd miss the sun."

As if she knew better than I would what I'd like. I hated that she'd even assume it. I was actually kind of excited about the idea of winter; I'd only seen snow in Tahoe, and it wasn't the same. California was so bland with its near lack of seasons. "There are some really great schools out there. And it's not like I couldn't come home and visit."

"It will be harder than you think," Mom said. "It's not like you could just come home for the weekend and do laundry."

"I can do my own laundry."

"And the time difference—we'd have trouble finding time to talk."

I was tempted to point out how little we talked even with me living here, given how much time the two of them spent at work, but I didn't want to make them mad.

"Well, you do what you have to," Dad said. "As long as it's not Harvard!" He said it jokingly, but I had a feeling he was serious.

"What's wrong with Harvard?" I asked, though I knew the answer. I'd been hearing them complain about it for years.

"It has one of the best math programs in the country."

Dad shook his head. "Listen, I'm not saying it isn't a great school. But you have to understand its reputation out here. It's one thing to go off to college someplace far, but there are so many jobs out here for someone with your skills, and if you want to come back, that degree comes with a lot of baggage. People here just don't respect it the way they do out east. And Stanford grads are very loyal—they'd be skeptical that you chose Harvard over Stanford, especially since you're from here and both of us are alums."

"Besides, we were so happy there," Mom said. "We just want you to be as happy as we were."

"Just because something made you happy doesn't mean it will work for me," I said.

"You've got a little time to think about this," Dad said. "How about we have our nice dinner and talk about it more later, when we're done celebrating your wonderful accomplishment?"

My wonderful accomplishment that required taking illegal drugs and had led to me getting blackmailed? Sure. I almost laughed at the thought of telling them, but then I felt kind of sick. It wasn't funny; it was awful. But I didn't want them to know that. Maybe I could avoid dealing with this for a while. Maybe Blocked Sender would leave me alone.

"Let's get dessert," I said.

15.

I woke Saturday morning to the sound of the doorbell ringing. "Kara, it's for you," Mom called out.

I hadn't even gotten out of bed, let alone started SCAM. "Give me a minute!" I yelled back. It was probably Alex; I'd texted her last night that I'd be home today, and we'd talked about hanging out. I threw on jeans and a sweatshirt, ran into the bathroom, and got ready as fast as I possibly could.

But when I came downstairs, it wasn't Alex hanging out in the kitchen with my mom, drinking coffee and chatting. It was Raj.

"What are you doing here?" I blurted out, before I had a chance to think about it.

"Kara, that's not how we greet company," Mom said. "I've been enjoying getting a chance to meet one of your new friends."

Did that mean Raj was my friend again? "I thought you

might want to go talk," he said.

"Uh, sure," I said. "Let me get my coat." I ran back upstairs and put on a jacket.

Raj was waiting by the door when I got downstairs. "I didn't know you had a car," I said, for lack of anything better to say.

"I borrowed one from my parents," he said, clicking the remote so the doors unlocked. The car was gray and bland and very adult, nothing I'd imagine Raj would pick out for himself. He went around to my side and opened the door for me. It was such a nice, unexpected moment of chivalry that I almost wanted to cry. Who did that? Especially someone who was mad at you?

"Thanks," I said. I looked away as I buckled my seat belt so he didn't see me tearing up.

He got in and put on his seat belt, not turning the car on right away, and not turning to me. "Look, I know Alex and I talked about us all meeting up together, but I thought it might be easier for us to talk one-on-one. It seems like what's going on is more about you, anyway."

That was true, and there was no need to tell him that the whole mess at his house was kind of Alex's idea. I didn't want to get her in any more trouble with Raj than she was already in. "You're right about that," I said. "I'm really sorry about what happened. I can explain."

"I'm ready to listen."

I hoped he really meant it. "I appreciate it," I said as he started driving. "Where are we going?"

"I thought we could probably use some coffee."

"Philz, then?" It was pretty much the only place anyone from school hung out.

"Too many people we know. There's a place the next town over that's not bad—okay if we go there?"

"Wherever you want." I was so relieved he was willing to talk to me that I didn't care where we went. In my head I rehearsed explaining what happened, though I wasn't sure knowing the whole story was going to make him any less mad.

We rode quietly for a while, down El Camino Real, past strip malls and car washes and fast-food places, until we got to a small café called Mary's Place. It was run-down and mostly empty, with little tables in front and a row of booths in the back, which was perfect. I ordered a mocha and Raj got a black coffee and we sat in a quiet booth where no one who came in could see us.

Best to just launch right into it. "I've been getting these text messages," I said. "Pictures of us at that party, when I got the Novalert from you, and other stuff too." I got out my phone to show him, watching his face as he skimmed through the texts to see if I could read anything in his expression. I had a feeling I'd learn more from that than anything else.

And I was right. No shock, no confusion. A nod of recognition. Just like Alex.

"This is happening to you too," I said. It wasn't a question.

"It was," he said. "I should have realized what was going on. This is all my fault."

Wait, what? Had I been wrong again? Was it his fault because he was responsible for this somehow? I opened my mouth, but I wasn't sure whether to ask questions or start yelling. My instincts had been wrong before, though, so instead I just took a sip of my coffee and waited.

"My turn to explain," he said. "I'll start at the beginning." He took a deep breath. "I started getting texts maybe a few months after I got here. I'd had some problems in England, and somehow this person seemed to know about them."

"Problems?" I asked. Raj seemed so carefree; it was hard to imagine him having real problems.

"Some school stuff. Things I didn't want my parents to know about. I don't know how he found out, but he knew, and he knew my parents were doctors and told me to find a way to get drugs from them that I could sell to kids at school. Then I'd have to get him a cut."

"That's crazy," I said.

"I know, right?"

But I hadn't necessarily meant it that way. The story sounded so crazy I wasn't sure I believed him. I waited for him to keep talking.

"Every month I'd leave money in an envelope somewhere in school, and when I went back to check, the money was gone. I tried hanging around and waiting to see who came, but I never managed to catch the person in the act."

So far, I wasn't getting a sense of why any of this was his fault, though I was starting to worry about what Blocked Sender was going to ask me to do. And what he might know. What if he somehow had pictures of the monster? The thought of people seeing my actual face wasn't as scary as the thought of going to jail, but it was still horrible. My stomach started feeling all twisted up.

"A while ago I got instructions to start sending the money online."

Now at least some of the pieces were starting to add up. I wasn't sure what Alex had told him, if anything, so I didn't mention that this had probably happened when Alex helped Blocked Sender set up his finances.

"It was this whole horribly complicated thing, but I did it. Except . . ." He stopped and took a sip of his coffee, then put the cup down and started picking at his fingernails. I hadn't noticed the torn cuticles before. I guessed we all dealt with our stress in different ways.

"Except?" I prodded.

"Except recently I stopped sending money," he said. "Or rather I stopped selling. I think that's why he came after you—to get me to start again."

"I don't understand. Why would coming after me make you start again?"

"Because I think he thought you'd ask me for the prescription. And he must have known why I stopped, though I can't imagine how."

"Well, why did you stop?"

He looked away for a minute, trying to decide what to say. I remembered reading about microexpressions and ways to tell people were lying, but I couldn't remember which direction they'd look in when they weren't telling the truth. Finally, he turned back to me. "I stopped selling because of you."

"What?"

He started picking at his nails again. "I know Alex always jokes about how I'm this big flirt, and she doesn't take me seriously. I asked her about you right after we met, whether you could ever be into me. She told me drug dealers weren't your type."

That was horrifying. I'd said that to Alex in confidence; I'd never meant for him to find out. I'd thought she was someone I could trust; I'd thought we were really starting to become friends, even if it would never be the same kind of friendship I'd had with Becca. "We were joking around," I said.

"Oh, I know. She thought she was teasing me. But it hit me really hard—I liked you as soon as I met you, and you weren't going to take me seriously if I kept doing what I was doing. So I stopped selling."

"Because of me." I had trouble believing that too, though

I was pretty close to convinced that he was telling the truth about the other stuff now.

"Because of you. Or the idea of you. You're smart and independent and lovely and you don't seem caught up in any of the stupid things other kids at this school are into. I liked being able to help you with your SAT problem; you seem like someone who doesn't ask for help all that often, and I liked how it felt to be useful to someone in that way. And maybe I'm not the guy for you, and maybe we'll just be friends, but I didn't want anything to get in the way of the possibilities. I don't want to be that guy, the one someone like you couldn't be with because of all this sordidness."

I didn't know what to say. I'd believed Alex when she said he was a big flirt, and even when there had been signs that maybe he really was into me, I'd brushed them aside. I hadn't thought about how that might have made him feel. "I never meant to make you feel bad," I said. I was tempted to reach out and touch his hand, but that didn't seem like a good idea. Somewhere in the back of my mind was a flutter of excitement that he really did like me, a flutter that threatened to turn into a whole flock of butterflies if I thought about the implications of what he was saying. He'd been blackmailed into selling drugs; he wasn't a dealer by choice. Which meant the only thing that had kept me from admitting how much I liked him was gone. But now wasn't the time.

"I never thought you had," he said. "But you see it now,

don't you? How me quitting handing out pills and sending money to some stranger set all this in motion?"

"So that's what you meant in saying this was your fault." I was relieved to hear it; I finally understood his logic, at least. But he was falling for the same thing Alex and I both had at first, thinking that we were the center of everything. She'd thought she was the only one being blackmailed until I told her what was happening to me; I'd immediately started suspecting old friends who had nothing to do with any of this because I felt guilty about lying to them. The more I learned, the more I was sure we were all wrong. "I don't think so," I said. "I think it's bigger than that. But I don't know what to do about it. Maybe it's time for us to come clean."

"We can't do that!" He sat up straight, like I'd just poked him with a Taser or something.

"God, whatever Blocked Sender's got on you must be pretty bad," I said.

"It's not that. I just can't put my parents through more than I already have."

"It doesn't sound like you put them through anything so far—you said you were trying to keep them from finding things out."

"It's not quite that simple," he said. "If you don't mind, I'd rather not talk about it right now. I feel I've revealed enough for the moment, don't you think?"

He had; he was a whole lot braver than I was, that's for

sure. I knew the nice thing to do would be to tell him that I might be starting to have feelings for him too, to tell him that he hadn't done all this for nothing, but I wasn't sure I was ready to follow through on what could come after that. I was too worried about the whole Blocked Sender situation to think about what I could finally acknowledge was my own stupid crush. "I really am sorry about all this," I said instead, hoping he understood at least some of what I was trying to tell him.

"I wish you guys had just talked to me," he said. "But those text messages are scary. I can't really blame you for not telling me."

"If it helps, it was partly because we didn't want to get you in trouble," I said, which was sort of true.

"Too late for that now. But maybe I can fix this. I'll start selling again, and then maybe this Blocked Sender person will leave us both alone."

"No way," I said. "You didn't want to get into this in the first place, and now you're out. Staying out is good. Besides, do you really think Blocked Sender is going to drop all this, just because he's got you back? He's got another person on the hook now."

"He'll probably just come back to me anyway. Why settle for just one dealer when he can have two? Or more?"

He was right. Once Blocked Sender had us, there was no reason for him to let us go. "What are we going to do? At least you have the option of just getting back in if he forces you to. I've been given this mission and I'm not going to be able to complete it." I didn't want to remind him that it was because I'd failed to steal from him.

"Will this help?" He reached behind him and got his wallet out of his back pocket. Inside, folded up into a tiny square that he opened like a paper flower, was a prescription. For Novalert. Already signed and everything.

Relief swept over me, followed by guilt, followed by the knowledge that he'd brought it with him, even before he'd heard what I had to say. He was a better person than I'd given him credit for, and a much better person than I was. But I knew I shouldn't take it. "You said you weren't going to do that anymore."

"I'm not doing for it myself," he said. "I'm doing it to help you. You're right that even if I started selling again, it's no guarantee that this Blocked Sender person would leave you alone, and I don't want you to have to take the risk of finding out what happens if you don't do what he says."

I looked at the prescription, with its wrinkles from where he'd folded it. Now I actually had to go through with it, whatever it was. "I'm scared."

"You'd be foolish if you weren't," he said. "How about we resolve to find a way out of this, somehow? Make it be over?"

"Without us getting in trouble?" I asked. "Without our secrets getting out?"

“If there’s a way,” he said. “If there’s a way, we’ll find it.”

He reached over and squeezed my hand, like I’d wanted to before, and I really did feel better.

Until the next day.

Time to fill that prescription. Walmart, Redwood City, between 1 and 5. Await further instructions.

And one more text, after that.

Tell no one. Or face the consequences.

16.

"What am I going to do?" I asked. My voice sounded whiny, even to me. As soon as I saw the text, there was no question I'd ignore the part about not telling anyone; it was much too late for that. I'd called Alex and she came over right away. She'd never been to my house before, but we needed a quiet place, and her parents were home while mine, as usual, were working. We sat in the living room while I drank cup after cup of coffee as if I needed it to keep me alive.

"I don't see what choice you have. You do what the text says. Unless you've come up with some way to get around it."

"I'm not sure I can go through with this," I said. "Getting the pills just for me was one thing, but this is a whole other level of trouble."

"I understand," she said. "But you need to think through what will happen if you don't do it. Get out your logic brain and let's figure it out."

I sat up straight, or as straight as the couch cushions would let me. "Okay. We've only seen Blocked Sender threaten people; we've never seen him come after someone who didn't do what he said. Although . . ." I told her about my conversation with Raj, how he'd stopped doing what Blocked Sender asked and how he assumed that was what had sent Blocked Sender to me. "I hope it's okay that I'm telling you—Raj doesn't know you're involved too yet, right?"

"No, but he should. We should get him over here." She texted him and we waited for him to respond.

Be there in ten.

I had a panicky moment when I realized I was practically still in pajamas, with only enough makeup to cover the monster, but I had to let it go. There were more important things to worry about at the moment.

"Do you think there's a chance Blocked Sender would let it go if I just didn't do it?" I asked.

"I don't know," Alex said. "But if Raj bowing out sent Blocked Sender to you, then it only makes sense that the least bad thing that could happen would be Blocked Sender picking on someone else."

"He'd probably go right back to Raj," I said. "Which is not what I want. Or someone else, and then someone else would be going through this and it would be my fault. That's worse than it happening to me."

"He could also just follow through on the implied threat,"

Alex said. "He could send the pictures to someone. To anyone. Post them online, social media, whatever. Given your rep, word would get out pretty fast. People would love to see Perfect Kara show how not perfect she really is."

I hadn't realized the dreaded nickname had made it to Alex. Apparently everyone knew it. Which meant she was right—everyone would love seeing me humiliated like this. I imagined Julia Jackson laughing about it with the Brain Trust at lunch. And then I remembered my other fear, that somehow Blocked Sender had a picture of my actual face. So many ways to show the world I wasn't perfect.

"So I have to do it. I have no choice. I don't even know how, though. I've never gotten a prescription filled by myself. Am I supposed to use my own insurance card? Isn't that not a good idea? And how much does it cost? If I pay with a credit card, they'll know who I am. And aren't there video cameras at these places? Do I have to show my ID?" The more I thought about it, the more I realized that there was no way I could do this without getting caught.

"You're spiraling," Alex said. "One step at a time. Raj will be here any minute—he'll know the answers to these questions."

She was right. I focused on my breathing to calm myself down and drank another cup of coffee, even though it would probably have the opposite effect.

Raj showed up even sooner than he'd said. I was relieved

to see that he hadn't gone to any great efforts to groom for us, either—he was in sweats and a heavy coat, and his dark hair was rumpled in a way that was clearly more from sleep than styling. "Thanks for coming over," I said. "We could use your help."

Alex interrupted before I could explain. "Before we get to that, I just want to say I'm sorry again for what we did at your house. It was my idea, and I was totally wrong, and I'm glad you and Kara have talked it out, but I wanted you to know that she would have done things differently."

I wasn't expecting that. I wasn't sure she was right—she'd come up with the plan, but it's not like I had any better ideas. And I'd gone along with it. She was trying to take the bullet for me, going way above and beyond what she needed to tell him. But she wasn't done.

"She told me it was happening to you too—not to break your confidence but because I'm in this up to my neck, just like you guys." She explained to him about the poker, and the money.

"The timeline makes sense," he said. "Thanks for telling me this."

"Sure, yeah, but does that mean you forgive me? Us?"

I understood her concern for saving their friendship, but I still didn't understand why she was trying so hard to help me. Did she really want me and Raj to get together that badly?

"I do forgive you," he said. "Both of you. I was angry that

you hadn't trusted me, but I understand. It's not like I told anyone when it started happening to me."

Sitting in the living room, just the three of us, I was suddenly reminded of hanging out with Becca and Isabel, how comfortable we were as a trio. How nice it was to have friends. Strange to be thinking about that at a time like this.

"So what kind of help do you need?" he asked. "Not another prescription already."

"No, I just need to know how to fill it." I didn't say that my mother had always filled prescriptions for me in the past; no need to sound like an idiot, even though I felt like one. I ran through my lists of questions.

"All right," he said. "I can tell you what to do. You don't need insurance—you can just pay cash. That avoids the credit card problem too. You don't need an ID, so no need to worry about that. You're right about the cameras—I usually go to small places that don't have them, but you don't have much of a choice here. It's an easy fix, though—just cover your hair, wear sunglasses and different clothes than you normally would, and look at the ground as much as possible."

With every sentence I started to calm down. Raj made it sound manageable. Scary, still, but manageable.

"I can help with the outfit and stuff," Alex said. "And we'll come with you. Right, Raj?"

"Of course," he said.

"No way. I'm not risking anyone else getting in trouble

for this. I'll meet you guys after."

"There's a diner not too far from the Walmart called the Bayview," Raj said. "We can meet up there. We won't see anyone we know. I'll drive us to Alex's so you can change, and then we'll wait for you while you fill the prescription."

Now that we had a plan, I felt better. I wasn't in this alone.

We went right to Alex's house—I wanted to get this over with, so I wanted to be ready to go right at one. Raj took Alex's massive desk chair while she and I dug through her Closet of Wonders for a disguise. We settled on all black for the pants and shirt, covered with a denim jacket and topped with a scarf to cover my face. I wore my hair in a bun and put on a baseball hat and enormous sunglasses. "Unrecognizable," Alex pronounced.

It only took about twenty minutes to drive to Redwood City, but it felt like forever. This will be over in under an hour, I reminded myself. Except technically it wouldn't—there could still be more favors to come, after all. I pulled down the mirror in the sun visor and checked myself out. My face was almost completely hidden. I was tempted to get a face wipe and take off my makeup—that would make me look totally different, for sure—but there was no need to go that far. I looked a little ridiculous, but if the parking lot was any indication, the Walmart was pretty crowded. If the cameras caught me, there wasn't all that much of me to see.

The front of the Walmart was decorated with wreaths

and holly, and there was a giant blow-up Santa waving gently in the breeze. I heard the bell of a Salvation Army volunteer ringing as the electric doors opened. The store was full of Christmas shoppers, their carts full of ornaments and fake plastic trees. I'd never been in this Walmart before, but the layout was pretty basic. Though the store was huge, there were signs above all the aisles explaining what I could find in each one, with an enormous arrow pointing toward the pharmacy.

The thing with stores like Walmart, though, is that they rarely let you get anywhere easily. I had to zigzag through aisles of stuff I didn't want that Walmart hoped I'd buy anyway, just because it caught my eye: consumer electronics, bath towels, hair products. But I barreled ahead, thinking about all those people on reality TV competitions who insisted they weren't there to make friends—I wasn't here to shop. And I didn't want to risk the cameras or run into anyone I knew, so I kept my head down as best as I could.

The pharmacy was in the back corner of the crowded store, of course, and there was a line. Two, actually: one for drop-offs and one to pick up. I got out my phone and started playing games while I waited. The line moved slowly; there was only one person taking orders, and he was moving between the two lines. I kept my head down until I reached the front and heard the pharmacist say, "What can I do for you today?"

I looked up and saw someone I wasn't expecting.

Justin.

I'd done a good job with my costume—it took him a second to realize it was me, and then his eyes widened in a way that probably mirrored mine. My head started whirling with so many different thoughts, I got dizzy. Did this mean Justin was Blocked Sender? Or knew who was? Or was he being blackmailed like the rest of us? Or was it possible that this was random? I had a million questions I wanted to ask him, but I had a job to do and a camera to avoid.

"Hi," I said. "I need to fill a prescription." My voice shook, and my hand started shaking to match as I handed Justin the piece of paper.

He'd recovered faster than I had. He reached out smoothly and took the paper, giving it a quick scan and a nod. No acknowledgment that we knew each other, which told me that randomness was off the table. I realized he had an assistant's tag on, though that didn't really clear anything up. "I'll take care of this right away. Give me a minute." He disappeared in the back; I could hear people muttering in line behind me, wondering why Walmart didn't hire more staff for the pharmacy if it was going to get this busy.

Finally, he returned, followed by a much older man—I figured that was the actual pharmacist—who handed him a little orange bottle full of pills. Justin quickly stuffed it in a bag and stapled it closed. "Cash or credit?"

I noticed he hadn't asked me for insurance. He knew I was coming. No, he'd been surprised to see me—he knew *someone* was coming, but not that it was me. This whole situation was getting weirder and weirder. "Cash," I said, and gave him the money, which ended up being three hundred dollars for the thirty pills. Only half of what Raj had told me it was, back when I bought those pills from him, but that was the markup, I supposed. Even with the cheaper price I hoped I wasn't going to have to do this often, because I didn't have that kind of cash lying around. Three hundred dollars was already a big chunk of my savings from years' worth of birthdays and allowance.

"You're all set," he said. "Next?"

"Um, thanks," I said, then turned around and zigzagged my way back out of the Walmart as fast as I could. Once I was safely in my car, I put my key in the ignition and just sat there for a while, trying to process what I'd just learned. Yet another one of my new friends was somehow involved in all this.

It wasn't a coincidence. It couldn't be.

I waited until my hands felt under control and then drove to the Bayview Diner. It was just south of Redwood City, a few towns away from Marbella, but it might as well have been in a different world. The town wasn't nearly as affluent, and the diner was literally on the wrong side of the tracks—it was made out of an old train car, and it wasn't all that far from the train itself. The décor was all retro: Formica tabletops, leather booths that had once been shiny but now had holes with the stuffing popping out, waitresses who wore wrinkled pink dresses with white aprons. A waitress whose real name was definitely not PINKY, despite her name tag, pointed me to a table where Raj and Alex were already sitting. They must have come early—they had a big plate of cheese fries in front of them and were drinking shakes.

"How did it go?" Alex asked.

"That depends on your perspective," I said. "I got my prescription no problem. From Justin."

Raj almost choked on his shake. "I'm sorry, did you just say Justin was working at Walmart?"

Alex looked even more surprised than Raj. "He's in on this too?"

"He was working the register at the pharmacy. His tag said he was an assistant. He's the one who got the prescription for me."

"That doesn't make any sense," Alex said. "He would have told me."

"It was definitely him," I said. "He didn't acknowledge that he knew me, though. That has to mean he's in on it too." I paused to think. "He seemed surprised to see me, but he knew exactly what to do. He was waiting for *someone*. I don't think he's Blocked Sender, but I can't be sure."

"No," Alex said. "Besides, Justin can barely work his cell

phone. He wouldn't know how to block his number."

"Besides, he's our friend," Raj said. "If anything, he got roped into it. Just like us."

"Maybe you don't know him as well as you think," I said. "Maybe he's got a secret life where he's an evil genius who knows how to hack phones. Maybe he's not such a good friend."

Alex looked skeptical. "People don't usually do a great job of hiding their inner selves."

I so totally disagreed with her I didn't even know where to start, except not with myself. "What about serial killers? Or even just people having affairs? People hide stuff all the time. Big things. Fundamental things."

"Okay, I get all that. But Justin hates hiding things. He came out of the closet when he was like five."

"He's hiding his secret boyfriend," Raj said.

"That's because it's fun."

"Is that really it?" I asked. "How long has he been hiding him?"

"A while," she admitted.

"So why would you think he'd tell you about Walmart if he won't even tell you about the boyfriend?"

"Because—" She stopped. "You're right. Maybe it was stupid of me to think that." She leaned back in her chair and folded her arms over her chest. I was getting confused. Alex had barely seemed fazed at all when I told her Raj was involved, and she seemed to be much better friends with him.

"We'll never know how he's involved unless we ask him. Can one of you guys text and tell him to meet us here after work? Blocked Sender gave me from one to five to pick up the pills, which I bet means Justin gets off work then. If he's in this like we are, he deserves to know what's going on. And if he's Blocked Sender, then we deserve to know that too. You guys know him better than I do—will you be able to tell if he's lying?"

"Maybe," Raj said.

"I'd like to think so," Alex said. "If I'm wrong about him, then I don't think I can trust my judgment about anyone."

She got out her phone and sent the text message.

Raj polished off the rest of the fries while we waited, but Alex just sat and nervously stirred her shake.

Finally, Justin texted back.

Be there at 5:30.

That meant we had hours to kill—it was only two—so we decided to go back to Raj's house and watch the rest of *The Usual Suspects.* Alex was right; I hadn't seen the ending coming. The creepiness of it made us all anxious, though, and we still had time, so we watched some dumb comedy to try to take our minds off things before we headed back to the diner.

Eventually it was time to go. We drove over together in my car, Raj in the front seat, Alex in the back, complaining about the radio station like a little kid. The music was a distraction, but it lasted only until we sat back down at the table we'd left just hours before. Not-Pinky-the-waitress didn't seem super happy to see us, at least not until we ordered more food.

And then we sat, waiting for Justin to arrive.

I was dying to know what he'd say.

17.

Five thirty came and went with no Justin.

"He's bailing on us," I said.

"He wouldn't do that," Alex said.

"You keep saying that. I don't understand why you're so sure. I mean, I haven't known him that long, but isn't he always bailing on stuff? He leaves parties early to go see his secret boyfriend, and he doesn't come out when you ask him."

"I know him," she said simply. "He'll be here."

And then, at six, he was. He took the seat next to Alex, across from me. I couldn't quite make eye contact yet. "I take it this isn't just a social call." He didn't look super surprised to be there, which didn't answer the Blocked Sender question, though it clarified that his presence at Walmart wasn't random.

"Don't be glib," Alex said. "Raj does glib better than you." She wasn't looking at him either.

"This is serious," Raj said.

Justin slumped back in his seat, chastened. "Okay, okay. Sorry."

I wasn't sure what to ask him first—I wasn't sure that Justin could be Blocked Sender, but even if he wasn't, I didn't know whether confronting him right away was the way to go. Alex wasn't about to wait for me to decide what to do, though.

"What's the deal?" she asked. "Do you just happen to have a job at Walmart you never told me about, or did someone get to you?"

"As soon as I saw Kara, I had a feeling it was all about to hit the fan," he said.

"Please, just tell us what you know," I said. "Tell us what's going on."

He ran his hands through his hair. "I don't know what you know," he said. "How about you guys tell me first?"

It was one thing for me to tell Alex and Raj what was happening, but I didn't know Justin very well. "I think you have a better idea of what's going on than we do," I said. "And you didn't seem all that surprised to see me. Not as surprised as I was to see you."

"Oh, I was surprised," he said. "You were the last person I expected."

"But you expected someone."

He sighed. "Okay, fine. I started getting these text messages about a month ago from someone who knew things I didn't want them to know. A smartass, too—said if I was such a good actor, I'd find a way to convince Walmart I was a pharmacy student so I could get an externship. I was supposed to get the gig and then await further instructions."

Await further instructions. I'd heard that before. He was one of us, then. If he was telling the truth.

"I basically just finished training and today I got another text telling me to do a good job on my first official day of work. I didn't know what it meant until I saw you, Kara. I'm assuming that Novalert prescription wasn't for you?"

"Not exactly." I didn't want to say anything else, though. This whole situation was getting weirder with every new thing we learned.

"So this started a month ago?" Alex asked. "That's it? What does Blocked Sender have over you, Justin?"

"I'd really rather not talk about it." He looked away from Alex when he said it, though, and she sharpened her gaze.

"Why not? Keeping more secrets? Or is this about that boyfriend of yours?"

"Like I said. Not talking about it."

"Even with me," she said. I watched them argue. Were they that close? Justin frowned and leaned back in his chair, clearly not ready to talk.

"Let's just skip the airing of laundry for now and move on to exactly what's going on here," I said. "I haven't been hanging out with you guys for that long, but it's clearly not random that the four of us all got roped into this."

"And we don't know that it's just us four," Alex said.

"Or who's behind it," Raj added.

"Can't help you there," Justin said. His leg was bouncing so hard I could feel the table vibrating.

Alex banged her hands on the table. "Come on. I know you know more than you're telling us. You think I can't tell when you're lying?"

"I've got nothing. Really."

For someone who was such a good actor, he wasn't doing a great job of sounding convincing.

"What are we supposed to do now? We're no closer to figuring this out than I was when I thought it was just me," I said.

"What's to figure out?" Justin said. "We're screwed. Whoever this person is has us just where he wants us. He knows everything about us, and we know nothing about him. And it doesn't seem like anything bad has happened to us so far. All our secrets are safe. Aren't we better off just going along with it?"

"That's not going to work for me," I said. "We need to figure out who's doing this."

"I don't think that's such a good idea," Justin said. "We don't want to make him mad."

"Wow, whatever he's got on you must be big," Alex said.

Justin ignored her. "I'll do whatever I have to. And I need you guys to do the same." He was almost pleading now. "If one of us doesn't follow directions, the rest of us could be in trouble. That can't happen."

"Sounds a little like a threat," Raj said.

"That's not what I meant," he said, as my phone buzzed. There was no question who it would be.

Leave pills behind the copies of The Mystery of Edwin Drood in the library by end of school Monday. Tell no one.

All eyes turned toward me.

I put my phone in the middle of the table, and they took turns reading it. "That's the spot," Raj said. He glanced at Justin. "Or it was, before."

Alex and I nodded. "Before what?" Justin asked.

"Nope," Alex said. "No info from you, no info from us. You want in, you have to pay up."

Justin frowned. "Fine. I'll stay out of it, then. You guys do what you have to, as long as you don't get me involved."

"You're already involved," Raj said.

"I'm happy to be a bit player in this little drama. I'll see you guys at school." He got up so fast he almost knocked over his chair, and then left without looking back.

"That went well," I said.

Alex was fuming. "God! Why was he being so unhelpful?"

"Because he doesn't trust us," I said.

"Yeah, I get that," she said, with more bitterness than sarcasm.

"Maybe his stuff is just worse than ours," I said. "Our

secrets are all things we want to keep from our parents, but Justin seems more concerned about keeping things from us. Different category."

"That could be true," Raj said.

"Easy for you to say when we don't know what Blocked Sender has on you," Alex said.

"You don't have to tell us that," I said. I wanted to know, but not just because Alex was mad. Alex and I had shared our secrets voluntarily; making someone spill his who didn't want to made us almost like Blocked Sender.

"No, you're right," he said. "I've avoided telling you guys because it doesn't make me look so good. But I'm in the same position you are. What Blocked Sender had on me was something I didn't want my parents to know. We moved here because I did terribly badly on some exams that I needed to move on to the next level at school, and instead of moving on, I flunked out."

"Like the SATs?" I asked.

"Kind of. Similar enough, anyway. My parents were humiliated and convinced that I had no future in England, so they panicked and decided to move here so I could start over. My sister was furious—she'd been doing great in school and had lots of friends, and she hates it here. I don't think she'll ever forgive me."

"I don't get it," I said. "Your parents already know you flunked out."

"That's not the problem. Blocked Sender somehow found out that I'd tried to cheat on those exams. I hadn't studied at all. Instead, I'd arranged to buy a copy of the test, but it turned out to be a hoax and I'd memorized all the wrong answers. I was totally unprepared for the actual test, which is why it went so poorly. One of my teachers told me the school knew what I'd done but were helping my parents save face by just throwing me out for failing instead of for cheating. I can't ever let them find out what really happened. My parents moved to another country to help salvage my future—they'd be devastated if they realized why." He looked back and forth at Alex and me. "So, have you both lost what little respect for me you might have had? Do you see why I didn't want to tell you?"

Alex had leaned forward while Raj was talking, the angry expression slowly leaving her face. "We're hardly in a position to judge you, Raj."

"But what I did was so much worse than anything either of you have done."

"Your family obviously loves you a lot, to make this kind of sacrifice," I said. "I understand why you don't want them to find out, but they'd forgive you."

"Maybe my parents will. Especially now that I've discovered I share their love of science. But my sister never will. Anyway, I think Kara's right that our secrets are all in the same family, pardon the pun, and it seems clear that Justin's are not. That changes things. I don't think he's our Blocked Sender, though."

I wasn't so sure. Not yet, anyway.

"I don't think so either," Alex said. "I don't know about the boyfriend, though. This has to be about him in some way. We've been teasing him about it all year and he's never slipped. Not once."

"Do you think the boyfriend might be Blocked Sender?" I asked.

"There's only one way to find out," she said. "We've got to catch Blocked Sender in the act."

"How are we supposed to do that? I'm not about to stick around in the library after I drop off the pills. Blocked Sender's not stupid."

"I could do it," Raj said.

"That won't work. Blocked Sender knows that you and I know each other. Remember the pictures? But we don't know how much he knows about us as a group."

"We should assume he knows everything," Alex said. "It's safer that way."

"That means none of us can be there, then," Raj said.

"Exactly," Alex said. "This is where I get to be helpful, finally. We're going to watch the pickup from the comfort of my bedroom."

"What, you're going to set up a video camera?" I asked. "That's not exactly inconspicuous."

"Oh, my dear Luddite Kara, you have no idea what changes the world has brought. Cameras have gotten super tiny—didn't you see that thing on YouTube where a squirrel picked one up and climbed a tree? It was adorable. We'll hook something like that up in the library." She was getting excited.

"Wouldn't we have to go back and pick it up later?" Raj asked. "And aren't they quite expensive?"

"We can stream it. They're so cheap we wouldn't even have to go back and pick it up if we didn't want to."

My shoulders finally unclenched. I was grateful to have a friend who was so much smarter and savvier than I was. "You're a genius," I said.

"Hardly. But at least we'll know who's doing the pickup. If it's Justin, we'll need to have a very different conversation than we did today."

"And if it's someone else?" Raj asked.

"We'll either have another member of our little Scooby gang, or we'll learn who Blocked Sender is. Either way, we'll know more tomorrow than we do now. And isn't that the point?"

The point was for all this to be over, and we were nowhere near it. But this was a start.

18.

Monday morning came way too fast. Alex, Raj, and I met at lunch in the cafeteria to walk through our plan; Justin knew enough to stay away, at least for the day. Alex brought the camera with her and showed me how it worked—it was just a little square with some adhesive on the back, so I had to find a shelf or a spot on the wall with a good line of sight and stick it there. It was so tiny that no one would notice it. Or so I hoped.

I got a bathroom pass during study hall, clutching my stomach to make clear that I was planning to be gone a while, then headed to the library. The high school's librarians were mostly recent library science grads from local universities, hipsters with thick bangs and glasses with equally thick frames who would rather have been working in an archive. The library's checkout system was completely automatic, so the librarians just sat around looking bored and waiting for people to come in for help with research projects. They smiled at me hopefully when I came in and then ignored me when I walked right past them.

The library contained a broad expanse of open space in the middle, filled with tables where students could study, though right now they were deathly quiet. I headed toward the back right, where signs informed me I could find the fiction section. There were three copies of *The Mystery of Edwin Drood* in the back; I'd had to look up the book online to learn that Charles Dickens had written it. Ironically enough (or maybe purposefully?) it was a book about drugs and murder. All three copies looked relatively new and untouched, especially as compared to the surrounding books—there must have been twenty copies of *Great Expectations*, all battered, as were the copies of *David Copperfield.* They'd probably been assigned for an English class.

I didn't want to end up on camera myself, so I decided to drop the pills right away. I pulled out the center copy of *Edwin Drood* and placed the bottle of pills behind it. I could see why Blocked Sender had chosen the spot; the bookshelves were lined up in rows, so while the Dickens books were on a shelf that faced a wall, there was a shelf of books behind them that shielded the back of the bookcase from the rest of the room. It was a private little spot. I replaced the book, leaving it sticking out just a little so it would be clear to Blocked Sender where I'd been, without it being obvious to anyone else.

Now for the hard part: setting up the camera. "Think of it as a replacement for your eye," Alex had said. "Make sure you've got a clear line of sight." I used my finger to trace a line between my eye and the book as I walked back and forth, searching for a good spot. The key was to get a good angle so we could see the face of the person who picked up the pills.

Finally, I found a spot on the adjacent wall that had a bunch of posters tacked up already. The camera wasn't so conspicuous when I stuck it in between a couple of different flyers, and it lined up perfectly, as far as I could tell. I made sure it was securely fixed there, pushing on its sides to test that it was really stuck.

And then I ducked out of the library as fast as I could.

Once school was over, Alex, Raj, and I piled into my car and headed back to her house. Having the two of them in my car was starting to feel comfortable; the front seat was already moved far back to accommodate Raj's long legs, and Alex tapped my shoulder from the backseat in what had quickly become the signal for me to turn the radio on to the indie station she liked.

"Any problems with the camera?" she asked.

"Nope. I think I found a good spot."

"We'll find out soon enough," Raj said.

We stopped at the store to pick up junk food for our afternoon of waiting, since we had no idea when the person would come get the pills, or even if it would happen today.

Armed with snacks, we settled into Alex's lair while she set up the feed on her computer. The camera worked amazingly well—the video quality was a little fuzzy, but I'd picked a good location, and we had a clear view of not just the bookshelf itself but the whole row, so we could see when people walked by even if they weren't the people we were looking for. Alex had set it to record, too, so the first thing we did was to rewind back to right after I'd set it up, just in case.

We scanned through the hour and a half of video that had accumulated since I'd dropped the camera, but no one had come. No one had even walked through the stacks. "This does give some context for why I never have to wait for any of the books I want," Raj said. "One would have thought a school of this quality would have some students interested in classic literature." He shook his head in feigned despair, his dark hair flopping over his eyes. I was tempted to brush it back, but I didn't want to start something I wasn't prepared to follow through. And right now, all I could think about was Blocked Sender. Well, almost all.

"Watch the judgment there," Alex said. "Just because you're British doesn't automatically make you classy."

"Compared to you lot? Please."

"You're responsible for tabloids and at least half of the boy bands."

"That's true," Raj admitted. "But we're much better at chocolate. Right, Kara?"

"Don't bring me into this," I said. I didn't want to fight with friends even over little stupid things. You never knew when those small arguments could turn into bigger problems before you'd realized it was happening.

We sat in silence for a while, watching the video.

Until.

"Check it out." I pointed to the screen, where a dark figure had entered the frame. The person was wearing all black clothes and a black baseball hat, kind of like the outfit I'd worn to Walmart. It wasn't clear right away whether it was a boy or a girl, let alone who the person actually was. The figure walked right up to Dickens and, head still bowed, pulled back the copy of *Edwin Drood*, and reached for the pills.

"This is a disaster," I said. "All this work and we're not going to be able to tell who it is."

"Patience," Alex said. "This is definitely someone who's trying to be stealthy, but they don't seem to know there's a camera—they're not avoiding it specifically. We just need to wait."

I wasn't convinced, but I kept watching anyway. The person looked at the bottle of pills, then opened it and took one out to inspect it. The person put the pill back and replaced the lid on the bottle, then straightened up. We couldn't see the whole face, but we could see the bottom half, and a slight smile.

"Well, that's not going to be enough," Raj said.

"Actually," I said, my voice cracking, "it is."

I knew that face.

"That's Isabel," I said.

"The one who's in all the plays with Justin?" Alex asked.

"That's the one."

"She was on your list."

"What list?" Raj asked.

"Early on, we tried thinking about who might be involved," I said.

"How did you come up with her?"

"We used to be friends. A while back."

Alex started singing the *Veronica Mars* theme, that old Dandy Warhols song.

"Now is not the time, Alex," Raj said.

She stopped singing. "She knows Justin. There could be a connection there."

"Like they could be Blocked Sender together?" I asked. "I thought we wrote him off."

"Well, maybe we shouldn't have. They could be working as a team. We've been assuming this was one person, but maybe it isn't."

"Do you really think Justin would do that? To you, especially?" Raj asked.

Alex looked uncomfortable. She'd had the same expression on her face when we'd first realized Justin was involved.

And there were all those cryptic comments she'd made about how well she knew him. Alex and Justin clearly had more of a history than I knew. But why wouldn't she have just told me? "I don't know about the whole Justin thing," I said, "but Isabel and I are not on good terms. I can't imagine her being Blocked Sender, but maybe she knows who is. I have to talk to her."

"I don't think ambushing her is such a good idea," Raj said. "It didn't work so well with Justin."

"Well, what are we supposed to do, then?" I asked.

"I say we keep playing detective," Alex said. "If she's not Blocked Sender, then she's got to be bringing the pills to someone. We should follow her and see where she goes."

"That's crazy. We have no idea when she would do it, and we can't just tail her every day. I need to confront her."

"What are you going to do, just wait for her outside rehearsal and start screaming? It's not the best strategy."

Alex was right. I had to make a plan. "Can we get screen shots from that video?"

She nodded, smiling. "Of course. That's a good start." She turned to the computer and started going through the video, clicking away.

"Should we go talk to her together?" Raj asked. "Like we did with Justin?"

"That didn't go so great. I should do this alone." Besides,

I wasn't sure what she would say, and not just about Blocked Sender. I was better off on my own.

He looked at his watch. "You guys can handle things from here? I have to get home."

"No problem," Alex said. "You go. We'll see you at school tomorrow."

Raj left as Alex was putting together an online folder of pictures. We'd stopped watching as soon as I recognized Isabel, but the camera had still been playing, and there were some great shots that made it very clear who we were looking at. Alex had arranged the screen shots like a narrative: Isabel coming up to the bookshelf, getting the pills, inspecting one, putting the bottle in her pocket, checking to make sure no one was watching her, and then heading out. The story was pretty clear, at least to me.

"I'm emailing these to you. Do you want the video too?"

"This should be enough."

"What are you going to say?"

That I hadn't thought through yet. "I don't know."

"It's worth thinking about," she said. "I should have strategized better when you told me about Justin, but there wasn't enough time."

"You did seem really surprised about him," I said. "And maybe I was reading things wrong, but . . . you seemed pretty angry, too. I mean, we're all pissed off about everything, but it felt different with you guys."

"It was. We've known each other for a long time." She paused, and I waited for her to say something else, but she didn't.

I guess we all still had our secrets.

19.

I decided I'd wait for Isabel after rehearsal the next day and find her before she left. She'd be exhausted, I was sure, and maybe it would be better to catch her off guard. I wasn't optimistic that it would be easy to get her to open up to me; it had been so long since we'd talked. I didn't know how long rehearsal would go, though, so I sat on the linoleum floor outside the entrance to the auditorium and waited. Which gave me a little too much time to think. And of course, since I was waiting for Isabel, I thought about her and Becca. Mostly Becca, though.

After I'd ditched swim tryouts freshman year and Isabel and Becca had started sitting with their new friends at lunch, I'd worried that I'd ruined everything. And for a while, it seemed like I had; though I'd called Becca a bunch of times to apologize, she was really mad. I pulled Isabel aside and asked what she thought I should do, but she said, "Just give her some time," and so I did. I stopped calling every day and settled for sending text messages every so often, and I stuck to my lonely lunches with the Brain Trust.

Finally, after a couple of weeks, I decided I needed to do something more drastic. I wasn't about to let things end this way. So I showed up at Becca's house when I knew her parents were out and she was home, gathered my courage, and knocked on the door.

I wasn't sure if she would answer, but she did. She opened the door and just looked at me. "Hi," I said. Now that my plan had worked, I realized I didn't actually have much of what I wanted to say figured out.

"Hi," she said.

"Can I come in?"

She just turned around and went back in the house, but she hadn't closed the door on me, so I figured I was supposed to follow her. She went back to her room and sat on one of her armchairs; it felt weird to sit in my normal spot, so I took Isabel's usual place on the loveseat.

"I'm really sorry about tryouts," I said.

She stayed silent, waiting for me to say something else. Something that would explain, that would make everything make sense.

I had no idea what that was. Other than the truth, which somehow was wrong. I couldn't make her understand how awful my skin problem made me feel, how I left the house every day terrified that something would happen and everyone would find out. If I told her that was the reason I couldn't swim anymore, I worried she'd think it was petty. And maybe it was. But not to me.

"I didn't know how to tell you I didn't want to try out," I said. "Classes are already really hard, and swim team is superintense. I was afraid I wouldn't have enough time to study, and I don't love swimming like you do. I'd have to work twice as hard as everyone else if I even made the team, and I didn't think I could do both."

"I understand that," she said, but her voice was hard. "I understand a lot of things."

"You do?"

"Yeah, I do," she said. "What I don't understand is why you didn't tell me. Why you've been hiding so many things. We've been friends for how many years now? Why didn't you just say something? I was worried about you."

"You were?" I'd been so fixated on her being mad that it hadn't occurred to me. And what else did she think I was hiding?

"I thought something happened. I thought maybe you got into a car accident. It never for one hot second occurred to me that you would just blow off tryouts and not tell me. Do you have any idea how much that hurt, when I realized it? I seriously considered never speaking to you again."

"I bet Isabel was totally on board with that." Everything that had happened since we'd started high school only served to confirm my sense that she'd be happier being a duo with Becca.

"Don't do that," she said. "Don't put me in the middle of you guys. Yes, I've known her longer, and I get that you and I are closer than you are with her. But I'm sick of being the one in the middle. She's not the problem here. You are."

Becca had always been direct; it was something I'd always admired about her. She wasn't mean like Isabel could be; she just said what was on her mind. I envied her for it, really. Of course, at the moment, I wished she was a little less direct. I was the problem, but hearing her say it made me feel kind of sick.

"I get that," I said. "Can you forgive me, though?"

"You realize this is the second time you've bailed on me," she said. "Don't think I've forgotten about the hair."

I stared at the floor, which made my hair hang in front of my face. Not the best move. "I know."

"You knew you weren't going to try out then, didn't you?"

"I wasn't sure," I said, but I was getting tired of lying. "I'd started worrying about school, but we hadn't started classes yet. I didn't know for sure until later." It was close enough. "I'm sorry about that too. You know I am."

"Yeah, I do," she said, and she finally sounded like herself again. "But we can't keep doing this. You not being honest with me, and then being all sad and apologetic and asking me to forgive you. We never used to be like this. I don't want high school to change us."

I didn't say that it already had, or that it wasn't just high school, or any of the things I should have said. I just said I'd never do anything like that again; if I did, I knew I wouldn't be able to come back from it.

And for a while, we were fine. We weren't great, or even good, but we were fine. I went to her swim meets when I could, and we met up to go to Isabel's shows, and once in a while the three of us went out for coffee or even hung out at Becca's house, like in the old days. But whenever the two of them wanted to go out at night, to parties or clubs in San Francisco, which was their new thing, I begged off. I wanted to hang out with just them, but they were more interested in meeting guys, which I knew was something I should want too. I even had a crush on a guy in my math elective, a junior named Drew who was totally out of my league. The thought of actually getting together with him, or anyone else, was terrifying. What if he found out what was under my makeup? It was one thing to walk the halls looking normal; it was a whole other thing for someone to come close enough to touch my face and feel the roughness underneath the smooth illusion.

Becca kept trying to get me to go anyway. "It's not like you have to get with anyone," she'd say. "We'll have fun no matter what."

But I went with them once or twice, and it wasn't fun. I'd end up sitting by myself or dancing alone while they were off with the boys they liked; even worse was when guys I didn't know would come up and talk to me, or try to get me to dance with them. It made me anxious—not as anxious as the thought of swim tryouts, but I wasn't interested in learning how much more anxious I'd feel if I kept doing the kinds of things they wanted to do. I didn't want to meet just anyone; if I was going to get over my fears, it would be for Drew and no one else.

I started to remember how things got really bad sophomore year, but before I could dive back into those memories, people started coming out of rehearsal. I stood up quickly so Isabel wouldn't be able to avoid seeing me, turning away when I saw Justin. He'd had no interest in being involved in the plan to find out who Blocked Sender was; I had no interest in explaining why I was hanging around outside the auditorium.

Isabel was one of the last people to leave rehearsal. She was as glamorous as ever with her short skirt and high boots, hairdresser-enhanced blond hair falling in waves around her face. She was talking animatedly with a couple of other girls; I hated interrupting, but I had no choice. She wasn't paying attention to me at all. "Isabel," I called out just as she passed me by.

She stopped walking and turned around to face me.

"Look who we have here," she said.

"We need to talk," I said.

"Do we, now?" She gave me her old up-and-down look and then sniffed, as if I hadn't met her standards.

I nodded. I wasn't going to let her scare me off.

"Do you want us to wait for you?" one of the girls asked.

"Nah, I got this," Isabel said. "I'll see you guys tomorrow." She waited until they'd walked away. "What's up, Kara?"

I got out my phone and opened the photo stream we'd pulled from the video camera, then handed the phone to Isabel. She frowned at me but took the camera and looked at the first photo.

"Keep going," I said.

She scrolled through the pictures, her frown deepening.

"Got anything you want to tell me?" I asked.

"Where did you get these?" she asked, sounding more scared than angry.

"It doesn't matter where I got the pictures," I said. "I just want to know why they exist."

"Not here," she said. "Come on."

I followed her into the auditorium, up a small set of stairs onto the stage. She took a left back through the curtains. They smelled musty as I walked behind her. She wound her way down a hallway lined with gray concrete blocks until she reached a door, got out a set of keys, opened the door, turned on the lights, and motioned me in.

She'd taken me to a dressing room in the depths of the theater. The walls were completely lined with posters from shows the school had done over the years, designed to look like Broadway playbills: *The Wizard of Oz*, *Our Town*, a whole bunch of Shakespeare, and lots of shows I'd never heard of. It was the first time I'd ever felt like Marbella High had a sense of history—the school had been completely renovated before we got there, and everything was so new and shiny and high-tech that I'd forgotten it had actually been around for decades.

Isabel locked the door behind us and then pulled two chairs close together. "All right, talk."

"Me? I'm here to talk about you, not me."

"You already know something about me, if you've got those pictures. How did you get them?"

"We set up a camera in the library."

"Who's we?"

"Nope," I said. "I need more from you first."

"Fine. I was there to pick up whatever was behind those books. Pills, apparently."

"I know that already," I said. "I'm the one who put them there."

"Perfect Kara? With drugs? How the mighty have fallen."

"Don't call me that," I said. "Just tell me who told you to get them."

"You want me to share my secrets with you? That's pretty

ballsy, considering you've never been willing to share yours."

"I don't have secrets," I said. More lying. Would it ever stop?

"Oh, please," she said. "You and your little transformation?" She motioned toward my face.

"What do you mean?"

"You're not the first person who ever had to cover up a zit. You think we didn't figure out what was going on? We were your friends. We knew everything about each other. You might not have wanted to tell us why you started letting your mom give you makeovers, but it was totally obvious."

"Are you kidding me?" There was no way they could have known all along. It wasn't possible.

"You went from makeup-is-the-devil to being able to do a contouring video in like two point five seconds. And then no swimming? Come on. It might have taken us a while to figure it out, but that's only because you never said anything. Did you think you were too good for us when you started getting all hot? Or were we just not smart enough for you?"

"That's not what happened," I said. I couldn't believe she and Becca had known about my skin but had read everything else so wrong.

"We tried to understand," she said. "And we tried to keep the threesome together. But you didn't want to do anything we wanted to do. And then you flipped out the night we went to that guy's house and wouldn't tell us why."

It was the night I'd tried so hard not to think about anymore. It had been after the disastrous PSAT, when all Isabel and Becca wanted to do was go out and party. I still wasn't over the panic attack I'd had, and even the thought of a party made me feel the nausea and headache that signaled something was wrong. I was afraid of what would happen if we went somewhere and things got bad.

I was right to worry.

It wasn't even a party, really. It was just a night at Drew's house, and a case of beer and some drinking games. It didn't sound so bad. Better than the clubs, anyway. Becca and Isabel both had their eyes on some of Drew's friends, and Drew was paying attention to me in exactly the way I'd always hoped he would. The beers were gross, but I drank them, and after a couple I understood why people drank; my whole body felt looser and a little tingly. I started to relax. My breathing came easier, and I even started to think I might have fun.

"What do we have to do to get these ladies to dance?" one of the guys shouted.

Someone hooked their iPhone to the speakers and music started blasting. Someone else shut off the lights, and all of a sudden it was like we were in a different place. Everyone was dancing. I drank another beer and felt like I could fly. I wasn't worried about freaking out anymore.

I was shaking my hips with my arms in the air when I

felt hands on my waist. "I'm glad you came," Drew said. "You look really good tonight." His hands felt sure and strong as they slipped under the tank I was wearing to settle on my bare skin. Thank goodness the zits didn't travel that low. He pulled me backward toward him and we danced like that for a while; then he flung me around so we were facing each other, hips still moving together, and though I was already sweating, my body flooded with warmth. If it hadn't been so dark, I'd have been worried that he was close enough to see past the makeup, but I barely had time to think about it before he moved his face so close to mine that it would be so, so easy for him to just lean in and kiss me.

And he did. His lips were tentative at first, as if he wasn't sure if I'd push him away. But when I didn't, he kissed me harder, opening my mouth with his tongue, and somehow I knew how to respond, even though I'd never done this before. His hands moved from my waist to the small of my back, farther up my tank top, until I worried he'd pull it off right in front of everyone. I pulled away for just a minute to yank it down, and then he started kissing me again.

But he moved his hands. To my face.

That's when the panic set in. I pulled away, maybe too abruptly, because even in the dark I could see that he looked confused. "Stop!" I shouted.

"I thought—"

My head was pounding and the room was starting to spin. Was I panicking, or was I just drunk? Did it matter? "You thought wrong," I managed to say before I ran off to find Becca and Isabel. More people had come while I was dancing, though I had barely noticed, and the small room was crowded with people, mostly paired off, mostly using the dark to make out. Where were Becca and Isabel? Why had they left me alone?

I hated the idea of interrupting them, but I had to. I had to get out of there. Through the crowd, I spotted Becca dancing with a guy I knew she liked. I grabbed her arm. "We have to leave. Now."

"Why?" she asked. "What's going on?"

"Let's just go."

"Are you okay? Are you sick?" She looked worried, but she also wasn't moving. She didn't want to leave; that much was clear.

But I was starting to feel the same way I'd felt during the PSAT, when I'd left the room to keep from fainting. I was sure now that it wasn't the beer.

I was having another panic attack.

I didn't want to faint here. I didn't answer Becca's question; I just ran outside and collapsed on the lawn, hoping no one had seen me. Becca didn't come out right away, which gave me enough time to get myself together and sit up. I waited for a while trying to figure out what to do. Should I just call my parents and get a ride home? Then they'd know I'd been drinking.

Finally, Becca came outside, with Isabel. "What's going on?" Isabel asked. "Why did you just run out of there?"

Looking back, it's obvious I should have just told them. Becca already knew about the PSATs; if I just said I was having a panic attack, they'd understand. But it was one thing to freak out over a test; it was a whole other thing to freak out because the boy I liked had finally kissed me and I was afraid he'd see who I really was. Which meant explaining to them about the monster. I couldn't do it.

"I'm not having fun. I want to leave," I said, standing up.

"So we're all supposed to just pick up and go?" Isabel asked, her voice getting louder. "We keep trying to get you to hang out with us, to have fun, and the minute we're all actually having a good time, you get to decide it's over?"

I turned to Becca, hoping she'd understand without me having to explain, but she looked just as mad as Isabel. Like I was abandoning her. Please, I thought. I tried to say something, anything, but standing up had made the nausea worse, and now I was so dizzy I felt like I might fall down again.

"You've got nothing you want to add here?" Becca asked. "Last chance to explain."

That's when I knew I'd lost her.

They dropped me off at home—Isabel was a little older

than the rest of us, and had gotten her license the minute she was allowed. I heard later that they went back to the party without me.

That had been what finally did it. I guess Becca viewed that as my third strike, and I was out. She gave up on me, and Isabel followed suit.

"I was having a panic attack," I told her now. "Like at the PSAT. I didn't want you guys to know. I didn't want to ruin the party. But I should have told you. I'm a horrible person who lied to my friends, and now you know every last one of my secrets. Okay? So now tell me yours."

She stared at me for a minute. I'd said something she hadn't expected. "Fine," she said.

"Fine," I said.

"It's a long story."

"I've got time."

She let out a deep breath, and then she was ready to talk. "I've been getting these text messages . . ."

"From a blocked sender," I said.

"You know about that too?" She sounded genuinely surprised. At this point I wasn't.

"We're all in the same boat," I said.

"Are you going to tell me who this *we* is you keep talking about?"

"We'll get to it. What does Blocked Sender have on you?"

"That's none of your business," she said.

"It is now," I said.

"I don't think so. Why should I trust you? How do I know you're not behind this?"

"How do I know *you* aren't?" I hadn't really thought so before, but the Justin connection gave me pause, and hearing her talk about how mad she'd been at me wasn't helping.

"Don't be ridiculous," she said.

"Look, I know you're still angry, but you don't seriously think I would do this, do you?"

"I don't know. I don't exactly know what's going on with you these days. You obviously have secrets, or you wouldn't be in this mess."

"I could say the same thing about you," I said. "I'll tell you mine if you tell me yours."

"Fine." She sat back in her chair and crossed one leg over the other. "You first."

So I told her everything. About the stress, the panic attacks, the Novalert, the pictures. Everything except the people. There would be time for that, but not yet.

"The panic attacks didn't go away, then."

"Nope."

"You should have told me. You weren't the only one under stress, you know." She uncrossed her legs and leaned forward. "The theater stuff is hard, and there's so much to do and so little time, and so much competition for the drama programs in college. I've had audition after audition and it's just exhausting."

I thought about my competition with Julia, and how hard I had to work just to get into the schools I wanted. Maybe Isabel was going through the same thing. It had never occurred to me.

"At first it was just a couple of bumps at a party," Isabel said. "The drama kids were always all about coke, and it was no big deal. But the energy rush was amazing, so finally I just got some for myself and started doing it before shows. Not a lot; just enough to get me going. And then it played out pretty much like it did with you—a photo of me backstage, damaging enough to make me want it to go away."

"But it didn't go away."

"Hasn't yet," she said. "But this all just started."

"What are you supposed to do with the pills?"

"I don't know yet. I'm waiting for—"

"Further instructions," I said.

She nodded.

20.

Isabel and I sat together quietly for a while, something we'd never done back when we were friends. We'd never spent a lot of time one-on-one, really; Becca always served as the filter between us. Our friendship had been almost completely dependent on her. I'd always thought being a trio was like being part of a triangle, but now I realized that the three of us had been more like one of those playground seesaws, Becca sitting in the middle while Isabel and I took turns moving up and down, vying for her attention.

Although she probably thought it was more like tug-of-war, and she was the rope.

"What do we do?" Isabel asked. I'd never heard her sound so uncertain.

"We have to make it stop," I said. "Will you come talk to the others with me? I'm supposed to meet up with them after I've talked to you."

"I don't like the idea of other people knowing about what happened," she said.

"I won't tell them. If you decide you want to, that will be up to you. There's one other person who's been kind of close-mouthed about everything, so you're not alone."

"Okay, then. Where are you meeting them?"

"Good question." I got out my phone and texted Alex. **Done here. Isabel's in. Make Justin come. Where are we meeting?**

Alex texted back right away—she must have been waiting for me. **We're at Amerigo's**.

"Pizza," I said. "Want to ride with me?"

"I'll meet you there."

"You'll really come? Do you want my number, just in case?"

"I never deleted you from my phone," she said.

I'd never deleted her, either.

By the time I got to the restaurant, Alex and Raj were already digging into an enormous pizza with the strangest array of toppings: anchovies, pineapples, green peppers, mushrooms.

"I know it looks weird, but it's delicious," Alex said. "It's got that whole salty-sweet thing going on."

"I bet Kara only likes plain pizza," Raj said.

That was true, but I didn't want to admit it.

"Try it—it's really good," Alex said.

"I'll take your word for it." I wasn't hungry, though I was dying for something to drink. I went up to the counter and ordered a Diet Coke the size of a Big Gulp, in an enormous clear red plastic cup. Hardly anyone was sitting at the tables around us; Amerigo's was more of a takeout place than a sit-down restaurant. The red-and-white-checked plastic tablecloth was worn and fastened to the table with binder clips.

I sat down next to Alex. "Did you text Justin? Is he coming? I think it's time for us to make a plan. Isabel's got the pills, and she's waiting to find out what to do with them. I think we should do what we did with her and set up a camera once she finds out where to drop them off."

"Assuming it's in a place where that makes sense," Alex said. "Justin's on his way, but he isn't happy about it. I had to call in some chips."

"He owes you a favor?" I asked.

"He owes me lots of things," she said, and took a bite of her disgusting pizza.

I guzzled my Diet Coke while we waited for Isabel and Justin to show up. I was curious to see how they reacted to the group—I believed that Isabel had no idea who would be here, but I wasn't as convinced Justin would be surprised to see her. I was sure he knew more than he was telling us.

Isabel got there first, and relief washed over me as I realized I hadn't been sure she'd really show up. She'd changed into jeans and pulled back her hair; that must have been why she'd taken a little longer to get there than I had. She sat next to Raj.

"Hi, gorgeous," he said. "Sorry to be seeing you again under these unfortunate circumstances."

Gorgeous? It was true, but I felt a pang hearing him say it. I wondered whether they'd ever gotten together; if they'd been going to all those fancy parties, it was definitely possible. Or maybe he was just trying to show me that I didn't have to worry about me not telling him that I liked him too, after he'd opened up to me and I'd given him nothing back.

Or maybe he was trying to make me jealous. If he was, it was working.

"It's much more fun hanging out with you at parties," she said. "So is this everyone?"

"We're waiting on one more," I said.

We didn't have to wait long; Justin was crossing the parking lot as I said it, and I could see him out the window. He had a stern, determined look on his face as he opened the door, but it fell away as soon as he saw Isabel. "Oh, shit, not you too." He sounded genuinely surprised, though I reminded myself that he was an actor. He sat at the end of the table, grabbed a piece of pizza, and started picking anchovies off it. "So the gang's all here, then?"

I turned to Isabel, curious what she'd say. She kept her

cool, though. "Please tell me someone here has an idea what's actually going on."

"I wish I could," Raj said. "I don't know how much you know, but I'm guessing we don't know a whole lot more than that."

"Speak for yourself," Alex said.

"What?" I asked.

"Not talking about me. I think there's one person at the table who knows more than the rest of us." She looked at Justin. I guess we'd had the same idea about him.

"What, me?" he asked with his mouth full.

"Gross," Isabel said.

"Spill it," Alex said. "If you value our friendship at all, it's time to start talking."

Justin put his pizza down, wiped his face with his napkin, and leaned forward. Apparently he was ready to talk. "Okay, here's the thing. I might not have been completely honest with you guys when I told you I first started getting those texts a month ago."

"Yeah, we got that," Alex said. She pressed her lips together as if to keep herself from saying anything else.

"This all started about a year ago. Do you guys remember the student teacher who covered some math classes last fall?"

We all shook our heads. I'd never been in any classes with Justin, and apparently no one else had, either.

"His name was Mr. Schultz, and he was hot. I'm telling you, just super super cute. He was finishing up his undergrad at SF State, getting a teaching certification. Anyway, he taught my class for a while, and we got to talking. Pretty soon we were meeting for coffee, then dinner, though always nowhere near here."

"Wait, you mean—" Was I understanding him right? He made it all sound so casual.

"I think we both knew we were into each other right away," he said. "And, I mean, he was only twenty-one. Five years is nothing."

"So this is why the mystery boyfriend's stayed a mystery," Alex said. "A teacher!"

"I couldn't tell anyone, not even you, Alex. He'd get in so much trouble. Which is how this all started. We were super careful when he was working at Marbella High, but after he got his degree and graduated, it didn't seem like such a big deal. Someone must have seen us, though, someone who knew we'd met when he was my teacher, because late last year I started getting these text messages. Just like you guys—from a blocked number. Pics of me and Mark, holding hands, kissing—enough to cause problems. The person said he'd need some favors."

Oh, I knew all about that.

"It was weird, though—at first the favors were just answers to questions about kids at school, and mostly gossipy stuff. Who was hooking up with who, who was in charge of getting booze for parties, that sort of thing. But then the questions got a little more specific. Who was doing drugs, who was getting them. I didn't really know, but apparently I was supposed to find out."

"So you basically educated this person about all the kids at school and what they were into," Alex said. "You're the reason Blocked Sender knows all this stuff about us? You told him our secrets?" When she'd teased him about the teacher, I'd thought maybe she wasn't so angry with him anymore, but I'd never heard her sound so mad.

"I had to," he said. "I had no choice."

"You always have a choice," Alex muttered, but she'd turned her body so she didn't have to look at him.

"Does that mean we're dealing with someone who doesn't know us at all?" Raj asked.

"I don't think so. The person seemed familiar with some of the names. And they knew what kinds of questions to ask, that's for sure." He looked down.

"What did you tell him?" Isabel asked. "You told him about me, didn't you? I figured it had to be someone in drama, since no one else knew."

"Knew what?" Raj asked.

"Not now," I said, feeling weirdly protective toward Isabel.

"I answered every question they asked me, but toward the end it really was all about drugs. And I never told them anything about you," he said to Alex. "I swear."

"Whatever," she said.

"You have to believe me. The rest of you guys, yeah, I told him about you. But I didn't have a choice. You have to know that, now that all of this is happening to you too."

"Because of you," I said.

"Look, the texts started talking about statutory rape laws in California. I'm not eighteen yet—Mark could get busted for being with me. I can't let that happen."

"Guess you learned how to use your camera phone app, then," Alex said. "Good job selling us all out."

"Lay off," he said. "Mark and I are really serious. I'm in love. Do none of you understand what that's like?"

"Love shouldn't have to mean turning on your friends," Alex said. "And I notice you didn't deny your new camera skills."

"Enough!" I said. "Alex, I get that you're mad. Justin, I get that you think this is some kind of romantic drama and you're the hero for saving your boyfriend from getting arrested, but I hope you can understand that none of us care about that even a little bit. We need to come up with a plan here. Are we all agreed that we want this to stop?"

I looked around to see everyone nodding.

"Excellent. Justin, is there anything else you can tell us? Do you have any idea who this is or how many people might be involved?"

"I don't know much," he said. "Except you'd be amazed how many people I was able to get dirt on. This is a lot bigger than just us."

"Let's clarify the facts, then." I went into logic mode. "Here's what we know: Justin gave Blocked Sender enough dirt on anyone who's ever done anything bad at Marbella High to set up some sort of drug empire. He's been making money through Raj and whoever else, using what Alex taught him to hide the money. He brought in the rest of us as a backup plan when Raj bailed. And he must have another source of information, if Justin didn't tell him about Alex."

"Not holding my breath to find out who that is," Alex said under her breath.

"What else?" I asked. "Is there anything else we can put together? Anything else we know?"

"There's one more thing," Isabel said, holding out her phone. "I got a text message on the way over here. We know where I'm supposed to drop off the pills."

21.

"You could have brought that up a little earlier," I said.

"Maybe I was a little more interested in hearing what Justin had to say," she said. "Kind of seemed like the most important thing."

I could see her point, I supposed. "Well, where are we supposed to bring them?"

"A mailbox," she said. "The address is 1744 Ridgewood Drive."

"That complicates the surveillance operation," Alex said.

"You sound like a seventies movie," Justin said. "Didn't we all watch *The Conversation* at Raj's house? During our Coppola weekend?"

"Oh, you remember?" Alex wasn't letting Justin off the hook anytime soon. I'd realized that our movie night at Raj's wasn't the first time Alex had been there, but I hadn't known that the three of them watched movies together. The list of things I didn't know was getting longer all the time.

"It just means it will be harder to set up a camera than it was at the library," Raj said.

"It's a cheap camera," Alex said. "It won't work that well in the dark. We're better off just following Isabel and watching her ourselves."

"No way," she said. "We don't know what will happen if I get caught. And I'll be the only one out in the open."

"We can take Kara's Prius," Raj said. "It's perfect for this sort of thing—so quiet."

"It'll be kind of tight with all of us, though," I said.

"I don't want any part of this," Isabel said. "You guys do what you want, but once I drop those pills, I'm out."

"Well, that solves the car problem," I said. "And we can make sure to stay far away until you're gone. It's not like Blocked Sender will come get the pills immediately. He won't want you to see him."

"What makes you think the person who picks up the pills will even be Blocked Sender?" Alex asked. "So far he's been making other people do his dirty work."

"Then at least we'll know one more person who's involved. We'll be one step closer." I hoped that was true, anyway. "Isabel, when are you supposed to drop the pills?"

"Tomorrow," she said.

"I think we're getting ahead of ourselves," Alex said. "I get the impulse to follow people around, but maybe we should do some investigation first. We have an address, so let's do some research."

"Do you think the address is actually Blocked Sender's house?" Raj asked.

"Nope," she said. "Given how careful he's been to keep everyone isolated, there's no way he's going to make himself that easy to find. But there's a chance there's some connection between whoever lives there and Blocked Sender, even if that connection won't be obvious right away. It would help to know a little something before we stake the place out."

"And then what?" Justin asked. "We watch the drop-off and confront whoever does the pickup?"

"Who's 'we'?" Alex asked. "We've got it from here." She wasn't even trying to hide her anger at him.

"No way," he said. "We're all in this together now."

"Fine, whatever. We'll pick you up tomorrow. Isabel, what time's the drop-off?"

"Nine. Look, I'm fine with you doing this whole following me thing, but do me a favor and make sure you don't get caught, okay? I don't want this to get any worse than it already is."

"None of us do," I said. "We'll be careful. I swear."

"Just tell me what happened after, okay?"

I promised I would.

"That's everything, right?" Justin asked. "Can we get out of here now?"

"Soon," I said. "But don't we need to think about what we're going to do when we find out who's picking up the pills?"

"That will depend on who it is, don't you think?" Raj asked. "It's not like we're going to just ambush the person on sight."

"I know you always like to have a plan, Kara. Sometimes we have to wing it," Alex said.

"I guess." I wasn't so sure, though. But I could tell everyone was ready to be done talking. Alex and Raj had already paid for the pizza, and between them and Justin it was nearly gone. Time to go home. It had been a long day.

I knew Alex was planning to do as much research as she could before I had to pick everyone up, so at school the next day I asked if I could come over and help. We hadn't had a lot of time to hang out alone, and I wanted to make sure she was okay. She'd gotten so furious with Justin, and I still didn't understand why. Especially if he hadn't told Blocked Sender her secret, which I really did believe he hadn't.

We got to her house and settled in at her desk. Alex started pulling up websites and databases and typing faster than I could keep up with her. "I got a head start last night," she admitted. "I'm not just doing this off the top of my head. Normally I'd just enter the address and follow it wherever it led, but I thought I'd try to be more like you. You know, methodical. When I got home last night, I researched the best way to find out information from an address, so I bookmarked a whole bunch of stuff to get ready."

I was flattered that she thought I was methodical. Which I knew would not be something other people might consider a compliment. Pages were still flying by; all the movement was on the main screen, but every so often Alex would move something over to one of the side screens. "What's happening? What are you finding?"

"I started with the address itself, and everything I could find about the house I'm putting over here on the left. It's been owned by the same person for years: Nora Sinclair. Everything I learn about her I'm putting on the right."

"That is very methodical," I said.

"I do my best. Nora Sinclair's owned the house for years and years, long enough that the previous owner probably doesn't matter much. Given how long she's owned the house, I'm guessing she's in her seventies or eighties. She has basically no internet presence at all that I can find, which makes sense if she's that old."

"What about the house?"

Alex was typing and talking at the same time. How did she do that? "The house is actually more interesting than she is. It's been on the market for a really long time, which is unusual for Marbella, since houses usually sell quick here. But the house is listed for an enormous amount of money, and from Google maps it looks like it's just a crappy little place. I'm pulling up property records to see if there's anything else we can find out."

"Can I do anything? I brought my laptop, just in case." I reached into my bag and took it out, moving aside some papers to make room on the desk.

"That would be great. Can you get on social media and do some digging for Nora Sinclair? I don't think she'll be on there herself, but maybe someone else might reference her?"

"Sounds good."

We both sat typing and clicking away, companionable in silence for a while. It was nice to have someone I felt so comfortable with, and all the frenzy of the last few days, and the group activity that accompanied it, had made me miss her.

"I found something," Alex said. "This house has a really weird history. Those first listings are way out of date—there's some sort of lawsuit happening. It looks like someone got Nora Sinclair's power of attorney and tried to sell the house, and someone else is trying to block the sale."

"Any names?"

"None that look familiar. You having any luck?"

"Nothing when I search people, like you thought. I'm going through photos now." I kept clicking through the list, hoping to find someone old. Finally, I saw a picture of a woman who could be the right age. There was a middle-aged woman standing next to her, and the caption read, "Getting my mother-in-law ready for the nursing home," with a sad face emoticon. "This could be it." I showed Alex.

"Whose page is it?"

"Barbara Sinclair."

"That's a bummer. Doesn't match any of the names in the lawsuit." She spun around in her desk chair and groaned. "We're not getting anywhere."

I looked at the picture again and saw a location tag for Palo Alto. "I think it's her," I told Alex. "How many Nora Sinclairs are headed for Bay Area nursing homes?"

"Okay, so let's say it's her," Alex said. "Now we know she doesn't live in the house anymore. It's nothing we can use."

"We still might find something later tonight," I said. "We can't give up hope yet."

"I know. This is just all so depressing, though."

Depressing? I couldn't help but think that if Alex was right about having set up her whole financial empire in a way that would keep her from getting caught, then most of us had it way worse than she did. And "depressing" wasn't really the word I'd use to describe what was happening here. She seemed more upset and angry than scared, which didn't quite make sense. I wondered what was really going on. Maybe it was time to find out. "Listen, I know you said you didn't want to talk about this yet, but I'd assumed that you and Justin weren't super close. But as soon as you found out he was involved—"

"I flipped out?" She grinned. "Yeah, I know it must have seemed extreme."

"Well, not entirely. I mean, he is the one who sold most of us out. But it did seem like more than that."

"I'm not even a little bit convinced that he didn't sell me out too," she said. "But you're right that there's more to it. I've known Justin since preschool. We've been friends my whole life. We were inseparable—that whole thing I told you about me not having many girl friends? That's because Justin was pretty much my only friend growing up. I didn't think I needed anyone else. And I thought he didn't either—even when we started high school and we both got into guys, we were more in it to have fun. We had a great time, but we always had each other, and that was more important. Things shifted a little when Raj moved here—they had some classes together and Justin's always been into soccer, so they bonded right away, and for a little while we were a threesome."

I thought about triangle friendships, and seesaw friendships, and I wondered whether Justin felt like he'd been in the middle, like Becca had. But Alex and Raj seemed to have their own friendship, so maybe there was more balance. "Was that okay? Was it hard having things not just be the two of you?"

"That's the thing—it wasn't bad at all. It made me wonder why we'd been so against hanging out with other people. Raj is really great, and we'd have movie nights at his house, and go to parties together, and it was fun. But then Justin met this Mark person, though of course I had no idea who it was at the time, and he basically disappeared. It was like he'd made friends with Raj so I'd have someone to hang out with when he bailed on me."

"I'm sure it wasn't like that," I said, though I understood why she might have thought so.

"I know. That's just how it felt."

"Did you talk to him about it?"

"I tried. He just said I needed to grow up, which really pissed me off. We had a huge fight and didn't talk for a while, and eventually we got to where we could be civil and hang out in groups, but it's not the same. I really miss him." I could hear the anger in her voice fading to sadness.

"I know what you mean," I said. "It's not the same thing, but I told you I used to hang out with Isabel and Becca. Becca was my best friend, but she was best friends with Isabel too—the three of us were kind of a trio, but it was more that Isabel and I were friendly because we both wanted to be around Becca."

"What happened? I remember you said there was a blowup."

"It was my fault," I said. "I screwed it up. I wasn't a very good friend, and I wasn't honest. They finally decided they'd had enough of me." That was pretty much it, really. The details didn't matter. I felt a pang of embarrassment remembering our argument out on the lawn in front of that party, and another remembering Isabel telling me that they'd known about the monster, had known all along. It made me look back at everything differently.

"Well, if it makes you feel any better, you've never been like that with me."

Except that of course I had. "I'm trying to be better."

"I wish Justin would. I'm sure this Mark person is all magic and unicorns and hotness, but that's no reason to give up a friendship. Or to ruin my life."

"He sounded so convincing when he said he hadn't told Blocked Sender about you, though."

"That's what he said. But he is literally the only person in the world who knew how much drama there was in my family when my uncle got arrested. It was awful, and I was completely miserable. He's the only one who knows I still talk to my uncle and that I'm terrified of my parents finding out about that and all the poker stuff, and he's the only one who knows what I think will happen if they do."

"I know that too," I said.

"But you didn't, not when Blocked Sender started texting me. That information could only have come from Justin. The fact that he used our history to save his relationship is unforgiveable. Once this is all over, he and I are done."

She'd reached her limit, just like Becca and Isabel had reached theirs with me. I understood, but I wondered whether that would really make her feel better. Even though Isabel and I had never been independently close, just being back on speaking terms with her was making me happy.

Despite the circumstances, of course.

22.

I picked everyone up at eight thirty that night, and by a quarter to nine we were headed over to Ridgewood Drive. No need to sit around too long, I'd figured, and we wouldn't need that much time to get there. "I don't see why you put the tall people in the back," Justin whined. "Alex is tiny. She doesn't need so much legroom."

I didn't tell him that Alex had insisted on sitting in front. "If we're in the backseat together I can't make any promises about his survival," she'd said. "I don't want to look at his stupid face."

So she had shotgun. Justin was sitting right behind her, and though the very long-legged Raj had been the last person to sit in front, she hadn't moved the seat up at all. Small victories, I supposed. I'd moved mine up as far as I could stand it to accommodate Raj, but I was sure he was uncomfortable too. I didn't feel all that bad for him; he'd been the one to suggest taking my car, after all.

We rode over to a neighborhood I'd rarely been in before, one with houses that were older and more run-down than the ones we all lived in, houses that hadn't been renovated in any of the real estate booms that had hit the Bay Area in the last however many years. The neighborhood was between the freeway and the train, and we could hear noises coming from either side of us as we snaked through back streets to find the house.

Finally we located it, a small, one-level bungalow covered in chipped stucco, in the middle of a street that ended in a cul-de-sac. It was dark outside and some of the streetlights were broken, so I couldn't tell what color the house was, but it might have been pink. Hard to see how it could ever have been attractive; now it just looked shabby. Poor sweet Nora Sinclair, presumably now settled into her nursing home, had really let the place go. I wondered how she linked up to all of this.

We parked a couple of houses away, next to a house that appeared to be under construction, just far away enough to see Isabel as she drove up and got out of her car. She was wearing a trench coat and sunglasses even though it was completely dark out, hair wrapped in a scarf. She looked like a spy from some old movie—unrecognizable but completely glamorous.

Alex could barely hold back a laugh. "Really?"

"Always the drama queen," I said. "I'm surprised she kept things so low-key when she went to get the pills." It made me smile, though. I liked the idea that Isabel was the same person I'd always known, even though time had passed and things had gotten complicated.

Isabel dropped off the pills in the mailbox in front of the house, looked around quickly to see if anyone was there, and then got back in her car and drove away. It happened so fast, it was almost like it hadn't happened at all.

"And now?" Justin asked.

"Now we wait," Raj said.

"And what then?"

"Then we follow."

We sat and watched for cars, but the only one we'd seen was Isabel's. We could hear the sound of the train, and traffic on the freeway, but no one drove by. As I watched, though, I could see someone walking down the street, heading toward the house.

"Someone's coming," I said.

"A car?" Alex asked. "I don't see anything."

"A person," I said. Which was weird enough—no one really walked in Marbella. The more likely option was that the person had parked somewhere else. Maybe so they wouldn't be spotted going up to that mailbox.

We watched as the person kept walking down the street, inching closer to the mailbox. The person was wearing dark clothes and a baseball hat, like Isabel had on the video, like I had at Walmart. Apparently we had our own uniform. I couldn't even tell if it was a boy or a girl.

Justin could, though. He started yelling as soon as the person closed the mailbox, bottle of pills in hand. "That's Mark!" he shouted. "That's my boyfriend!"

Before we could stop him, Justin jumped out of the car and started sprinting toward Mark. "So much for trying to follow him," Alex muttered.

"So much for no ambush," I said. "What do we do?"

"Give him a minute," Raj said. "Clearly he wasn't expecting this."

With everything that had been happening, I had trouble believing Justin was somehow surprised, but whatever. We watched as Justin caught up to Mark and grabbed his arm. We weren't close enough to see the expression on his face when Mark realized who'd found him, but we saw him put his finger to his lips. Did that mean he was worried that whoever was in the house would hear them? They whispered together for a while, Justin's arms flailing; Mark eventually reached out to hold them down, trying to calm him. I supposed Justin was starting to understand how the rest of us felt; it almost made me feel bad for him. But not quite.

Finally, Justin headed back for the car. Mark turned around and walked in the opposite direction, back to where I assumed he'd parked. Justin slammed the door behind him as he returned to the backseat. "Don't even say it, Alex," he hissed. "I get it now, okay?"

None of us asked him what he got. We knew.

"Did you learn anything?" Raj asked. "What does he know?"

"More than we do," Justin said. "He wouldn't tell me anything other than that his life would be over if he gave up who was behind this, but he did say we could follow him. He's doing the drop-off now. He said he can't have anything to do with what we decide, but if we follow him, we'll get all the information we need. He says he didn't know what was happening to me, to all of us, but I'm not sure I believe him."

I looked in my rearview mirror and saw a tear run down his cheek. I hoped Alex would stay quiet; now wasn't the time for her to say what I knew she was thinking. I started the car.

"He's around the corner, in a blue Civic," Justin said. He'd wiped his face and was trying to sound like his usual snarky self. "He said we can just follow him. Get your camera phones ready, people. He told me he'd make sure we have a good shot."

This was it. This was really it. My head felt like it was full of buzzing mosquitos. I could barely focus on the road as I drove down the street and turned the corner. Mark had waited for us, his car idling by the sidewalk. When he pulled out, I followed, trying to stay close but not too close.

"I don't think you need to worry about distance," Justin

said. "It's not like whoever it is will be expecting us."

"Did Mark tell you anything at all? Even a hint about who we're going to see?" Raj asked.

"Nothing. Just that he was sorry. Apparently he thinks this is all his fault."

"It is, isn't it?" Alex said. I knew she wouldn't be able to stay silent forever. "He's the reason you're being blackmailed, and you're the reason the rest of us are. Maybe he's behind this, or in league with whoever is."

"No way," Justin said. "He wouldn't have told us to follow him, and I know he wasn't lying. Not about that."

"We were going to follow him anyway," Alex pointed out.

"Enough! I know you're mad at me, but you have to trust me on this one. It's not him. He's just as stuck as the rest of us. I'm sure of it."

"You're still defending him?"

"Guys. Let Kara drive," Raj said.

They actually listened to him. I wondered whether he'd taken the middle role on their seesaw. He was good at it, that was for sure.

Mark had gotten on the freeway. I'd have to follow more closely to make sure we didn't lose him, though he seemed to be keeping track of us as well. We left Marbella and headed north, getting off the freeway in Redwood City, a route that was all too familiar to me.

And to Justin. "We're not seriously going to Walmart, are

we?" he groaned. "Bad enough I've been forced into that stupid job, but being here late at night when I'm not working is just too, too sordid."

It was actually smart, though. I pulled into the parking lot and realized Walmart was open later than I'd thought it would be. There were a fair number of cars in the lot, but it wasn't crowded at night, so there was an empty back corner that was perfect. Mark parked in one of the spaces; we parked a couple of rows behind him, not sure what the best angle was for taking pictures.

Justin's phone beeped. "Mark just texted," he said. "Someone's meeting him here but they're not here yet. We should wait." Another beep. "Person usually parks to his right."

"That means you and Alex will have the best shots," I said. "You guys ready?"

"Got the zoom all set up," Alex said. "Do we know how long we're going to be waiting, though?"

Justin started typing, then we waited for his phone to beep. "Could be a while," he said. "Mark says there's a window."

"How much of a window?" I asked. "It's already almost ten." I hadn't left my parents a note that I'd be out; I'd thought I'd be back before they got in from work. But they were always home by midnight. I got out my phone and shut off the ringer so I'd have an excuse for why I didn't answer if they called.

"He didn't say."

"Well, we might have some time then," Raj said. "Anyone have any predictions about who we're about to see?"

We all sat silently. At this point I really had no idea. Pretty much the only person I'd never suspected was Alex, and I'd spent so long thinking it was Justin that I'd lost track of my list. Becca seemed so unlikely, as did the Brain Trust. It had to be someone I didn't know. That would be better, anyway.

"Not sure why we're trusting Mark at this point," Alex said, finally. "This could all be a trick."

"Stop it," Justin said.

"I haven't been able to think of anyone specific," Raj said. "But I heard rumors that some of the kids who sold pot weren't thrilled when I started selling pills. Maybe it was one of them, trying to get in on the pill action."

"That would be better than finding out it was someone we knew," I said. "Though I don't know how much getting a picture is going to help us there."

"We don't know whether a picture will help with anyone," Justin said. "But it's all we've got right now."

"I guess. You have a theory?" I asked.

"Not really," Justin admitted. "I've tried not to think about it too much, to be honest. It's not like knowing who it is will make me feel any better about what I've had to do."

I wondered whether knowing that Justin felt guilty would make Alex any more sympathetic toward him. Probably not.

"How about you, Kara?" he asked. "Got any thoughts?"

I was saved from having to answer by the sound of a car coming up behind us. It was a beat-up silver SUV that had probably been nice a few years ago. The car parked two spots down from Mark.

"Here we go," Justin said. "Lights, camera . . ."

"Don't be an asshole," Alex said, but she got her phone ready. We all took ours out, just in case.

The driver's side door opened, and we saw a leg emerge. A cowboy boot, covered partly by a flowing flowered dress.

"Oh, no way," I said. "I know who that is."

It was like a thousand alarms started blaring at once, deafening me and making my head pound. But there were no alarms; everyone in the car had fallen silent. We all knew who it was. We finally had our answer.

Except now, of course, we had a million more questions.

23.

Ms. Davenport was clearly visible in the parking lot lighting. Our collective moment of silence didn't last long; after that first moment of recognition, everyone started yelling at once.

"I had her for trig," Raj shouted, while Justin and Alex started spewing curse words nearly in sync.

I felt like I was going to throw up. Mark hadn't actually said Ms. Davenport was Blocked Sender, but it sure seemed like it. Still, maybe she was one of us. Maybe there was someone behind her. I imagined those Russian nesting dolls, layers and layers between the outer doll shell and the secret tiny doll heart. I didn't want that heart to be Ms. Davenport. Especially since she knew even more secrets of mine than Blocked Sender had threatened to reveal. So far, at least.

"Pictures, people," Justin said. "Let's not forget the mission."

Justin started snapping pictures furiously, while Alex took video. Raj and I didn't have a clear shot, so we just watched as Mark got out of his car and walked over to Ms. Davenport. Thank goodness he knew we were there; he made sure the bottle itself was visible as he handed it to her, rather than palming it like I imagined he'd have done if he'd been alone. She didn't seem to catch on, though; she just took it, nodded, and got back in her car.

"Did you guys get that?" I asked, hoping they couldn't hear how shaky my voice was.

Justin scanned through his shots as Alex watched the video. "I've got a good one," Justin said.

"The video's a little grainy," Alex said. "But it might be enough."

"We've only got her getting the pills," Raj said. "If someone watches this, they might just think she's buying. It could get Mark in more trouble than Ms. Davenport."

"It's still illegal," I said. "It's a start." I didn't want to state the obvious, which was that going to the police would be terrible for Mark at this point, but Justin didn't say anything. He must have been really mad. It wasn't my main worry, though; I was still trying to wrap my head around the reality of what we'd just learned. How was this even possible? Ms. Davenport was a teacher. And not just any teacher. She was the one teacher I actually confided in. She knew more about me than anyone at school, including my friends.

And if she really was Blocked Sender, she'd used that knowledge against me.

I wanted so badly to believe it wasn't her, but the more I thought about it, the clearer it seemed that it had to be. I started getting angry. Rageful, even. I'd never felt anything like it before—not when I got mad at my parents for their absurdly high expectations, not when Becca and Isabel cut me out of their lives, not even at the doctors who couldn't do anything about my skin except to keep giving me drugs that did nothing.

I hated her. I wanted her to pay for what she'd done.

"I think we should go to the police," I said.

"You've got to be kidding," Justin said.

Alex knew how close Ms. Davenport and I were, though. "I get how upset you are—"

"Upset?" I yelled. "Upset does not begin to cover it. Upset is the coffee shop being out of croissants. Upset is not acing a test you studied for. I'm not upset. I'm fucking furious."

"I think that's the first time I've ever heard you swear," Alex said.

I was so sick of people thinking I wasn't capable of being anything but logical. I could get pissed off and irrational just like everyone else. "Maybe you just don't know me that well," I said.

"So not the issue right now," Justin said. "Look, Kara, I'm just as mad as you are. But I'm not seeing how all of us getting arrested is going to fix things."

"It'll take her down," I said. "I don't care about anything else."

"Right now you don't," Raj said, gently. "And we understand, really we do. But you have so many good things to look forward to. If you try to get her this way, you'll take yourself down with her."

"And the rest of us," Justin said. "Don't forget about that."

"We'll find another way," Alex said. "I promise."

"I'm all for a strategy session, but I've got some things I need to know now," Justin said. "Like whether my boyfriend was also being blackmailed, or whether he's just a lying, blackmailing scumbag who is most definitely not my boyfriend." He started typing on his phone, though Mark was just sitting in his car.

"You really want to have that fight now?" I asked. "Are we supposed to drop you off somewhere?"

"Oh, I have no problem having that fight in front of all of you. And I'm sure he's got things to tell us that we'd all like to know. It's just a question of where it should happen."

"My house is out," Alex said. "Parents are home, and I don't think they'll leave us alone if there's going to be a lot of screaming."

"How about that place we met up last time?" I asked. "After Walmart? It's not too far from here."

Justin texted Mark to meet us at the Bayview Diner and

got a beep back quickly. He read it and laughed. Well, it was more of a sardonic chuckle. "He'd rather be alone. As if. Come on, let's go."

"What if he doesn't come?" I asked.

"Then we'll eat eggs, talk about what an asshole he is, and decide what to do about Ms. Davenport. All this anger is making me really hungry."

"Works for me," Raj said.

I was surprised to find that I was hungry too. And I knew Alex still wanted to kill Justin, though I wasn't sure what that would do to her appetite. I started the car back up and headed for the diner. It looked exactly the same as we'd left it; we even had the same waitress.

Mark walked in as we were looking at the menus. "Justin, what am I doing here with these people?" he asked, as if we weren't even there.

"Nice to meet you, too," Alex said.

"Just sit," Justin said, and Mark did.

We were off to a great start. I put down my menu and looked over at him. Now that he was sitting here, I had a vague memory of seeing him around school, though I'd thought he was a student. He had messy dark hair but was clean-shaven and wearing a button-down shirt with a T-shirt underneath. The T-shirt had a cartoon on it. The whole outfit didn't really add up, but he didn't look like a teacher, that was for sure.

"The way I see it, you've got some things to say that all of us want to hear," Justin said.

"This is between you and me," Mark said.

"Not even close," Alex said.

"Look, I helped you guys," Mark said. "You got a picture, right? You guys basically own me now. Isn't that enough? Can I please just go talk to Justin alone?"

"You're right that we own you." Even just hearing the words come out of my mouth made me feel powerful. It was an unfamiliar feeling, and I liked it. "Feels pretty terrible, doesn't it? Now you know what we've been going through."

"As if I didn't already? You think I was doing this on my own?"

"It's possible," Justin said. "And we don't even know the extent of 'this' yet." He made little air quotes with his fingers.

"Don't you know me better than that by now?" He was looking only at Justin, his tone and his eyes both pleading.

"I thought I did. Now I'm not so sure."

Mark sat up straight in his chair and looked off to the side. He seemed to be working something out in his head. "If you're not sure, then I guess I have to convince you."

"Exactly," Justin said. "Start talking. Don't leave anything out."

"How much do these guys know already?"

"Enough."

The waitress picked that perfectly inopportune second

to come back and take our orders. We ordered pancakes and omelets and coffee, so much food I think we even impressed the waitress. "Late-night snack, huh? You kids and your metabolisms."

"Nothing for me, thanks," Mark said.

"He'll have a water," Justin said. "Wouldn't want you to get a dry throat, from all that talking."

"Message received," Mark said, as the waitress walked away.

We waited for him to start, but he was looking off to the side again. Thoughtfully, though, not like he was avoiding us. I didn't know Justin that well, but Mark didn't seem like his type at all—he was much quieter, lower key. But maybe that was it; maybe Justin needed someone like that, to balance him out.

"First, I just want to say that I never meant for any of this to happen. Especially not to you"—he looked over at Justin, whose expression didn't soften at all—"but not to any of you. I didn't mean to get in a relationship with a student, though I'm not sorry about that at all—"

"Maybe you should be," Justin said.

"Come on," Mark said. "Just let me apologize. Yes, I get that getting together with Justin opened the door to Samantha's blackmail—"

"Samantha?" Raj asked.

"Ms. Davenport," I said. So we had it. Confirmation that

she was Blocked Sender. I started to feel sick. Ordering food had been a mistake.

"But I never meant for any of this to happen. You have to believe me."

"Enough with the excuses," Justin said. "Just tell us the story."

"Okay," Mark said. "Here goes."

24.

The waitress came back with our drinks and told us the food would be ready in a minute. Given that we were the only people in the diner, I wasn't surprised; what else did they have to do? I hoped she'd take her time, though—it sounded like Mark had a lot to say, the way he was gearing up to talk, so we might be there a while.

"Like I said, I hadn't meant to get involved with a student, especially not during an externship. It's against college rules, and it's also a distraction for someone who's serious about teaching, like I was. Am. But I couldn't help myself." He reached out for Justin's hand, but Justin pulled it away.

"The heart wants what it wants," Alex said, practically singing.

"Seriously, Alex, cut it out," Justin said. "I get it. You're mad at me. You're welcome to have at me later, but now's not the time."

Mark ignored them, which I thought was a smart move. "Samantha was assigned to be my mentor for the externship, which at the time seemed like the best thing that had ever happened to me." His reserve fell away a bit there; he gave a sniff that I suspected was to keep him from saying something sarcastic. "She's a great teacher herself, as I get the sense some of you already know, and she seemed completely committed to her students, like I wanted to be. She'd come observe my classes and give me really helpful feedback; she'd meet with me in the teachers' lounge and go over lesson plans with me. She was dedicated and committed and perfect."

"What changed?" I asked.

"We became friends," he said. "I didn't confide in her right away, not during the externship, but when it was over we got to talking about our personal lives. She'd just gone through a really horrifyingly messy divorce, and I was in love—it was all I could talk about."

"You told her about me?" Justin practically jumped out of the booth, but Raj held him back.

"Not right away," Mark said. "She just knew there was someone; she didn't know who. But time passed, and you and I were still together, and she and I had become so close—I knew all about her ex, and problems she was having with her family. Her grandmother had raised her but now she was sick, in a nursing home, and Samantha was going to have to start paying for it when Medicare ran out. Her ex was supposed to be sending her checks but he'd stopped, and there was a whole bunch of drama with her mother about selling her grandmother's house."

I looked over at Alex, and she gave me a little nod. We'd found the right Nora Sinclair, then.

"And she was so frustrated with the school system, how little the teachers were paid in relation to how much money there was in the community. She was so open and honest with me, even her issues with the school, with students, that it didn't occur to me that it wasn't safe to be open and honest with her. About anything."

"So much for keeping things secret," Justin said.

"Obviously that was a mistake, in hindsight. But it didn't seem like it at the time. At the time she was a perfect confidante—she was sympathetic and helpful. We stayed in touch after fall semester when my externship ended, and she wrote me the recommendation that got me my current teaching job. She was basically the best friend I could imagine."

"Because she was imaginary," I said, starting to understand. "None of it was real." Ms. Davenport had made Mark think they were friends, and he'd poured his heart out to her. Just like she'd made me think she was just trying to be a good teacher and counselor for the rest of us, convincing us—convincing me—to tell her things I wouldn't have told anyone else.

It was all a lie.

"Well, maybe some of it was real," Mark said. "I think the stuff about her mother and her ex-husband was. And her money troubles, and how frustrated she was getting with school. The best liars keep their falsehoods to a minimum; it makes them more convincing. And she was probably the best liar I'd ever met."

"When did you figure it out?" Raj asked.

"Not for a while. I don't know whether she'd had plans all along, or whether she finally just lost it when her grandmother's Medicare ran out and she started missing mortgage payments on her grandmother's house to pay the nursing home bill. Either way, she called me one day and said she had an idea for how to make things better and she needed my help. She was my friend—I'd have done anything to help her. Or so I thought."

"She told you everything?" I asked, getting excited. Now maybe we'd really have something we could use.

Mark gave a harsh laugh. Almost not really a laugh at all. "Hardly. I just got the barest outline. She had a scheme, she said, and the less I knew the better. The spoiled students would support her, she said, and they'd get what they deserved."

I was having trouble reconciling the bitter woman Mark was describing with the teacher who'd helped me so much. The person who helped Mark with his career, mentored him, guided him—that person I recognized. But this one?

"I told her I thought she was being too harsh. The students I'd met at Marbella were great—thoughtful and focused on their work, not too mean to someone who was a sub as far as they were concerned. 'Sure, you like them,' she said. 'You're sleeping with one of them.' I hadn't expected that. She'd always been so cool and understanding about Justin before. She sounded like a different person, someone I didn't really want to know. 'Whatever your plan is, I'm not interested,' I told her. 'We'll see about that,' she said."

"That sounds kind of terrifying," Alex said. She sounded less cold and more forgiving toward him than she had toward Justin.

"It was," Mark said. "I told her I understood she was going through hard times, but it wasn't the students' fault. And she could call me if she wanted to talk, if she'd stop whatever she was planning. All she said was that she'd see me around, and that was the last time we ever hung out."

"But that's not the end of the story," Justin said. He didn't sound any warmer than he had before. I wondered whether it was that he didn't believe him or that it didn't matter what Mark said.

"I didn't hear from her for a long time." Mark was deep into the story now, and he seemed to get that this wasn't only about Justin anymore. "I hoped that meant she'd dropped whatever it was she'd been planning, but I knew her well enough to know she didn't just drop things. I figured radio silence meant she wasn't going to include me in it, which was exactly what I wanted. I missed my friend, but that's how things go sometimes. Sometimes we lose friends, and we miss them, but we have no way to get them back."

I hoped that wasn't true.

"Samantha called me a few months after I told her not to," Mark said. "She told me her plan was off to a good start but she needed some help. I reminded her that I wasn't interested, but she said that wasn't an option. And then she reminded me of everything she knew about me and Justin. I'd had no idea she was willing to sink that low. She told me she'd done some research into California's statutory rape laws, and I knew I'd do whatever she said."

"To protect yourself," Justin said.

"Yes, to protect myself," Mark said. "And you—I didn't want you to get involved in a scandal, but yes, I also didn't want to go to jail. It's a pretty big risk I take, being with you, and I'd rather still be with you than be an unemployed registered sex offender when they let me out of prison. Does that make me such a horrible person?"

Justin didn't say anything to that, just drank his coffee and avoided eye contact with Mark.

The waitress came over with the food and unloaded big platters in front of us. We all stared at them. Our anger-fueled hunger had faded; I knew I couldn't manage a bite of the pancakes I'd ordered.

"Anyway, I didn't see what else I could do but what she said. I told her everything I knew about everyone I'd heard about."

"Including me," Alex said.

"Justin talked about you all the time," Mark said. "You sounded so fascinating—I was dying to meet you, when the time was right. But Samantha became obsessed with you once I told her about the money. I might have pushed Justin for more about you in particular, and I'm sorry about that."

So it was Justin's fault that Ms. Davenport had gone after Alex, but not for the reasons Alex had thought. I wondered whether that would make a difference to her. Justin clearly didn't care, though. "You don't seem to feel too bad about setting me up. She made me tell her about all the other kids at the high school."

"I didn't know what she was going to do," he said. "And I did it for you. Maybe if you'd told me what she was asking, I could have done something, but you never did. Even when you got that stupid Walmart job, and I was sure it was because of her, you never told me why. Just said you were trying to get in character, some method acting kind of thing."

I almost laughed. That wasn't a bad story.

"That's everything I've got, okay?" He turned to face Justin. "Can we go somewhere and talk now, please? Can we not hash out our whole relationship in front of your friends?"

Justin finished his coffee with a slurp. "I have some thinking to do," he said. "I'll call you."

"So I'm dismissed, then," Mark said.

This time I couldn't help it—I giggled at the irony of a teacher saying that to a bunch of students. I immediately regretted it, though, when I saw how sad Mark was. "Before you go, do you have any ideas about what we should do now?" I asked. He was an adult, after all. Maybe he'd come up with something better than we could.

"I don't really know what you can do," he said. "I tried to think of ways out myself—she's smart enough to know she's walking a real tightrope here, and I'd thought it would be easy to push her off. But then I went through the options, and they all involved getting myself in trouble too. I'm not sure how much she even cares about getting caught; if she got arrested she'd be off the hook for the bills, and there's always a chance she could turn on all of you to get a lighter sentence. You guys care a lot more about your futures than she does."

He made it sound so hopeless, and I said so.

"I wish it weren't the case, but I think that's where we are," he said. "Justin, I hope when the dust settles we can talk. We went through a lot to be together—don't let Samantha ruin it." He waited to see if Justin would say anything, but when there was nothing but crickets, he left.

"You sure you don't want to go after him?" Raj asked, ever the romantic.

"He can wait," Justin said. "It's more important for us to talk about what's next."

Alex got out her phone and pulled up a still of Ms. Davenport and Mark and the pills. It was a pretty good picture, really—Mark's face was in shadow, but Ms. Davenport's was clear as day, and the streetlights glinted off the orange bottle. "We've got her, and she's got us," she said. "So what do we do now?"

25.

I knew what I wanted to do now, which was to have a complete meltdown. But I wasn't about to do it in front of everyone. I excused myself and went to the restroom.

I almost turned around and walked out as soon as I opened the door. The ladies' room had three stalls, all with broken locks, and two were clogged. I got that this wasn't the most popular place, but did they not even think it was worth cleaning the bathrooms at all? It made me furious.

Except of course that wasn't why I was furious. I wanted to scream or run or hit something, but if I punched the concrete bathroom wall I'd probably break my hand, and someone had already taken a shot at the paper towel holder—its metal had a fist-shaped dent in it. I had so much anger and nowhere to put it, and it made me so frustrated that I finally started crying.

I hated crying.

It wasn't just the snot and the sniffles and the smeared makeup that I'd have to fix before I went back out to the group; it was the embarrassment of knowing that something had broken me. Or, in this case, someone.

Ms. Davenport was everyone's favorite teacher. She was so young, so supportive, so good at explaining even the hardest concepts. She'd been counseling me ever since freshman year. She was the only teacher I'd ever exchanged cell phone numbers with. I'd told her about my skin, about my panic attacks. I'd told her everything.

And what I hadn't told her, Justin had.

She was Blocked Sender.

I choked back another sob. How could she do this to me? I'd trusted her. She was an adult; she was one of the people who were supposed to be looking after us. And I wanted her to pay.

The door opened behind me, slowly. I was still facing the dented paper towel holder, so I grabbed a towel and dotted my face with it before I turned around, hoping my waterproof foundation had held up.

It was Alex, of course.

"Are you okay?" she asked. She hesitated before taking another step toward me, then stretched out her arms as if to give me a hug.

I pulled back a little. "I'll manage," I said. "This all just kind of threw me."

"Kind of?" She moved back too, but I couldn't tell if she was hurt. "That's quite an understatement. But I know you guys are close, so I get that this would hit you pretty hard."

"Were close," I said. "That's over now. I want to take her down."

"I know you do. We all do. You ready to come back and talk about it?"

I looked in the mirror. My mascara had run but I fixed it quickly; otherwise, I needed one more blot with those horrible stiff brown paper towels and I'd be good to go. "Okay," I said.

When we got back to the table, I didn't waste any time. "I really think we should go to the police," I said.

"I thought we agreed—" Justin said.

"Hear me out. It was one thing when we thought we were dealing with another high school kid. We'd all be in the same boat; some of us did worse things than others"—I avoided looking at Raj—"but basically we're in a similar position, and we're all minors, right?"

They nodded. "Cutting it pretty close, though," Raj said. "My birthday is coming up soon. Don't forget it!" He didn't have his usual jokey energy, though. It was getting late, and we were all kind of exhausted.

"Mine's coming up too," I said. "But that's not the point. Ms. Davenport is an adult. And not just any adult—she's a teacher, one of the people responsible for helping us grow up, and yet she's put us in this horrible position. She's magnified the things we did wrong and taken advantage of us being young and weak compared to her. I don't want to have to admit everything, and it will probably ruin my life, but maybe if we go in together we can get some kind of deal, and then we can be sure her life will be ruined worse." I didn't know if it was necessarily the best idea—I'd lose everything I'd ever wanted, after all—but I didn't know what else to do. Besides, there wasn't much chance they'd go for it, anyway.

"No offense, Kara, but that sounds more like revenge than justice," Alex said. "We have no idea how many people she has dirt on. If she decides to trade her story for something on everyone, wouldn't the police be better off nailing a big group of us, rather than her?"

"I'm with Alex," Justin said. "Believe me, we're talking about a sizeable crowd here. I think the cops would go for numbers over just one person, even if she is the ringleader."

I hadn't thought this through. I always prided myself on being logical—Alex's saying I was methodical was the best compliment I'd ever gotten—but being logical and being methodical weren't always the same thing, and I was learning that sometimes I sacrificed one at the expense of the other. What was logical for me might not work for other people. And sometimes I got my logic wrong.

"What if we came up with another strategy?" I asked. "We could call in an anonymous tip. One of those Crimestoppers-type things."

"Doesn't solve the problem," Justin said. "She could still use us as leverage for a better deal."

"We need to be completely on top of who knows. Telling the police means we have no control over how they might use what we've learned," Raj said. "That's a recipe for all of us landing in jail."

We kept throwing around ideas. I knew they'd reject anything that involved the police, but I appreciated that they were at least willing to talk it out. For a minute I sat back and watched while Alex and Raj debated the pros and cons of telling our parents, and Alex and Justin even managed to talk to each other without getting into an argument. Even as we were fighting about strategy, I felt something I hadn't felt in a long time, at least not like this: I belonged. These were my friends. It was a strange time to acknowledge it, but in the moment, that's how it felt.

I remembered having a similar feeling back when I was hanging out with Becca and Isabel. We'd be in Becca's room, fighting over what we should do over the weekend or which boys were the cutest, and in the midst of all the yelling, I'd feel this sense of warmth, this security in the knowledge that these were my friends, that we could argue and disagree and still have each other's backs. It hadn't turned out to be true, but that was at least partly my fault. I found myself wishing Isabel were here and remembered that I was supposed to tell her what happened, but it was really late. I'd call her in the morning, or find her at school.

It was after midnight when Raj suggested an elaborate scheme involving burner cell phones and counterblackmail attempts, with packages of documentary evidence ready to send to newspapers if Ms. Davenport didn't do our bidding.

"You've been watching too much TV," I said. "I don't think we're going to figure this out tonight. Why don't we all go home and get some sleep and think about it tomorrow, and we can meet up later on and decide what to do? There's got to be something better than what we've come up with so far, and right now, none of us have any tasks scheduled for Blocked— I mean Ms. Davenport." Hard to get used to saying her name in this context.

We agreed it was time to go. I dropped Alex off last. "We have a lot more information than we had yesterday," I said. "Do you think it might be worth doing more research? I could come over after school and help."

"It's worth trying," she said. "See you tomorrow."

It had been a bizarre and terrible day, but now it was finally over. Or so I thought.

Mom and Dad were sitting in the living room when I came home. "Glad you decided to join us," Dad said.

Uh-oh—Dad sarcasm was always a bad sign.

"We called you several times," Mom said. "We texted, too. Why didn't you answer?"

"I'm so sorry," I said. "I was studying, so I shut off my ringer. I'm exhausted, though." I faked as big a yawn as I could manage, complete with the over-the-head arm stretching. "Can we talk tomorrow?"

"We're all here now," Mom said. "Though we would have preferred to be sleeping. Do you realize what time it is?"

"I don't, actually. I kind of lost track of time."

"It's nearly one in the morning," Dad said. "You're being very cavalier. I know we've never given you a curfew, but I didn't think we needed to."

"You didn't need to because I didn't have any friends to go out with," I said. "I thought you wanted me to be more social."

"We want you to go hang out at the mall with your girl friends on a Saturday afternoon," Mom said. "We don't want you going who knows where all night on a Wednesday."

"I told you, I was at Alex's," I said. "Studying." Even though I was in the wrong, even though I was lying, I found myself wanting them to feel guilty. The truth was that I'd never have gotten into this mess if I hadn't felt so much pressure, and some of that pressure came from them.

Mom frowned. "I know you're anxious about keeping up your GPA, but we're worried about you. The SATs are over and you did a wonderful job. Can't you relax a little before you have to start turning your attention to college applications? You're a lock for Stanford with that score and your grades. You'll be fine."

Funny how even when she was supposedly taking the pressure off she added just a little bit more. How could I explain that to get into Harvard, I needed to be better than fine? How could I make them see how badly I needed to be as far away from Marbella as possible? "I thought that's what you wanted. Perfect Kara and her perfect GPA."

"We never expected you to be perfect," Dad said. "Where did you get that idea?"

"Are you kidding? You've been pushing me to be perfect since I was a little kid. Ever since Mom started bringing home those logic problem books, it's been all you-can-do-better-Kara and you-just-need-to-work-a-little-harder-Kara. I wish I'd never seen one of those books in my life." Logically, I recognized that it was not my parents I was mad at. But logic wasn't ruling the day anymore. And I was beyond mad, and they were here.

Dad was starting to sound mad too. "Don't talk to us like that," he yelled. He almost looked like he wanted to stand up.

Mom didn't seem angry, though. She put her hand on Dad's knee as if to keep him sitting down. Her voice was quiet, all the more noticeable because of Dad's yelling. "Evan, calm down. Kara, I'm sorry you feel that way about the logic problems. I bought those books because I thought you enjoyed working on them with me. I remember those times as some of our happiest, and I thought you felt the same way."

Great, now I had to feel guilty on top of everything else. "I do. I'm sorry. I was upset. I get such mixed messages from you guys. You want me to study hard and be smart and do well, but you also want me to have friends and be social and not worry so much. You don't want me to have panic attacks, but you don't want me to take medication for them, either. You want me to go to college and be happy, but only the college you want, because the only happiness that matters is the kind that you have. And even if I'm not happy, I should act like I am so people don't figure it out. God forbid anyone realize that we're not perfect." I'd been talking so fast I was out of breath.

They both stared at me for a minute, their mouths hanging open a bit. I understood why, too—I never spoke to them like that. Sure, once in a while I'd get what Mom called "a little snippy," but I never just laid out how I was feeling.

I'd never, it turned out, been fully honest with them.

It felt great.

"I didn't realize we'd been doing that," Dad said. He wasn't yelling anymore, and he'd clasped his hands together, placed his elbows on his knees, and rested his head on his hands. Mom reached over and rubbed his back. She was in her nightgown, not her work-Mom clothes or her Marbella-yoga-Mom uniform, with no makeup and her hair loose from its usual updo. She looked softer, but also older, than when I pictured her in my mind. They both did.

I hadn't meant to make them so upset, but it was my fault. I could only imagine what learning about the Novalert would do to them. Alex, Justin, and Raj were right. The police were not an option. No one could ever find out.

"I didn't mean it to sound so harsh. I love you guys, you know that. But sometimes it's just kind of hard to be me around here."

"We thought we were doing what you wanted," Mom said, leaning back into the sofa. Almost like she was giving up. "We thought we were pushing you to do the things you wanted for yourself. If that wasn't true, I wish you'd said something. We would have stopped. I hope you know that."

It was all so confusing. They weren't wrong—I did want to be valedictorian, and I did want to work hard and excel and go to a great college. Everything they wanted for me, I wanted too. But I'd thought they'd wanted it first, and they'd thought I had. Did it matter, ultimately? "It was true. It is true," I said, finally. "I think maybe I didn't see that before. Can we talk more about this later? I'm really, really tired. I swear I didn't mean to stay out this late."

"We were just worried," Dad said.

"Are you going to give me a curfew?"

They exchanged a glance. Mom raised an eyebrow; Dad gave a little head tilt. It was fascinating—they were totally communicating and I had no idea what they were saying.

"No curfew," Mom said. "But we want a better idea of where you are, so we want texts or notes when you're out at night, and if you're not going to be home by midnight, you need to check in. Fair enough?"

"Totally." I went over to the couch and kissed them both good night, then went upstairs. I couldn't believe I had to get up for school in just a few hours. I was going to be exhausted. School would be horrible.

But sitting through math class would be worse.

26.

Math class was at least as awful as I'd imagined it would be. At first I wasn't sure I was going to make it. I kept my head down, staring at my desk, sure that if I made eye contact with Ms. Davenport, she'd instantly know that I knew, and something terrible would happen. I couldn't even imagine what, but it would be bad.

But today's class was all about prepping for winter finals, and Ms. Davenport spent most of the time writing equations on the board, equations I had to look up to see so I could write them down in my notebook. She wasn't paying any attention to me, which meant I could pay attention to her.

She wore her usual funky outfit, a vintage checkered dress with red cowboy boots that matched her lipstick, and I thought about how hard she tried to act young and cool like a teenager, even though as I studied her face more carefully than I ever had, I could see the beginnings of lines forming.

She wasn't quite as young as I'd always assumed she was, and now her outfit looked more like a costume. Or camouflage. She was dressed to attract the outsiders, the kids with problems, the ones who were most likely to be doing things they didn't want other people to know about.

I'd thought she was hip; now I wondered if she was just manipulative. She used her look and her position to convince kids like me she was someone we could trust, and then took that knowledge and destroyed us with it. I got angrier and angrier as I thought about what a betrayal that was. I wanted to hurt her as bad as she was hurting me. I just didn't know how.

I glanced over at Alex, sitting on the other side of the room. She, too, was staring at the board and frowning, like I knew I was. I bet she was thinking some of the same things, though she and Ms. Davenport didn't have the same relationship we did. She felt betrayed too, though not on the same level.

It's not like we both hadn't been hurt by people before; despite the fact that what had happened with Becca and Isabel was mostly my fault, I still wished things had gone differently, that they'd somehow understood me better and stuck around even as I'd made things difficult. And Alex had to deal with Justin ditching her for a guy, and then sharing all her secrets with him, even if he hadn't known how badly that would turn out.

But neither of those things was nearly as horrible as what was happening now.

"Ugh, the whole class I just wanted to go up and punch her in her stupid face," Alex said after class, when we were a safe distance away.

"I know. I was like two seconds from going to the bathroom and never coming back."

"It's killing me to just sit here and do nothing," she said.

"There has to be more we can do," I said. "You know, we haven't actually researched her yet. Maybe we can find some dirt."

"Totally," Alex said. "There must be something we can use. Then we can get some leverage."

"That would be helpful." I still wasn't convinced going to the police was a bad idea, but if we could make this go away quietly, everyone would be happy.

"We should go now," she said, pausing outside the door to our econ class.

"Now? We have two more classes left."

"So we'll ditch," she said, like it was nothing.

But to me, it wasn't nothing. I'd never skipped a class before. My attendance record was nearly flawless. But what was the worst that could happen? Absences didn't affect grades until you'd been out a bunch of times, and since I'd never skipped before, no one would assume I was skipping now. I could tell my teachers tomorrow that I'd gotten sick and gone home, and they would believe me. Maybe they wouldn't even ask for a note. The fact that I'd been honest before would make me a better liar now.

"I'm in," I said.

We went to Alex's house and got ourselves set up, her on the big computer screens, me on my laptop. Her room now felt as much like a second home to me as Becca's had; I no longer superimposed Becca's love seat and chairs into Alex's workspace every time I came over. Being around Alex, I realized, made me miss Becca less. She wasn't a replacement; it was more that I related to what Alex had said about thinking it was enough to have Justin as her only friend. It didn't have to be that way. I'd been holding back with Alex as if us being truly close was some kind of betrayal of Becca, but there was no need to. That wasn't how it worked.

"Where should we start?" I asked.

"I have no idea," she said. "My brain is so full of rage I can't think. You're going to have to do the thinking for both of us."

I was mad too, but it was making me feel focused. Maybe I didn't need Novalert to get things done; maybe I just needed blind fury. "Well, I've got one idea—remember how Mark said that Ms. Davenport went through a divorce and then had to pay for her grandmother's nursing home and mortgage? I think Mrs. Sinclair is her grandmother. Can you get into some legal databases and find out more about the lawsuit? And the divorce?"

"Definitely," she said.

"Great. I'll do the social media thing again and see if there's anything there."

"Bonus points for whoever finds the name of her ex first?"

"Yes!" A contest! I loved contests. I had the easier job, I was sure, so this one I could win. I started with Google just to see what I could come up with and found that Ms. Davenport was all over social media; she had accounts on all the major sites. But I quickly found that her privacy settings were locked down, and I could access almost nothing but the occasional photo.

"Brick wall," I told Alex.

"That was fast." She was typing as quickly as ever, and all three of her screens had documents on them, some of them with numbers down the left side.

I peered closer and saw that they were from courts. She'd found the lawsuit and the divorce decree, which was from just a couple of years ago. "'It is therefore ordered that the marriage of Jonathan and Samantha Fisher be dissolved,'" I read. "Jonathan Fisher. He's the ex. I win!"

"How do you win? I'm the one who found that doc," Alex protested. "And we don't even know for sure that it's them."

"You might have found it, but you haven't read it yet."

"That is totally not how this contest works. Proof first, then the win."

"Okay, but what should I do about the social media stuff? Can you hack into her accounts?"

She frowned. "I could, but it would take forever, and there's got to be a better way to find out what we need to know."

I thought about it for a minute. "I'll look for pictures where she's tagged. Everyone screws up their privacy stuff every once in a while, right? And then I'll see if her ex is online too."

"Worth a shot," she said, and turned back to her screens.

I got back online and did a search for pictures, and I hit pay dirt fast: a whole bunch of photos from a couple of years ago and beyond, posted by her ex. And in one of them, Ms. Davenport was wearing a wedding dress.

"We found the right guy," I said. "I win!"

"You couldn't have done it if I hadn't found the divorce stuff," she said. "I'll take the draw, though."

As much as I liked winning, I liked how much fun it was working with her, as a team. "Okay, fine."

"Excellent. Now let me see him."

Alex looked over my shoulder and we went through the photos. Ms. Davenport's husband was good-looking, though he was completely different than what I'd have expected. He had short, neatly styled brown hair and wore suits or business-casual clothes in all the photos. In a way, he kind of looked like my dad. "I'd have thought she'd be married to a hipster," I said.

"Totally," Alex said. "And he's older than I thought."

We looked at his profile, which was completely open. He was a banker who lived in San Francisco, thirty-five years old, and from what we could tell, he and Ms. Davenport had gotten married eight years ago. The big surprise, though, was seeing his most recent photos. Most of them were pictures of a baby. And not a newborn, either—the baby was a few months old.

"Whoa," Alex said as we scrolled through his timeline. There was another wedding picture there, from just over a year ago. "So he got married less than a year after the divorce?"

"Looks that way," I said. "And either the new wife was pregnant already or it happened pretty quick."

"Ms. Davenport must have been furious. Unless this was some crazy whirlwind thing, this guy was cheating on her."

"That sucks," I said. For a minute, I tried to imagine what it might have been like, to be Ms. Davenport. To be married to a banker who clearly had a lot of money—his cover photo was of his house in San Francisco, and it was gorgeous—and then to have it all end, most likely in an awful way. With all those nursing home and mortgage payments, I bet she was broke, while her husband was living it up with a new young wife and baby. "She must be so angry. Maybe it made her crazy."

"I'd say it's understandable, except most people who are mad about getting divorced do things like sell their husband's fancy cars on Craigslist for pocket change, or try to hook up with one of their husband's friends. At least that's what they do on TV. I don't think they start crazy blackmail schemes."

"I know. I'm not saying it makes sense. It's more that she must have felt so betrayed. Someone she trusted, going behind her back like that." I knew how she felt. Her betrayal had gutted me; ironic that the feelings of hurt and anger were helping me understand her better now.

"So she turned around and did the same thing to us? Don't get soft on me now."

"I'm not." And I wasn't, really. But there was this moment when I could see where someone could just lose it and do things they'd never thought they were capable of. Which didn't make it okay. Just because I got how this could happen didn't mean I was any less angry. I still wanted her to pay.

And I wanted to find a way to end this nightmare.

We plugged away, me searching through Jonathan Fisher's timeline, Alex using his name to see if she could come up with a connection to the house. "I've got it," Alex said. "It's easy now that we know her married name—it looks like she used it for everything but work. The lawsuit was filed against her by her mom. Said she tricked her grandmother into signing everything over to her before she went into the home, and then took out a second mortgage on the house."

"She's being sued by her own mother?"

"Isn't that the worst? Here we are thinking our parents are going to have fits over the stupid things we've been doing, and Ms. Davenport's actually in a lawsuit with hers."

"It was pretty hard to find that, though, wasn't it?"

"Once I had her married name, it wasn't," she said. "But yeah, there's nothing here that would link it to her now."

"I wonder if people know," I said. "I wonder if the lawsuit is something she'd want to keep quiet."

"We've found our leverage," Alex said.

"Exactly. We just need to figure out what we want and how to use the leverage to get it."

"We should tell everyone," I said. "Let's meet tonight. I want to get it over with."

"Okay. You want to text them?"

"I don't have Justin's number. I can take care of the other two."

Alex rolled her eyes. "Great. Fine."

"We're all in this together," I reminded her. As if she needed reminding.

I got out my phone to text them and realized I hadn't looked at it since I'd shut the ringer the day before. The signal was blocked in school, so I wasn't in the habit of checking my phone during the day. Because if I had, I'd have seen that in addition to the missed calls from my parents, I had new text messages.

A lot of them.

My head started pounding as I wondered how many of them were from Ms. Davenport, what she could possibly want now. But none of them were from her. They were all from Isabel. I'd forgotten to call her.

She was not happy.

I started reading through each text.

Where are you guys?

Did you find out anything?

I'm staying up until I hear from you.

WHAT IS HAPPENING?!?!

Okay, now I'm getting scared.

Seriously, you're freaking me out.

Just write even one word so I know you're okay.

I can't do this anymore.

And then the last one:

If you haven't texted me by the time I wake up, I'm coming up with my own plan.

"What's that supposed to mean?" Alex asked, reading over my shoulder.

"I don't know, but that's the last one I got. I'll write her back and apologize and hopefully that will be the end of it." I wrote and apologized and told her about our plan to meet up.

My phone buzzed with a text notification almost immediately.

Too late. Couldn't stand it anymore. Had to talk to someone.

Tell me you didn't, I wrote back.

No choice. Bringing her with me tonight.

I'd been hoping she didn't mean who I thought she meant, but as soon as I read her final text, I knew.

"Was that her?" Alex asked. "Is she mad?"

"That's not the problem anymore," I said.

"Then what is?"

"She told someone."

"She did *what*? Who did she tell?"

I tried to stay calm. Breathe, I told myself.

"Becca," I said.

27.

The problem with Marbella was that there weren't very many places for big groups of kids to go. Not if they wanted to have a private conversation, and particularly not if they wanted to talk about how they were going to take revenge on their blackmailer. Too many kids hung out at Philz; the coffee shop I'd gone to with Raj didn't have big enough tables; and we'd all come to hate the Bayview Diner, which we now associated with all this craziness.

Thank goodness for Raj, who took it upon himself to figure out a solution. It turned out one of the big chain restaurants on El Camino Real had private rooms you could reserve, as long as you ordered something. We'd have to suffer through terrible inauthentic Mexican food, but at least we'd be alone.

We arranged to meet at six, driving over in two cars. I picked up Raj and Alex, who reverted to their usual seats; Justin was responsible for everyone else. We rode to the restaurant in silence; for once, Alex didn't bug me about the radio.

Justin was pulling into the parking lot just as we were. We waited by my Prius as he got out of the car, followed by Isabel and Becca, just as I'd expected. I avoided looking directly at them, which conveniently allowed me to avoid seeing whatever expression Becca might have had on her face as she looked at me.

The restaurant was tacky inside and out. The front was painted in yellow and red and green, with giant ceramic cacti flanking the entrance. An overly chipper middle-aged man confirmed our reservation and led us to the back room, which was covered in murals in the same bright colors as the outside. We sat down at the table set for six: I took a chair at one end, Alex and Raj on either side of me, and Isabel sat at the other, surrounded by Becca and Justin. When there had been five of us, I'd felt like we were all in it together; now that we were six, it felt like we'd been divided into teams. I hoped I was wrong about that, but Alex and Raj pretty much wanted to kill Isabel for talking; they weren't having the same eye-contact issue I was, and their glares were practically verbal, they were so hostile. I wasn't too happy about it myself, but I understood, even if I didn't like it.

Instead of Not-Pinky, our cranky waitress at the Bayview Diner, we had a perky girl with a shiny blond ponytail. She looked young enough to go to school with us, but no one seemed to recognize her, and most Marbella kids didn't have jobs. At least not during the school year. She set down six enormous glasses of water and two big bowls of chips with sides of salsa and asked if we wanted anything to drink.

"We'll start with sodas, and a plate of nachos for the table," Justin said. "Everyone?"

We all nodded.

The waitress gave us a big smile and went off to get our drinks. I finally steeled myself to look over at Becca. She, thankfully, wasn't looking back at me; she was staring down at the table, which wasn't like her. I wondered if she was scared. I would be, if I were her. I already was, myself. Just being at the table with her made me nervous. I wondered whether it would rise to the level of panic, whether I'd get that head-throbbing feeling, but something about sitting between Alex and Raj made me feel a little better.

The six of us waited quietly for our sodas to arrive. Technically Alex and I had been the ones to call for this meeting, but it didn't feel like we were in charge now that Isabel had brought Becca into the mix. Once the waitress came back with our order and left, I waited for someone to start talking. But the silence continued, broken only by the sound of mariachi music piped through the speakers.

"Is anyone going to say anything?" Justin asked finally. "I feel like I'm the only one with nothing to volunteer here, so someone get this party started."

"Not me," Raj said. "I'm in the same position you are. Though I'm very curious to hear from Isabel." He could have cut himself shaving on the sharpness in his voice.

"Fine," she said. "You all went off without me and did your little detective thing and forgot to tell me what was going on. So I took matters into my own hands. Becca's dad is a lawyer, and—"

"You did not tell Becca's dad what's going on," I said, horrified. I loved Becca's parents. The thought of them knowing what I'd done was almost as bad as my own parents finding out.

"I'm not an idiot. I told Becca everything I knew, and then I made Justin tell us the rest once I realized you were never going to call me back. She asked her dad about it as one of those things he likes, that thing lawyers always do, you know—"

"A hypothetical," Becca said. It was the first time I'd actually heard her voice in so long, but it was almost as familiar to me as my own.

"Like he wouldn't be curious why you were asking," Alex said. "Seriously. We're all so screwed I can't even stand it."

"She told him she was doing research for a school paper," Isabel said. "She's not an idiot."

"He didn't ask questions," Becca said, her voice low. "He just answered mine."

"What exactly did you tell him?" I asked. They were the first words I'd spoken to her in over a year, and they weren't the ones I'd imagined when I pictured us talking again. I'd pictured something more like an apology and less like an accusation.

"I asked what would happen if a teacher manipulated students into doing illegal things for her. Like selling drugs."

"It's not that simple," Raj said.

"I'm not done," she said. "He told me that what the teacher had done was a very serious crime, and the police and the district attorney would treat it that way. So I asked about the students, whether they'd get in trouble too. He said it was possible, but if they were all under eighteen and they all had basically the same story, then they'd probably be able to make a deal. Probation, maybe, and they could get the record sealed so it didn't hurt them later."

"You can't be sure of that," I said.

"And that doesn't factor in the possibility that she could turn on us," Alex said. "I don't think we're the only ones involved, by a long shot."

"You're not getting it," Becca said, and I recognized the tone she used when she got frustrated. "You guys are small potatoes here. Nothing any of you did is that big a deal. What she did is horrendous. She's a teacher, which means she's a state employee, and she's in a position of trust. Which she totally took advantage of." Her voice softened. "She had power over you, and she abused it. I get that you guys all feel bad about what you did, but you didn't hurt anyone."

I wasn't sure she was right about not hurting anyone. Who knew what kinds of terrible things might have come from what Ms. Davenport had made us do? I'd been lucky that I hadn't reacted badly to the Novalert, but that might not be true for everyone Raj sold it to. And we had no idea how big this whole thing really was.

But what Becca said about power spoke to me. She'd said what I was feeling about Ms. Davenport taking advantage of us, only better than I could say it. "I want to get the power back," I said. "And I think we can do it."

"I'm not going to the police," Isabel said. "I don't care what Becca's dad says about us not getting in trouble. I'm not willing to take the chance. And if you do it without me, I'll tell them you're lying."

"I get the no cops thing," I said. "You've made that clear from the beginning. But I don't think we need the cops to get what we want. Becca's right—what we have on her is way worse than what she has on us. We have the picture of her getting the drugs from Mark."

"That makes Mark look worse than her," Justin said.

"I thought you didn't care," Alex said.

"I may be pissed at him, but that doesn't mean I want him to go to jail."

"You're missing the point," I said. "That's just one of the things we have. There's also the texts, and the things we know she made us do, and Alex, you must have something on her whole money thing, right?"

"It's complicated," she said. "But I could come up with something."

"And Alex and I have been doing research, and we have some stuff about her family that she might not want to get out. So together, we kind of have a lot. We can use what we know to make her stop doing this. To us, and to everyone."

"How?" Isabel asked. "I mean, I'm all for taking her down, you know I am. But I'm not seeing how we do it yet."

"We do to her what she did to us," Alex said. "We send her a blocked-sender text with one of the photos we took the other night and tell her we need a favor. Then we have her meet us somewhere. We lay out what we know and we tell her to stop."

"What if she doesn't listen?" Raj asked. He was picking at his fingernails, like he had in the coffee shop when we'd talked. Raj was usually so confident, it was weird to see him nervous and unsure.

"She'll listen," Becca said. "I'm sure of it."

"Are we all supposed to go?" Justin asked. "I'm not sure I really need to be part of this confrontation. It might be better to have a smaller group involved."

"I kind of want to strangle her," Alex said. "Not sure I'm the best person for the job either."

I looked across the table at Isabel. "You know her the best out of all of us," she said. "I remember you were her biggest fan freshman year."

"Which makes it even harder to think about confronting her now," I said. "And I'm in her calculus class too." But she was right that I knew her better than any of the rest of them did. And I wanted to see this through.

"I'll go with you," Alex said. "I can restrain myself from violence. And I can scare her with what I know about the money stuff, if it comes to that."

"Thank you." I felt a sudden burst of affection for her.

"I'll come too," Raj said. "Just to make sure Alex keeps her word."

Justin sighed. "Am I the bad guy now? Again?"

"No," I said. "You're right that we don't need a big group. Three will do it. You guys are off the hook. We'll let you know when it's over."

"The sooner the better," Isabel said.

"We'll make a plan tomorrow," Alex said. "No sense in waiting."

"Then our work here is done," Justin said, getting up. He threw a few dollars on the table. "This should cover the soda and nachos."

"Dick," Alex muttered, as he walked away.

Isabel and Becca got up to follow him. "Wait," I said. "Becca, can I talk to you for a minute?"

She looked over at Isabel. They were doing a kind of silent communication, like my parents had done, with raised eyebrows and little head shakes.

Whatever Isabel didn't say helped me. "How about you give me a ride home?" Becca asked.

"Sure."

"Justin will drive me, Isabel, and Alex," Raj said, though Justin was already in the parking lot.

"No way," Alex said.

"You'll be fine," Raj said. "We'll sit in the back and you don't have to talk."

"So much drama," Isabel said. "And me and Justin are the theater people. Come on."

They all left the restaurant, and it was just me and Becca. "There are a lot of nachos left," she said. "Let's stay here for a bit."

"Okay." At first we both just stayed where we were, but it was kind of awkward trying to have a conversation with someone basically sitting diagonally from you. I was the one who'd asked her to stay and talk, so it only seemed fitting that I be the one to move. Baby steps and all that. I switched to Isabel's chair, so we were sitting next to each other.

"I'm sorry," we both said.

"Wait, what?" I asked.

"Isabel told me about what happened at Drew's house. That you had another panic attack. I was so hard on you that night. I should have figured out something was going on besides you just wanting to go home. I should have been a better friend."

"You're kidding me, right? I'd been lying to you guys since the summer before we started high school, ever since I found my first zit. And I was on my third strike."

"Your what?"

"I'd already screwed up twice before. You'd told me not to let you down again. Three strikes."

"I didn't mean it like that." Her eyes glassed over with tears. "You were going through something, and I wasn't there for you."

"Because I wasn't honest. And I was pretty miserable, too. I can't have been much fun to be around."

"It was never about whether you were fun." She blinked a couple of times, and I knew she was still trying not to cry.

"But I worried that we didn't have anything in common anymore. I couldn't swim because of the whole skin thing, and it made me scared about being with guys."

"Which is kind of all Isabel thinks about when we go out," Becca said, with a little smirk. She didn't look like she was going to cry anymore, which was good, because if she did I would have lost it.

"Which is a totally normal thing to think about," I said. "I made everything hard. I'm working on being more trusting, though this whole Ms. Davenport situation is not helping."

"I can't even imagine." She took a sip of soda.

"This is going to sound weird, but I'm glad you know everything now. I don't have to hide anything anymore. I really am sorry."

"Me too," she said. "I love how both of us were totally convinced it was our fault, but we were both too stubborn to do anything to fix it. Actually, I hate that, but it reminds me of us, when we were *us*, you know?"

I smiled. "Yeah," I said. "I do. Look, I know it's probably too late, but do you think there's a chance we could ever be friends again?" I felt nervous even asking, but it was worth a shot.

"You're working on the trust thing," she said. "I can work on the understanding thing. It won't be easy, and it's not going to be the same. But I'm willing to try if you are."

We both got up from the table and hugged each other, and I felt the pain of missing her all over again, even though she was right there. We'd lost over a year, and we would never get it back.

"Let's get out of here," I said. "Those nachos were terrible."

28.

The next day at lunch, Alex decided that we should have a movie night while we figured out how to lure Ms. Davenport into meeting with us. We agreed that she and I would be responsible for the snacks, and Raj could pick the movie. "PJs all around, this time," she said. "Can't have Kara showing up all fancy again."

I blushed, thinking about wearing pajamas in front of Raj. Raj didn't seem all that worried about it, though. "I'll wear my flannels with the duckies and bunnies," he said.

I hoped he wasn't kidding. I planned to go with leggings and a hoodie, which was what I normally wore to bed anyway. It wasn't all that different than what I was wearing to school—the leggings were jeans, and the hoodie was a sweater, but it was pretty close.

I just had to get through one more day of calculus before everything would be out in the open. I knew things would most likely only get harder, but at least I wouldn't have this fidgety feeling of hiding stuff all the time, along with the fear that Ms. Davenport would somehow look at my face and figure out what I knew. One way or another, I needed this to be over.

Today wasn't that day, though. I sat in class and daydreamed about what we would say to her when the confrontation finally happened. I couldn't quite decide on the right words, though I hoped they'd come at the appropriate time. Now it was just a matter of deciding what the appropriate time was. That was part of what we were going to figure out tonight.

I got through class without making eye contact with Ms. Davenport at all, and the rest of the day went by quickly. Alex and I did our junk food shopping and headed to Raj's house. I felt a wave of guilt as I remembered what had happened there the first time, but I reminded myself that we were well past that now. And Raj was not, to my serious disappointment, wearing ducky/bunny pajamas; he was in a plain white T-shirt and sweatpants, which didn't make him look any less cute.

Raj started getting the snacks all set up as Alex and I went straight for the couch, each one of us grabbing an armrest.

"Movie first, then talk?" Alex asked. "Or talk first, then movie?"

"I vote talk first," I said. "Let's get this mess over with. I made a list." I got my little notebook out of my bag.

"Of course you did," she said.

"What kind of list?" Raj asked. He brought bowls of chips and M&Ms over to us and set them on the coffee table, then plopped down in the middle. The couch was super comfortable but wasn't huge, which meant that Raj was just one cushion away, and I felt very aware of how close he was. Last time we hadn't been sitting next to each other; Alex had sat in the middle. I bet she'd changed her seat on purpose. Ever the matchmaker, even at a time like this.

"It's a list of everything we need to do." I looked down to read what I had written. "First, we have to decide when we want to set the meeting. And where. Then we have to figure out how to send a blocked message—"

"Covered," Alex said.

"Okay, but then we have to agree on what to write." I looked up. "Is that everything, do you think?"

"Very thorough," Raj said. "Most impressive."

"Any ideas?"

"We have to meet her someplace public enough that she can't make a scene, but not so public that people can overhear us," Alex said.

"Coffeehouse?" Raj asked.

She shook her head. "A little too public, I think."

"What about somewhere else downtown?" I asked.

"Those picnic tables near the park? They're set a little bit back from the street but not too far, and people walk by there all the time."

"Won't we be cold?" Alex asked.

"Not if we're doing it this weekend. It's supposed to be in the low fifties, and we can always bundle up."

"Okay, I can manage that," Alex said.

"That brings us to the second item on your list," Raj said. "The when."

"I think we should rip off the Band-Aid," Alex said. "Do it tomorrow. Don't give her a lot of time to think about it."

"Works for me," Raj said.

I nodded. The sooner the better. The stress was really getting to me, though despite it all I was having a good time, sitting with the two of them, planning how to make things better. I just wished we were talking about something else: where the next party was, or what we were all going to do after school, or whether going to prom was fun or stupid. Anything other than this.

"I was thinking I'd send one of the Mark pictures, and then say 'I'm going to need a favor. Await further instructions,'" Alex said. "You know, use her lingo."

"And then we wait until later to send the next one," I said. "Make her stress out for a while."

"Getting a bit vindictive there, are we?" Raj asked, but he flashed me a big smile as he said it.

"Believe me, I'd be happy to do worse," I said.

"Uh-oh, have we turned Perfect Kara into Carrie?" Alex asked. "That's totally what we should watch tonight."

"We'll do nothing of the sort," Raj said. "I have control over Netflix, and we're going to watch something charming and funny that will make us all forget our troubles."

"What did you pick?" I asked, forcing myself not to yell at Alex for bringing up Perfect Kara.

"Not until we're done," Raj said. "We're meeting tomorrow at the picnic tables, and Alex has the first text ready, but we haven't settled on a time."

"How about seven?" Alex said. "It will be dark, and there will be lots of people coming in and out of restaurants."

Raj and I both said okay, and we waited as Alex set up her phone and sent the first message.

"So anticlimactic," I said.

"Well, it's not like she can write back," Alex said. "Unless she sends a blast response to everyone involved, which doesn't seem all that likely."

Raj picked up the remote and turned on the TV. "Time to move on to the more enjoyable part of the evening," he said. "I present to you a movie about a girl who people think is perfect until she accidentally starts a rumor about herself that changes everyone's mind."

"So basically you're showing Kara her worst-case scenario," Alex said.

"Hardly. More like an alternate universe where the bad things happen without such terrible consequences. Come on, you'll like it."

He pressed Play and the movie started.

I was hyperaware of Raj next to me on the couch. We'd both stretched out with our feet on the coffee table; in the glow of the television I could see his socks, which did have the promised duckies and bunnies on them. Every so often our legs would brush up against each other, and it sent what felt like an electric shock all through my body. The sensation was even more exciting than that one kiss I'd had with Drew, way back when everything with Isabel and Becca had gone bad. For a minute I forgot about Ms. Davenport, forgot about the scariness of our impending confrontation, and I let myself daydream about how things might be different when this was all over.

The next night, I picked up Raj and Alex and we headed downtown. "Let me do most of the talking," Alex said. "Kara, you're too close to her, and we might need to get into the financial stuff to convince her she has to stop. I promise I'll keep the anger reined in."

"Works for me," I said. The less talking I had to do, the better.

"I trust you," Raj said.

Alex had brought along a folder with color copies of the

photos and some documents that explained the whole banking thing, as well as papers from the lawsuit. "It's not worth getting into," she said. "But she should be able to tell that these documents are evidence that I could show the police how to find stuff on her computer that leads to the money. And she'll see that we know about her family, too."

"Nice one," Raj said. "Did you save the video as well?"

Alex sniffed at him. "You think I'm some kind of rookie?"

He laughed. "No, I just didn't have you pegged for a reverse-blackmail expert. Sue me."

"Get serious, you guys," I said. "She could be here any minute."

But she wasn't. She didn't come early, anyway, and seven o'clock rolled around with nothing. At ten minutes past she finally walked by the picnic tables. Strolled, really. She didn't look scared, and I hadn't realized until then that I'd wanted her to.

"Interesting," Alex muttered. "Late, but not super late. She's a little worried, but she's not terrified."

"You can't know that for sure," Raj said as he watched Ms. Davenport scan the row of tables before she saw us.

I wondered how many people she'd sent those horrible text messages to, how many people might have been in the position we were in. But as soon as Ms. Davenport saw us, she headed for our table. She was dressed more casually than she normally was for school: she had on a T-shirt under a leather jacket and skinny jeans with her cowboy boots, her hair in two pigtails. At first I was reminded again of how young she looked, but then I inspected her face more closely and saw the lines again, under the layers of powder. She was good at pretending, but she wasn't that good. She wasn't as good as me.

She gave us an appraising look; I could see a hint of surprise when her eyes settled on me. How was she going to play this?

"You guys taking advantage of the nice weather?" she asked.

I wondered if she was hoping there was a chance this was some sort of coincidence. We just stared at her, waiting. Trying to look calm.

"I suppose you're expecting me," she said, and sat down. The three of us were all sitting on one side of the table, so it was almost like an interview. "Clever move, using a blocked number to get me here," Ms. Davenport said. "And in public, no less."

"We learned from the best," Alex said.

"How did you find me?"

"We don't need to explain ourselves to you," Alex said. "That's your job."

"Well, first perhaps you can tell me whether I should be expecting anyone else. Your compatriots? The police, perhaps?"

"That depends on how this conversation goes," Alex said.

"What do you want to know?"

"Everything."

"That's a tall order," Ms. Davenport said. She was starting to look a little smug; I wondered if she thought we didn't know all that much ourselves, yet.

"Tell us about the drugs," Alex said.

"It sounds like you think you already know. What more do you need from me?"

"Why are you doing this to us?" I blurted out. I knew I wasn't supposed to talk, but I couldn't help myself.

Alex glared at me.

"I'm not doing anything to you," Ms. Davenport said. "Nothing that you haven't done to yourselves. This isn't a big deal, and it's not personal, you know."

"It feels like a big deal to me," I said. "And pretty personal, too."

"I can understand why you'd say that," she said, and then her tone shifted. She leaned in toward us, nearly hissing. "You're all too naive to realize it, but Marbella High is filled with rich kids who just want to have fun and would find a way to do it with or without me. This school used to have to cover up drug arrests and overdoses; now no one gets arrested, the supply is clean. Things are under control now, and it's all because of me. This school needs me."

She was delusional. I could hear in her voice that she'd

actually convinced herself she was doing a good thing. "Why get us involved, then? If you had everything under control," I said.

"Everyone needs a little help sometimes," she said. She sounded less angry, as if she thought she'd convinced us. "And I only asked for help from those who'd already shown they were willing to bend or break the rules. Alex here, with her online gambling and offshore accounts; Raj, who'd been stupid enough to buy fake exam answers just so he wouldn't have to study, and then was dumb enough to tell his friend about it. And you, Kara—I have to say I never expected it. I had such high hopes for you. I thought you were different. I'd lost faith in everyone else, but you—you were so sincere, so dedicated. You were the one student who made me think it wasn't all pointless. To find out that you were just like the rest of them . . . I couldn't help myself. You had to be part of everything too, if only to teach you a lesson."

"Oh, you were trying to be a good teacher? And this was your strategy? You're a regular Good Samaritan," Alex said.

I appreciated her sticking up for me, but it didn't change the fact that Ms. Davenport's description of how things had played out made it sound like this was my fault, like I'd let her down. As if I didn't already feel bad enough about everything, now I was a disappointment to Ms. Davenport too? Ms. Davenport, who it turned out was responsible for making my life hell? This was all so confusing.

"You wanted to know everything. Did you want me to edit out the parts you don't like?"

"That's not what we meant," Alex said.

We'd started the conversation feeling like we had control, but we'd quickly lost it. I wondered whether we'd ever had it in the first place. We had to try again, and Alex was losing confidence. I turned to Raj to see if he would jump in, but he didn't seem to know what to do either.

It was all on me, then.

"Let's get back on track here," I said. "We would like you to stop doing what you're doing. What we'd really like is for you to move away from Marbella and never come back, but we get that doing that might look worse than you just finishing out the year and then getting a new job somewhere else. So that's what you're going to do, and you're going to wrap up all your little operations and never contact any of us again."

"That's what I'm going to do?" Ms. Davenport asked, amused. "You want me to shut the whole thing down, not just the parts that involve you guys."

"How much more is there?" Raj asked.

"Does it matter?"

"No," I said. "And yes, you're going to shut it all down. And after the school year is over you're going to stop working at Marbella High. If teaching has made you this awful, then maybe you should find something else to do. Go ask your rich ex-husband for money."

She frowned at this. Good—I'd finally said something that rattled her, even a little bit. "What do you know about that?" she asked.

"I know about the new wife, and the baby. And you of all people should know that I can do math. The timeline doesn't quite add up, right? Is that what made you such a horrible person, or were you always like this?"

I was getting to her. "You have no idea what that kind of betrayal can do to someone," she said. "And you have no idea what it's like to be broke in Marbella, spending all your time dealing with lying, spoiled kids, or your senile grandmother with her nursing home that costs more than my apartment, and the mortgage she never paid off—"

"You mean the one you took out after you tricked her into signing her life over to you?" Alex asked. "That one?"

"You've been doing your homework," she said, grudgingly impressed. "That lawsuit is a lie. But that doesn't matter."

"No, it doesn't," Raj said. "None of this excuses anything you've done."

"We've got the pictures of you and Mark," I said. "And we have Alex, who can explain to the police how you're stashing the money. We have people who are willing to testify against you, and if we need to, we'll find more."

"Testify?"

"That's what will happen if you don't do what we tell

you," I said. "Meet our terms, or we go to the police."

"You'd never do that," she said. "I'd tell them everything. I've got enough dirt on Marbella High to decimate the whole school. The DA would make a deal with me in a heartbeat."

"You really think so? You think it would look better for Marbella to go after its teenagers than to take down a teacher who blackmailed her own students?" Saying it out loud like that made me believe it more. Becca was right—we did have power.

And Ms. Davenport could feel it. "You're bluffing," she said, but she shivered. And it wasn't very cold.

"We aren't," I said, trying to sound powerful still. We were kind of bluffing, though. I definitely was.

"You all have bright futures ahead, sunny skies all the way." The bitterness was palpable. "I might be a bigger catch for the police, but my life is ruined already. You all have way more to lose than I do."

There it was again—that little window of sympathy I felt for my favorite teacher. Even if she was older than I thought, her life wasn't even close to half over, and she already thought it was ruined.

Alex had learned to read me well, though. "Don't even, Kara."

But I had to try. Making threats wasn't really my thing anyway. "Ms. Davenport, your life isn't over. Bad stuff happened, and you did terrible things in return. But if you do what we're asking, no one ever needs to know. You can start over, pretend none of this ever happened. I know there was a time when you were a good person—you're too good at playing one for it never to have been real. You can go back to that. We all can."

"Some things you can't come back from," she said, but she was starting to slouch down in her seat. To relax. It was almost over. I could feel it.

"People start over all the time. That's what I always thought college was—a place to become a new person. We talked about that, you and me. We talked about a lot of things. I trusted you then, and I have to be honest, right now I hate you for that. But you can make it better. You can make all this be over. Just promise us that you'll stop, that you'll go away and not do this to any more kids. Promise us that you'll try harder next time, find a way to be better."

"I'm not sure I can promise to be better," she said. "You don't really know me, after all. This is who I am. It always has been, in some ways."

"Well, what about the other promises, then?"

She pulled on one of her pigtails like a little kid. "How do I know you won't turn on me?" she said. "How do I know you won't make this deal with me and then go to the police anyway?"

"You don't," Alex said.

I shot her a look. I was making progress, and she was about to undo it. "She's right that you can't know for sure," I said. "Just like we can't know that you won't go off and do this to another group of kids at another school somewhere else. But we have the file on you, and you have everything you have on us. We may be willing to go to the police, but that doesn't mean we want to."

"You're basically suggesting mutually assured destruction, then. I do what you say, or you'll ruin me, but I'll ruin you right back."

"Sounds about right," Raj said. "Doing what we say is certainly better than the alternative."

"You haven't fully thought this through, though. Do you have any idea what's going to happen to the drug trade in this town with me gone? Someone worse is going to step in." She was sitting straighter again. I hoped that didn't mean she was changing her mind. We'd been so close.

"We'll let the police take care of it," I said. "Are you in or not?"

"I have to shut down everything? And leave in June?"

The three of us nodded.

"No police involvement?"

We nodded again.

"How will I know you'll keep your word?"

"The same way you'll know we've kept ours. We'll just have to trust each other."

Trust. That word was nothing but trouble.

"I suppose we've got a deal, then," Ms. Davenport said.

29.

I didn't know how to feel. Was I supposed to be relieved? My head was reeling from the mix of emotions I'd gone through, talking to her—I'd been so angry, but once she was in front of me I had trouble processing her as Blocked Sender and she went back to being my teacher, someone who was disappointed in me in a way that I still found meaningful. I'd had that brief sense of power, and I wanted it back, but I couldn't find it. And there was still the problem of making it through nearly half the school year in her class, but I would find a way.

"We did it!" Raj yelled.

"Quiet," I said. "We're still in public."

"It's finally over," Alex said, and I could tell she was holding back from yelling too.

But it didn't feel over to me. "I hope so."

"We got what we wanted," Raj said.

"Yeah," I said. "Mutually assured destruction. Which

contains the words 'assured' and 'destruction.' The whole plan could go south at any time."

"But it won't," Alex said.

"You can't be sure of that."

"You know this is the best outcome we can manage. We went over this, like, a million times."

"I know." And I did know; I was just having a hard time convincing myself that knowing was the same as it being true. "We should tell Justin and Isabel."

"I'll text them," Raj said, and got out his phone.

I felt a momentary pang at the knowledge that Raj had Isabel's cell phone number. He'd been so flirty with her that first time we all met up—was that just Raj being Raj, or had they had a thing? Was I actually jealous? I thought about the night before, the jolt of our legs touching. Yes, I was jealous. There was no point in denying it.

"We should get out of here," Alex said.

"I agree. Let's go somewhere and celebrate," Raj said.

But I didn't really feel like celebrating. I was just about to say I wanted to go home when Alex's phone pinged with a text message. She picked up her phone to read it, and I watched a mix of emotions cross her face that I didn't really understand.

"What's up?" I asked. "You okay?"

"Justin wants to talk," she said.

"Did he change his mind?" Raj asked. "Is he not on board? I told him it was over—I thought he'd be excited."

"He is," she said. "But he broke up with Mark, and he apologized for not being honest with me, and he wants to see if we can fix things. I didn't think I could ever forgive him, but . . ."

"But maybe you can," I said. "You should go talk to him. We've all done some things we shouldn't have, and I think we've paid enough. Don't you?"

"Maybe. I don't know. It's worth a shot, though. Can you guys handle celebrating on your own?"

Raj and I looked at each other. "We can manage," he said.

"Do you need me to drop you off?" I asked.

"Justin's at Philz, right down the street. I can just meet him there. He wanted to be close by, to make sure that we were okay. That I was okay."

"That's a good-friend thing to do," I said.

"It's a start," she said, and left to go meet him.

"Do you want to go somewhere else?" Raj asked.

"It's kind of nice here, actually." The sky was pitch-dark now, and stars were visible through the trees in the little park where we were sitting. The temperature had dropped a bit, and the wind was blowing, making the leaves rustle and whipping my hair around, but I didn't mind. More important, we were sitting pretty close together on the picnic table bench, our legs touching again, and I didn't want to move.

"Winters here are much nicer than in England," Raj said.

"They were so dank and dreary and miserable. And cold."

"Was there snow?" I asked.

"Once in a while. But it got dirty and gray so fast. It wasn't pretty like you might imagine."

I'd imagined it a lot, especially since I'd decided I wanted to go to school someplace with seasons. "Do you miss it there?"

"Not in winter," he said. "But sometimes. Less than I used to, now that I've made some friends." He nudged me with his elbow, and I nudged him back. So we were friends, then. I felt a little twinge of disappointment, but I was the one who'd insisted that friendship was the only possibility, so I had no one but myself to blame.

"I'm so glad this is over," I said, and I was starting to mean it. "I feel like I can finally relax. Though I don't know if this makes sense to say, but being with you guys—it's been really fun. I mean, when it wasn't super scary and awful. Is that weird?"

"Yes, it's weird," he said, and laughed. I laughed too. "But I think I know what you mean. Listen, can I ask you a question?"

I felt myself tense up, but in a good way. "Sure."

"What you said to Alex, about us all having paid enough—did you really mean it?"

"Of course," I said. "Don't you agree?"

"It's not that. It's just—I keep thinking about what you

told Alex a while back. About what kind of person you'd want to be with."

"She should never have told you that," I said. "And I never should have said it."

"But on some level you meant it, didn't you? Be honest with me."

I decided I would. I was going to try to be as honest as I could with everyone, from now on. Lying hadn't made my life any better, that was for sure. "I meant it at the time," I said. "I had this really simplistic idea in my head about the kind of person who did what you were doing. Which was totally wrong. Not to mention that I ended up basically doing the same thing. And worse."

"Is it still true, then?"

"What I think about who I would date?" Was he really asking what I thought he was asking?

He paused, as if to decide whether he really wanted to say it. "What you think about me."

Well, that answered that question. "I thought you flirted with all the girls," I said. "I saw how you were with Isabel."

"No joking about this," he said. "I'm serious. I know this experience has been horrible and we all want to put it behind us as fast as we can, but I have to tell you, getting to know you has been the only thing that made all of this bearable. And if we're just going to be friends, that's fine. But if there's any chance, I want to know."

He was saying exactly what I wanted him to, and yet it kind of scared me. Why did the idea of being with him, with anyone, feel like such a risk? Was it really just about the monster?

"We still don't know each other all that well," I said. "There are still things about me you should know."

"We have time," he said.

"Not a lot. We're graduating soon." The thought of turning my attention back to college applications was laughable, though.

"You're fast-forwarding," he said.

He was right; it was the same thing I always did. I'd told myself to slow down, but moving ahead was a habit by now.

"I haven't dated all that much," I said. "Or hooked up, or whatever."

"Then we'll take things very, very slowly," he said. "Are these excuses? If you're not into me, you can say it. It's just that there were a couple of times when I saw you look at me and I thought maybe . . ."

I remembered what Alex had said when we talked about college. I'd decided not to enjoy high school, to put off living thinking my real life would start later, but that had led me to do something so stupid that I might never have gotten to live my real life at all. What was the point? What, exactly, was I waiting for?

I didn't need to wait for anything. And I needed to stop

being so afraid. I had to take a risk sometime, and here I was, sitting with a guy I really liked, who wasn't afraid to tell me that he liked me back. He'd taken a chance, and now it was my turn.

"You thought right," I said.

And then I leaned over and kissed him.

He clearly hadn't been expecting it; his head wasn't turned toward mine, so my lips landed on that space where his cheek and his lips met. But just when I thought I'd made a huge mistake, that this was the kind of super awkward moment I'd never get over, he figured it out. He pulled back for just a second, then realigned himself so we could start over, properly, our lips aligned. I was afraid for a minute that he'd reach for my face, like Drew had, but he just put his hands on my shoulders to pull me closer to him, and the moment went from being awkward to perfect.

"So we are celebrating after all," Raj said, after we'd both pulled away. He couldn't hide the big smile on his face, and I couldn't hide mine, either. I didn't want to.

"Not for long," I said. "I've put off so much because of all of this. I have to get back to work. I just don't know how I'm going to go back to just studying and dealing with college stuff again. That seems so far away. I don't even know if I want the same things anymore."

"What had you wanted?"

I told him about how I'd always wanted to go to Harvard,

or someplace east, and my parents' whole Stanford/Harvard issue, and how I still didn't even know what I was going to write my essay about. "I mean, I'm not exactly going to use this whole blackmail scheme to explain how I've grown as a person."

He laughed. "That would be hilarious, actually. And quite fitting. But probably not the best application strategy. I know I mentioned this to you before, but have you considered not going to college right away? Taking a gap year?"

"Not for a second," I said.

"Well, maybe it's time to think about it. It's common practice in England, and more people here take time off than you'd think. You could focus on school without worrying about everything else, and your SAT score will still be good next year."

"What would I do, though? I've never really done anything but school. I don't want to just sit around and hang out with my parents."

"People do all sorts of things," he said. "They travel, or get jobs or externships. They figure out who they are, and who they want to be."

"Why aren't you going to do one?"

"Because my parents went through a lot for my education, and I've started to realize that maybe their whole thing about wanting me to be a doctor like them wasn't just about them; it was about something they saw in me. I really do enjoy my science classes, and helping people, even if I went about it all wrong. If I want to be a doctor, I'll probably have to do an extra year to make up for not taking enough science classes in high school, and I don't want to wait to get started."

That was unexpected. We really did have a lot to learn about each other. "Wow," I said.

"I know, right? I'm going to be quite the respectable gentleman after all." He reached over and took my hand. "Just think about the gap year thing, okay? Going from all this pressure to a place like Harvard, or whatever fantastic school you choose, will be a lot. There's nothing wrong with making sure you're ready."

"I'll think about it," I said, and I knew I really would.

"But not tonight," he said. "Tonight we need to think about happy things, to let go of the worry and the stress and just enjoy ourselves, yes? Should we leave this picnic table and do something more memorable? This is our first date, after all."

"You don't think our evening's been memorable enough?"

"We can do better," he said. "Come on, let's go."

I took his hand, and we went off to find an adventure.

30.

"You didn't," Alex said.

"I did," I said. "I kissed him first and everything." I'd called her as soon as I woke up and told her she had to come over immediately. She was there within an hour, coffees in hand. She sat at my desk while I curled up on my bed; I'd only gotten up long enough to do super-basic SCAM. Just in case I changed my mind.

"You realize I've never seen your room before," she'd said.

"That's true, isn't it? You were just in the living room that one time. Yours is so awesome, there was never really any reason for you to come here." I thought about that for a second, and then realized I wasn't being completely honest. And the whole point of having her come over was that I was trying to be. "No, that's not really it. It's more that your house is fun—your parents are around a lot of the time, and you have your crazy kitchen routine, and it's just so loving and warm, and my parents work all the time, and I guess I didn't want you to know how cold it can feel here sometimes. Not that they don't love me. It's just—"

"I know what you mean," she said. "And I get it. Although you've deprived me of the opportunity to see how you live." She looked around at my room, with its lavender walls and violet comforter and fluffy white rug. "I hadn't realized you were such a fan of purple."

"It looks terrible on me, so I can't wear it. I decided it was better just to surround myself with it at home."

"So what's the big news?"

There were a couple of things I wanted to share with her, and questions to ask, too. Starting with the Raj story, of course. She'd kill me if I made her talk about Justin first. I told her everything: about the conversation, and the kiss, and the rest of the night, when we'd driven to Pacifica and walked along the water, just talking.

"Just talking? Seriously?"

"Okay, mostly talking." My face felt warm. I was not used to having this conversation. But that's what friends did. They talked about the guys they liked. I wanted to be a good friend, since if there was one thing I'd learned, it was that Alex had been a pretty great friend to me all along, even if it had taken me a while to recognize it.

"So what does this all mean?"

"Why does it have to mean anything?" I asked. "You and your Prospects—what do they mean?"

"This is not even a little bit similar, and you know it," she said. "Besides, I think I'm ready to ditch the idea of Prospects. Maybe consider something a little more substantial."

"Are you now? What brought that on?" I hoped by "something a little more substantial" she meant Bryan. He'd be good for her.

"I've been thinking about it for a while," she said. "I thought keeping things light was a good idea, back when Justin and I were friends. But now that I look back, I wonder whether I avoided getting into anything real so it wouldn't interfere with that friendship. I don't think it has to be that way. Or maybe I just don't want it to be, anymore."

"How did the conversation with Justin go?" I asked.

"As well as it could. I'm still really mad at him, and not just for what he told Ms. Davenport—I'd never told him how pissed off the whole secret-boyfriend thing made me. And I should have. I let things fester too long, and now we're in this place where we don't trust each other, and that trust will take a long time to get back."

"Do you want to get it back?"

"I want things to be better than they are now," she said.

It sounded like they were in the same place I was with Becca. Trust was everything in friendship, I'd come to realize. And now it was time for me to accept that, for real.

"Can you give me a couple of minutes?" I asked. "I want to show you something."

“I’ve got nowhere to be,” she said. “Take your time.”

The easiest way to do this was to take a shower. I put my hair in a bun so I didn’t have to wash it and turned the water on as hot as I could stand it. I scrubbed my face and body until I felt squeaky clean and then got out, toweled off, and threw on my clothes. Then I looked in the mirror.

Another day with no improvement whatsoever.

Be brave, Kara.

I walked out of the bathroom and back into my bedroom. Alex was still sitting at the desk, turned away from me. “Turn around,” I said.

She did.

I don’t know what I was expecting—some sort of horrified gasp, or for her to crack up, or even to pretend she wasn’t seeing what I knew she was seeing right now. But she didn’t do any of that. Instead, she looked at me. Just looked. But really looked, like she was seeing me for the first time.

“Okay,” she said.

“Is that all you’ve got? You realize I’m kind of baring my soul to you here.” My face turned red, and I knew she could see it.

“It’s really nice to see the real you,” she said. Which was pretty much the best thing she could have said, under the circumstances.

“Don’t even ask if I’ve ever considered going without makeup. It’s not going to happen. You know you’re the fourth person in the world to even see this."

"The fourth?"

"Mom. Dad. My doctor. You." I ticked them off on my fingers.

Alex pointed to me.

"What?"

"I'm the fifth person," she said. "You're not counting yourself."

"Ugh, is that supposed to be some kind of metaphor?"

"No, I meant it literally. You didn't count yourself as a person there."

She was right. I hadn't. But it was time to start.

Alex went home to start on some big cooking project with her dad. She invited me over for dinner, but Mom had left a note saying she and Dad wouldn't be working too late and asking if I wanted to have a takeout-and-TV night. After everything that had gone on, that sounded kind of nice. I wished they'd been home to meet Alex, but there would be time for that. There would be time for a lot of things.

They came home earlier than I expected and brought Indian food. I remembered Raj's skepticism about Indian food in America, how it was nothing like real Indian food. Maybe someday I'd have a chance to find out. Maybe even sooner than I expected.

"You look tired, honey," Mom said as we dished the food onto paper plates. "Everything okay?"

"Everything's good," I said. "Can I ask you guys something?"

"Of course," Dad said.

We took our food into the living room, plates settled on the coffee table. "What would you think if I said I wanted to put off college for a year?"

"That's kind of sudden," Mom said. "Is that what you really want?"

"I don't know," I said. "I just wanted to know if that was something we could talk about, someday."

"We can talk about anything," Dad said. "You know that."

Not anything, I wanted to say, but maybe from now on that wouldn't be the case. Maybe I'd have to commit to being honest with everyone. "It doesn't have to be now," I said. "I still have some things to figure out."

"Well, we're here whenever you want," Mom said. "Now, let's decide what to watch."

"*CSI* reruns?" Dad asked.

"Cute boys solving crimes?" I said. "Sure."

There was a marathon on cable, of course, so we watched episode after episode as we ate way too much food and sank deeper and deeper into the couch cushions. I closed my eyes for a while; I'd seen the show so many times, I could guess which cute boy would be solving the crime from just a few lines of dialogue. I didn't need to see it to know what was going on.

A scene ended, and commercials started, loud and blaring as always. I hated how the commercials were always at such a higher volume than the shows—it was jarring every time. But this woman's voice was so soothing, I almost didn't mind hearing her talk about some random drug and its scary side effects.

Then I heard the tagline.

"A new life. With Novalert."

I froze for a minute, as if the TV was speaking to me directly.

I thought about everything that had happened in the last few months, the last few years, and really, the last few days. How much things had changed. How much I'd changed, or at least how much I wanted to.

I didn't yet know that Ms. Davenport wouldn't show up for school on Monday, or ever again; that my parents would agree to let me spend a year traveling so I didn't have to stress out so much about school; that Alex would get into MIT early and Raj would get into Boston University late, and I'd make them promise to show me around when I did finally decide to go out east to college, since I finally had a legitimate reason to be there; that Raj and I would spend the rest of senior year together; that my new group of friends would include the reconciled Alex and Justin but also Becca and Isabel; that we'd spend the rest of our time in high school making up for all the fun I didn't have before.

I didn't need to know any of those things to know that, for some reason, the ad was hilarious. I couldn't help myself—I started laughing. And laughing and laughing and laughing, so hard that when I opened my eyes I could see my parents looking worried. But I couldn't stop laughing. Because, for me, the tagline had turned out to be true.

Just not the way they meant it.

ACKNOWLEDGMENTS

Thanks again to Melissa de la Cruz, Richard Abate, and everyone at Spilled Ink—I couldn't have done this without you, and I'm so grateful for the opportunity to work with all of you.

Thanks to the team at HarperCollins, especially my amazing editor Jocelyn Davies and my publicist Gina Rizzo, who have both been fantastic and exceedingly patient with me.

Extra-special thanks to Katherine Bell, who helped me more with this book than is reasonable for any one person to do, particularly given everything she was going through at the time. She claims the book was a welcome distraction; I choose to believe it because her help was invaluable. Keep sending pics of V, please.

Thanks to all my friends who've provided moral support and advice, both online and off: Rebecca Johns Trissler, Brandon Trissler, Nami Mun, Gus Rose, Vu Tran, Elisa Lee,

Caroline Sheerin, Mary Campbell, the Fearless Fifteeners, and the Group-That-Must-Not-Be-Named on Facebook.

Thanks to my high school friends, who were so incredibly supportive when my first book came out, after the acknowledgments had already gone to press. Vicky Morville helped me with web design; Nadine Levin created wonderful bookmarks, and Mary-Jo Rolnick, Elisa Goldberg, and Cristina Miedema were the best cheerleaders ever.

Finally, thanks, as always, to my family.